Her eyes were

Delamere took out
her chin still held b
hand, wiped her ey
she had been a child. Then, in the most
natural way possible, he leaned over and
kissed her gently.

'There now,' he said. 'Dragons must not cry,
you know.'

'Or shrews?' Anne said tremulously.

'Or shrews. But you are not a shrew, little
Miss Winterborne. A mouse, perhaps. . .'

Dear Reader

In COUNTRY MOUSE, we have the latest Regency by Petra Nash — a treat! Joanna Makepeace leaves Richard III for the Monmouth Rebellion in CORINNA'S CAUSE, an action-packed plot. Our American authors are Patricia Potter and Lucy Elliot, with THE ABDUCTION, set in the Scottish Borders of 1550, and PRIVATE PARADISE, featuring New York in the 1880s.

See you next month!

The Editor

COUNTRY MOUSE

Petra Nash

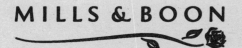

MILLS & BOON

MILLS & BOON LIMITED
ETON HOUSE, 18–24 PARADISE ROAD
RICHMOND, SURREY, TW9 1SR

First published in Great Britain 1993 by Mills & Boon Limited

© Petra Nash 1993

Australian copyright 1993 Philippine copyright 1994 This edition 1994

ISBN 0 263 78246 8

Set in 11 on 12½ pt Linotron Times 04-9402-74605

Typeset in Great Britain by Centracet, Cambridge Made and printed in Great Britain

CHAPTER ONE

THE morning sun shone valiantly, but the air that came in through the open sash — and round the edge of the ill-fitting old window — was cold. Anne Winterborne shivered a little, and wished she had thought to bring a shawl downstairs. The simple white cambric gown with its slightly faded pattern of printed flowers was scarcely warm enough for October. She had better look out her winter gowns today; would the poplin do for another year? she wondered. Well, it would have to. The income of one hundred pounds a year, though a fortune to some, invariably seemed to have dwindled to nothing before she could do more than buy herself a new pair of gloves, or some lengths of fine flannel for winter petticoats. And at the sensible age of twenty-five she had very little need of finery. She sighed gently, noting that the tablecloth on which rested their carefully preserved breakfast set was once again in need of darning.

'Oh, merciful heaven!'

This exclamation, mild though it was, made Anne raise the large hazel eyes that were her only pretension to beauty from the offending tablecloth which she had been studying with an anxious frown. That little frown still creased the pale skin of her smooth brow beneath the neatly dressed soft brown hair as she gazed at the rector across their breakfast table. Her brother, the vaguest and mildest of men, rarely reacted otherwise than calmly even to the most worrying or exciting information. The letter telling them of their brother Edmund's death at the battle of Vittoria, four years earlier, had whitened his cheeks but not unleashed his tongue. The victory at Waterloo, a year later, had likewise been received in silence. A man of sincere and simple piety, he would not normally allow himself the use of words that he regarded as verging on the blasphemous.

'What is it, James?' Anne swiftly ran through her mind the most likely candidates. Twelve-year-old Henry, the youngest of her brothers, she had seen only that morning when he left the house early to go with his bosom friend Charles for a morning of adventuring in the woods. He had been his usual cheerful self, with no undisclosed sins troubling the happy expectation of a holiday Monday. Charles, who was not as strong as his parents would have wished, came to the rectory daily for his lessons from James, who frequently allowed the boys their freedom on a Monday so that he could catch up with parish work after the rigours of a busy Sunday.

It must be William, then. At nineteen her other brother was starting his second year at Cambridge, and though he was dutiful in his studies Anne had frequently wondered whether he was really happy there. Once or twice, during the previous year, his energy and high spirits had led him to forsake his book-learning to indulge in pranks which made the authorities frown. Though such escapades had done no more than make James smile, Anne had been troubled. It was, she knew, very kind of her younger brother's godfather to sponsor William through school and university, and to offer him a place with his own practice at the end of it, but she knew that William found the law dry and uninteresting, and suspected that he viewed the plans for his future more in the light of a prison sentence than good fortune.

'He is very young,' she pointed out to her brother, who had returned to the beginning of his letter and was reading through it again, his lips compressed as if to contain any other expletives that his tongue might give utterance to.

'Very young? My dear sister, to the best of my knowledge the man is thirty at the least, if not more! Old enough to know better, at any rate!'

'More than thirty? It is not William, then, of whom you speak?'

'William? What can he possibly have to say in the matter?'

He was still frowning over the letter. Anne, who was accustomed to his absent-minded habits, reached across the table for his coffee-cup. She refilled it, adding cream and sugar until it was just as he preferred it, and put it back so that his questing fingers would find it when, as he presently did, he put out his hand without taking his eyes from his correspondence. While he emptied the cup and finished re-reading the letter she sat quietly, her hands folded in her lap, and waited as patiently as she could for his explanation. At length he laid down the letter, and raised troubled eyes to meet her own questioning regard.

'My dear, I wish you would tell me what is troubling you,' she said. 'I collect that it is not, as I had thought, anything to do with Will?'

'With William? No. I could almost have wished that it were. It is Arabella.'

'Arabella!' The possibility had not occurred to her. Her only sister, eight years younger than herself, had lived for so long with her maternal uncle and his family that Anne was inclined still to think of her as the small child she had been, rather than as the young lady of seventeen she now was. 'What is the matter with her? Is she ill?'

It seemed scarcely likely. The announcement of illness, however serious, would have made him unhappy and worried, but not shocked as he so obviously was. Arabella, besides, was blessed with a splendid constitution, and beyond the usual childhood ailments had scarcely known a day's illness in her life.

'No, she is not ill. She has, however, displeased her uncle and aunt very severely. So severely, in fact, that they are sending her home to us.'

'Sending her away, after all these years! Good heavens, what can she have done to deserve such treatment?'

'What indeed! Mr Littleton does not make himself very clear. He speaks in the vaguest of

terms. . .here, you had better read it for yourself.'
He pushed the letter across the table, and Anne
picked it up, scanning it swiftly. She could scarcely
make sense of what she read, so great was her
shock. Someone called Lord Delamere was mentioned — she supposed that he was the man who
was more than thirty that her brother had referred
to. The words 'ingratitude', 'indelicacy' and 'scandal' seemed to leap up from the page, but there
was no actual explanation. She laid down the letter
again.

'But I thought they were so fond of her! After
all these years, treating her as a daughter! And I
cannot see how she could have had a chance to
misbehave so particularly — she is not even out
yet! I know that her cousin had her first season
this year, but Arabella is still in the schoolroom!
Whatever could she have done?'

Her brother shook his head. His clever face
with its beaky nose and fine-drawn features was
sad. Anne pushed back her chair and went round
the table to him. Small and slightly built, she
looked much younger than her years, but she put
her arms round his bony frame and held him in a
comforting hug as if she had been his mother,
rather than his younger sister. He rested his head
against her for a moment, and she saw with
compunction that the thick hair which resembled
hers in its indeterminate brown colour was
streaked with silver.

'How could they treat her so? To send her home
in disgrace, when she has lived with them as a

daughter these last six years! And without any proper explanation!'

'It is very hard, certainly.' He put an arm round her slight form, and returned her embrace. 'We must not judge them too harshly, however, nor our sister. Certainly she must have displeased them, and I can only think that it must be something to do with Eliza. As she is their only child, you know, they are naturally over-anxious about her. They would be bound to react more violently where she is concerned.'

Vague and absent-minded he might be, thought Anne, but where human nature was concerned he was rarely mistaken. His parishioners in the small Dorset village where he was rector had implicit trust in his judgement, and so did his family. Anne dropped a kiss on the greying hair.

'I am sure you are right, my dear. We know them so little, after all. I do not think I have met them above six times. It is a pity they are not our own family; it would have been so much easier.'

'Yes. I always felt that Mr Littleton did not approve of his sister marrying our father. Of course you were only four then, so you would scarcely have noticed such things, but I was eight, and I remember how very cool he was at the wedding. And we only saw him and Mrs Littleton two or three times during our stepmother's lifetime, I think.'

The late Reverend James Winterborne, their father, had had the misfortune to lose his first wife, their mother, after only a few years of marriage. She had died of an inflammation of the lungs, leaving him with five-year-old James, and Anne and Edmund who were two and one respectively. He had mourned her sincerely, and three years later had married again, a beautiful young girl who had played with her stepchildren as if she were scarcely older than they, and had presented him with three more offspring before dying, in her turn, in childbed. He had survived her for only four years, a broken man, and had drifted thankfully into death leaving his younger children in the care of his eldest son.

At the age of twenty young James Winterborne had accepted the burden of his five sisters and brothers without question. Their father's income had died with him, and neither of his two wives had possessed more than a few thousand pounds, which had been divided among them. Fortunately he had been a well liked man, and friends and family had rallied round. James himself, who had been on the verge of following his father into Holy Orders, had been given his present living by Sir Robert Sudbury, their father's old friend. This gentleman, who lived in the great house outside the village and was its squire, had also bought a commission for Edmund, who had always dreamed of a military career. William had been helped by his godfather, and Mr Littleton had surprised them all by offering to take Arabella, then only nine years old and a pretty child, strongly resembling her late mother, his sister.

'She shall be a companion for her cousin

Elizabeth — there is scarcely two years between them,' he had boomed, standing before the fire with his legs apart and looking down his long nose at James and Anne. It had been an offer they could scarcely afford to refuse, for he was a wealthy man who lived in some style in London. Anne had worried, at first, that her sister might be treated as a charity case, but fortunately the lonely Eliza had been delighted with her pretty little playmate, and Arabella was soon treated as a valued member of the family. Her dutiful letters home had spoken of new gowns and pelisses, of outings to see the wild beasts at the Tower, the pantomime at Sadlers Wells and the performing horses at Astley's. Anne had sincerely rejoiced for her, and had happily taken up the role as her brother's housekeeper knowing that her pretty little sister's upbringing and future were secure.

Now, however, that secure future had been blown away like a candle flame. Arabella, the sister whom she had not seen more than twice in the last eight years, was being sent back to them in disgrace. Anne shook her head, as if to free her thoughts from the sticky cobwebs of might-have-been, and applied her mind to the practical.

'Well, it is of no use speculating,' she said with an attempt at cheerfulness. "We can know nothing more until she arrives. Ten to one it was all a misunderstanding, and we will be getting another letter to say that all is resolved!'

'I am afraid there is little chance of that,' her brother responded seriously. 'Her uncle speaks of her departure as quite settled, to take place almost at once. She will be arriving. . .when? Let me see the letter. On Monday. But that is today!'

'Today! Then we shall soon be in possession of the facts, and there is no time to be lost. I must see that a room is prepared for her, and be sure that the bed is properly aired. We so seldom have visitors! Not that she is precisely a visitor, of course, our own sister. . .'

'Poor child, she will be very unhappy. Whatever she has done, Anne, she must have our love and support, you know. Whatever she has done,' he repeated with emphasis.

'Of course, my dear,' agreed Anne. In both their minds was the frightful thought that neither could give voice to: the possibility that their little sister might return to them dishonoured, bearing a nameless child. . . Anne gave herself a brisk little shake.

'Now, I shall be busy,' she said briskly. 'You have a meeting with your churchwardens at eleven o'clock, do you not? Then I shall see you at luncheon.' She was pleased to see that the reminder had galvanised her brother into activity, and she whisked herself out of the room.

For the rest of the morning she attempted to concentrate only on practical matters, though the worry was always there, hovering like a dark goblin in the corners of her mind. At half-past twelve Henry returned, very muddy, and towing an equally bemired Charles behind him.

'Can you clean him up, Nan?' asked her scapegrace brother, reaching up to embrace the only mother he had ever known. 'And he may stay for luncheon, mayn't he? We're both starving, and if he goes home like this. . .you know how they fuss.'

'Anything, anything, if only you will keep your muddy hands off me,' she implored, backing away from him. 'Not that you should speak of Lady Sudbury like that, of course,' she added. 'Take him up and find him something of yours to wear, while those dry off. And heaven send you haven't caught cold, Charles!'

He assured her that he had not, and it was a relief to have them at the luncheon table, gabbling about their adventures of the morning and making good inroads into the cold meat, the cheese, and the fresh baked bread that made their simple meal. Charles said little, leaving most of the talking to his livelier friend, but Anne knew how much he enjoyed eating with them. At home he still ate most of his meals in the nursery, with his old nurse fussing if he did not finish every scrap on his plate. In the straitened circumstances of the rectory they had never bothered with nursery meals, and Henry had benefited, she thought, from taking his meals in their company. Certainly he was a lively companion, and cheerfully accepted his brother's quiet checks when his volubility became too great.

At the end of the meal, Anne mentioned Arabella's imminent return, giving the news as casually as she could and not referring to any of the problems. Henry accepted it without question: adults were still distant beings, who acted and reacted in strange, incalculable fashions that he did not attempt to understand. Charles, more thoughtful, looked at Anne.

'I had meant to take Henry back with me for the afternoon. Should he perhaps stay here instead, to greet his sister?'

Henry cried out at this, and Anne smiled at Charles. Singularly lacking in vanity, she did not know how her face lit up when she smiled. She thought of herself as small, pale and insignificant, but when she smiled her face was transformed, her hazel eyes glowing with golden flecks in their depths, her even teeth white as pearls within the soft pink of her lips.

'What a kind, thoughtful boy you are, Charles,' she said warmly. Henry groaned. 'Well, he is,' she said, frowning him down. 'But as it happens I expect that Arabella will be very tired from her journey. It is quite a long way from London, you know, and I expect she may want to go straight up to bed. So you may go with Charles, Henry, and see your sister in the morning, when she is rested.' Her eyes met James's, and she saw in them the mirror of her own relief that their youngest brother should be out of the way when Arabella arrived.

The worst of the mud had dried and been brushed off Charles's clothes by the time they left. Anne took herself to the sunny window-seat of the sitting-room, and resolutely set to work on another new shirt for Henry, who was able to turn them into rags in what seemed like a matter of days. James sat at the other end of the room with the account books and wrestled with the church accounts. Both of them were straining their ears for the sound of a carriage, but neither would admit it. By half-past three Anne felt as though her nerves were stretched so thin and tight that they would snap at the slightest touch, and it was a relief when the sound of horses' hoofs sounded on the gravel of the drive, and she might lay aside her sewing.

She stood up. She had changed the old cambric morning dress for one of white muslin, equally plain but brightened by the addition of a Kashmir shawl of her mother's, old but beautiful. Now she shivered a little, and pulled it around her, glancing up at James. His bony face was pale, but he smiled down at her.

'Well, here she is,' she said unnecessarily.

'Yes, here she is. Come, Anne, we must go and meet her at once. She must not think herself unwelcome here, her home.'

Jenny, their elderly maid, was already opening the front door, and James and Anne went out to where the carriage was halting in the drive. James reached up and opened the carriage door before the footman had time to get down from his seat beside the coachman. A cross face, prettily framed in an azure velvet bonnet, peered out of the dim interior.

'Arabella, my dear,' he said, holding up his

hand to her. The pouting lips quivered a little, and beneath frowning brows her blue eyes were wary. She did not move, and her hands remained tucked into a velvet muff of the same blue as the bonnet. 'Come, dear child,' he said gently. 'Here is your sister Anne waiting to greet you.'

By now the footman had climbed down and lowered the steps, and was waiting with an impassive face by the open door. The wide blue eyes flickered towards him, and at last Arabella took her hand out of her muff, and put it in her brother's. She stepped out of the carriage, holding up the skirts of her velvet pelisse that was of a paler blue than the bonnet and muff, and made in the very latest fashion. Anne found that she was looking up at her little sister, who was now at least three inches taller than she. She put out her arms, and felt the slim form quiver at her touch.

'Welcome home, darling,' she said, reaching up to kiss the cold face. 'I see I cannot call you my little sister any more! Come inside quickly, and get warm.' Hastily she drew the girl into the house, away from the avid gazes of coachman and footman. 'And did your uncle send you all this way alone, without even a maid to bear you company? I wonder at him, letting a child of your age travel so far by yourself!'

'He sent me in his own carriage, with John Coachman,' said Arabella. Anne was relieved to hear her speak. She took her sister into the sitting-room, where a small fire warmed and brightened the chill. Arabella stood like a lay figure while

Anne took off her bonnet, gloves and pelisse. The white silk dress she wore was cut and fashioned with exquisite simplicity. Anne looked at the slender body revealed by the flowing, high-waisted skirt and allowed her greatest fear to fade away. Surely that slim waist and small, delicately rounded bosom did not belong to a girl bearing a child. Even as she thought it James came in, and his eyes met hers in a moment of shared relief.

'The carriage is gone,' he said, coming forward to embrace Arabella. 'Now, my dear sister, can you explain to us what has been happening? Your uncle's letter has left us sadly perplexed.'

She broke at once into a storm of tears, and her words were broken by sobs so that they were scarcely intelligible. 'Unfair', 'unkind', 'cruel' and 'heartless' were the burden of what she said, and her cousin Eliza's name was mentioned, together with that of Lord Delamere. When they questioned her, her sobs grew more violent until they were frightened that she would make herself ill. James rang for brandy, and Anne sent for tea, and when both of these remedies had been administered, together with a dose of hartshorn and water that Anne fetched from upstairs, she grew quieter, and they were at last able to piece together her story.

Eliza, it appeared, had made her come-out that spring. A large girl, with no great claims to beauty, she had still achieved a certain success, partly because her father was a wealthy man, and partly because she was a pleasant, friendly girl. Her

greatest triumph, however, had been in capturing
the attention of Lord Delamere. At thirty-two his
title, his wealth, and his handsome face and figure
made him one of the most eligible bachelors in
London, who, though he had several times paid
desultory court to the hopeful beauties paraded
before him by anxious mamas, had never seemed
seriously interested in any of them.

Now, however, rumour had it that he was
wishing to settle down, and abandon his rackety
bachelor ways. Certainly he had been surprisingly
attentive to Miss Littleton; had three times taken
her driving in his phaeton, had danced with her at
Almack's, and had generally exhibited symptoms
of being decidedly *épris*. Until, that was, the day
when he had called at the Littleton house in
Mayfair and set eyes on Miss Arabella
Winterborne.

Looking at her little sister, Anne could scarcely
blame him. Even with a face blotched by tears
Arabella was startlingly lovely. Her dark hair
glowed with rich copper lights, her eyes were a
deep blue and fringed with impossibly long dark
lashes, her skin was petal-soft, white and pink as
a newly opened rosebud. Eliza's blonde prettiness
would have looked insipid next to her, and Anne
could well understand why Mrs Littleton had
insisted that Arabella was far too young, and
should not come out for another year, or possibly
two.

'They said I flirted with him!' wailed Arabella,
tears flowing once again from her impossibly blue

eyes. 'As if I were a kitchen maid, or something! And I didn't! I couldn't help it if I was prettier than Eliza, could I? And she didn't care for him, anyway. She was frightened of him, I know she was; she told me so. She didn't understand his jokes, and when he took her out in his phaeton she felt sick! So you see! It was a kindness to her, really! It was just Aunt Jane and Uncle John. They wanted her to marry him because he's a lord, and has a big house in Sussex.'

There was a great deal more, along the same lines. Anne let her ramble on, feeling that it was better to allow her to have the relief of speech. How far her sister was culpable she did not like to judge. Certainly, when questioned more closely, Arabella was evasive about the number of times she had met with Lord Delamere, and the circumstances of their meeting. Reading between the lines, Anne thought that her sister had probably slipped away from her governess several times to meet with him clandestinely. The whole thing had come to light when Arabella, flown with romance, had borrowed her cousin's domino and mask and attended a masquerade at Vauxhall with Lord Delamere and some friends. As might have been expected, her distinctive colouring had been recognised by one of her aunt's friends, and she had been dragged home in tears and disgrace.

'And that was certainly no place for a girl of your age to be,' said Anne gently. 'Of course your aunt and uncle were angry, I should have been so myself! Lord Delamere had no business to take you there, no business at all.'

'Well, he didn't know my age, exactly,' admitted Arabella. 'I mean, I didn't lie to him, but he thought I was the same age as Eliza, and somehow I never told him any different. . . After all, I *feel* the same age!'

'That is hardly the point. At this precise moment, I feel about fifty, but it doesn't mean I should be treated as though I were.'

Arabella wept again, and railed against the cruelty of her treatment. It did seem that she had been harshly dealt with, thought Anne, and though the child had been disobedient and wilful she did not believe that she had been as wicked as the Littletons seemed to think. They, it seemed, had called her a harlot, and kept her locked in her room until she left the house, as though she were a contaminating presence.

'Well, it is all over and done with now,' said Anne soothingly. 'Perhaps it is all for the best. Certainly James and I are very happy to have you at home with us again, and so will Harry be, when he comes home. Why, he hardly remembers you!'

'Yes, but what am I going to do?' Arabella wailed. 'I was to have made my come-out next year, if Eliza had got herself married. I should have had ballgowns, and a court dress with feathers, and everything! How can I do that now?'

James frowned a little at that, but Anne silenced him with a look.

'Well, I'm afraid we don't live quite in the

London fashion,' she said cheerfully, 'but we are
by no means without amusements, you know! The
Sudburys are kind friends to us—you remember
Sir Robert, who is James's benefactor?—and I
expect there will be parties this winter, and maybe
even a dance or two that you can attend. With all
your lovely gowns, you will be quite the belle of
the village, you know!'

Arabella, who had seemed less than thrilled by
the offered treats, brightened a little at this prospect. It was wrong, of course, to play on her
vanity, Anne knew, but for the moment it seemed
only kind to give the child something to look
forward to, at least.

By five o'clock Arabella was yawning widely.
They dined at six, but when Anne suggested an
early night, with a light meal in bed, her sister
seemed happy to accept. Anne took her up,
helped her to bed, and sat with her while she ate
a bowl of soup and some poached chicken. She
stayed until Arabella, curled up in the warmed
bed, was almost asleep, then made her way downstairs again. It was already half-past six, and James
would be waiting for her: there was not time to
change her dress; she must dine in her afternoon
gown. Since there would be only the two of them
it scarcely seemed important.

By a strong effort of will she had kept back the
fierce criticisms that were boiling in her mind, and
spoken no more than soothing nothings to her
sister. It seemed to her that the Littletons had
been much at fault. From what she had seen since

Arabella had arrived, the child had been spoiled
and over-indulged, her vanity fed by praises and
pretty clothes, her ideas allowed to be formed by
undirected reading and daydreams. And when, as
a result, she had acted so unwisely, she had been
summarily ejected from the family circle.

His lordship, too, had a great deal to answer
for. To encourage a young girl who, as he must
have known, was not even out of the schoolroom,
and to allow her to behave with such unbecoming
lack of decorum, was more than bad, it was
actively wicked. Anne's blood was almost boiling
in her veins as she ran downstairs, and opened the
door of the sitting-room.

Her brother was there, as she had expected, but
he was not alone. A tall, dark man, clad in
buckskins and a riding coat of impeccable cut,
with topboots that shone like mirrors, was standing before the fire. Anne looked at him in exasperation; of all times to have an unexpected visitor,
when she was longing to discuss the whole thing
with James! She glared at the stranger.

'Good evening,' she said with chilly civility. She
wished, not for the first time, that she were not
such a little dab of a thing, but could sweep
majestically into the room with queenly gait. The
man bowed, a graceful inclination. He did not
smile, and in the glow of evening light his strongly
boned face was disconcertingly handsome.

'Anne, my dear,' said James, 'this is Lord
Delamere. Lord Delamere, my sister Anne.'

His lordship bowed again.

'Your servant, Miss Winterborne.' His voice was deep, with a careless beauty that matched his person. Anne glared at him, her hazel eyes snapping.

'Well!' she said, not acknowledging his greeting. 'How you dare to show your face in this house, after what has happened! I have to say, my lord, that you are not welcome here!'

He raised a dark eyebrow sardonically.

'Anne, my dear. . .' James intervened.

'No, James. I'm sorry, I know it is not a Christian attitude, but I cannot forgive Lord Delamere for the way that he has behaved. A sister's life, perhaps ruined forever, certainly made miserable, and for what? So that his lordship might enjoy an evening's pleasure. No, it is not to be borne. You will kindly leave, and at once.'

'Certainly I will,' he spoke lazily. 'I came merely to ascertain that Miss Arabella had arrived safely. Feeling, as you might say, a certain sense of responsibility.'

'A certain sense of. . . As well you might, my lord. Though perhaps a trifle late in the day! Well, she is safe here with her family, as you may see, so you may stop worrying yourself sick, as I can see you have been.'

'Not at all,' he corrected her. 'Merely a momentary twinge of anxiety, no more. Well, I see that she is amply protected, if only by a diminutive dragon. I will wish you a good evening, Rector. And Miss Winterborne.'

He bowed again. Anne, frozen with fury in the

doorway, found herself put firmly to one side. Close to he was even larger than she had realised — her eyes were on a level with the middle button of that horridly well-made coat. She opened her mouth to speak again, but he was gone.

CHAPTER TWO

'You mean to say that he was here, and you sent him away? Oh, Anne, how could you?'

Arabella sat up in bed, looking enchantingly pretty with her dark curls tousled beneath her lacy nightcap. Her nightgown, too, was a miracle of pin tucks and more lace, and Anne tried not to be envious. It would be dreafully fiddling to launder and iron, she thought, and the laundry woman would almost certainly charge extra for it. That, however, was a minor worry compared with the nightgown's owner.

'Sent him away? I should think I did, and with a piece of my mind into the bargain. When I think of the harm he has done you, the unhappiness he has caused. . .'

She was cut short by Arabella's wail.

'But Anne, you don't understand!' The cry of every young person down the ages, Anne thought sadly. In fact, she understood only too well. A sober twenty-five she might be, an old maid long past her last prayers in Arabella's seventeen-year-old eyes, but she was far from forgetting the violent passions that could raise tempests in a young girl's heart. A man like Delamere, with all the advantages of wealth, position, age, and above all extraordinarily handsome, was made to be

26

hero-worshipped. And when one added the fact that he had never, as yet, shown a decided partiality for any female, his attentions would have been enough to turn the head of any sheltered schoolgirl.

Devil take the man! she thought. What could he have been thinking of, to follow her to Dorset in such a fashion? The best thing for Arabella would be to forget him as quickly as possible, to let him recede to that little secret corner of her heart where grown women stored the pressed-flower memories of their early loves. Anne wished it had been possible to keep his visit a secret, but she knew from past experience that there was no hope of persuading James to join with her in even the mildest kind of subterfuge. He was consitutionally incapable of making any kind of pretence, and would have been certain to give the game away at once.

Arabella was crying again, great glistening tears pouring from her lovely blue eyes. Anne noticed, a little enviously, that she still looked lovely, and that though her nose was a little pink her eyes were clear as jewels within the slightly swollen lids. Anne, whose eyes became red and bloodshot whenever she cried, felt that at times the Creator was a little unfair in the distribution of His gifts. She went to the bed and perched on the edge of it. Arabella turned away from her, and buried her face in the pillow.

'My dear, I do understand, you know, though you think I don't! It can do you nothing but harm,

at present, to have anything to do with Lord
Delamere. You must remember that as a girl not
yet out your reputation is all-important. As it is,
your sudden departure from the place which has
been your home for so many years is enough to
set tongues wagging. I only hope that Mr and Mrs
Littleton will not be so cruel as to allow any
rumours about you to spread. So far as the world
is concerned, we must put it about that you had
been a little unwell, and have come to see if
country air may not set you up again.'

'Nobody will believe that,' said Arabella
crossly. 'I am never ill.'

'Well, you will be if you continue to cry like
this. That will do nothing for your looks, though
just at present perhaps that is a good thing.'

Arabella stopped crying abruptly, and turned
back to Anne.

'A good thing, when Delamere might still be
here in the village! How can you say such a thing?'

'Very easily. I hope you will not need to see
him again.'

'Not see him? But he followed me down here!
That must mean. . .surely that must mean that he
loves me?'

'Has he ever told you so?'

A mixture of chagrin and pride passed over the
frowning face.

'No,' she admitted reluctantly. 'But I am sure
that he does. He paid me so many pretty compliments, you know! And he preferred me to Eliza,
I know he did.'

'That does not mean that he loved you.'

'Well, and that's where you're wrong. He had been going to propose to her, I know that for a fact. Of course, it was not precisely that he loved her. But his grandmother is an old friend of Eliza's grandmother, and they agreed the matter between them.'

'How very gothic. And he agreed?'

'I think so. I know I heard old Mrs Littleton talking to Uncle John about it, and saying what a suitable match it was and how it was time he settled down. But then he saw me, and at once he knew that it could never be! All of a sudden, like a. . .like a. . .'

'A hiccup?'

Arabella pouted.

'No! A thunder clap, though I was going to say it in French. I've forgotten the word.'

'*Coup de foudre.*' Anne spoke absently. So James had been right, and this was indeed the cause of all the anger. If Elizabeth had in truth been on the verge of receiving so very flattering an offer, it was scarcely to be wondered at that her parents should be furious at the cause of its loss. Whether a man such as the gentleman she had seen so briefly the previous evening would really have married a girl simply because his grandmother suggested it, of course, was another matter. But since the Littletons had believed that he would, they must indeed be disappointed that the matrimonial prize should slip through their fingers.

It was also, of course, possible that his lordship might be serious in his pursuit of her sister. The child was beautiful enough to catch any man's eye. It was just as likely, however, that he was merely amusing himself with her. Anne's lip curled as she thought disparagingly of the kind of man who could thus spoil a young girl's future simply for his own entertainment. Well, she had shown him that Arabella was not without those who would protect her from him. Doubtless he would be long gone, back to London to look for easier prey.

The first thing, in any case, was to pacify her sister.

'Well, it's a pretty little muddle, and no mistake. But you can be very sure, my dear, that if he does truly love you then he will not allow anything to prevent him from seeing you again. You are very young, of course, but if you should both be of the same mind in, say, a year's time I am sure that James will not stand in the way of your happiness.'

'A year!' Arabella was horrified. 'But that's. . . that's impossible! A whole year! Nobody could wait that long!'

'They can, and they do, believe me. For the moment, however, we must think only of you. I am afraid that a little pretence is necessary — even James agrees with me about that. The story that you have come down here for the sake of your health is what we must promote. That means, of course, that for a few days at least you must stay indoors. It is boring for you, I know, but quite essential. James has already written to your aunt and uncle, asking them to perform at least this small service for you. Since they can hardly wish to see their daughter spoken of as one who has been slighted by his lordship, it is in their interest to agree.'

Arabella hunched her shoulders.

'I don't care. I might just as well, if you will not let me see him. In fact, I might as well stay in bed.'

'No need for that.' Anne spoke bracingly. 'If you were that ill, they would hardly have sent you on so long a journey, after all! No, you are just a little tired with the vicarious excitement of your cousin's come-out, and in need of country air and quiet. A few days on the sitting-room sofa and you may be allowed to recover, I think. Come now, will you get up? The morning is already half gone, and Henry is so looking forward to greeting you when you come downstairs.'

Arabella put reluctant feet out from under the bedclothes.

'It is very cold in here,' she complained. 'Why is the fire not lit?'

'In general I try not to light the bedroom fires too early in the year — it is only the beginning of October, after all. If you need one, though, of course you shall have one.'

'No, it's all right.' Arabella spoke in martyred tones. 'Where are all my clothes?'

'I unpacked your boxes last night, after you were asleep. Everything is put away, in the drawers of the tallboy and in the cupboards. What do you want to put on this morning? You have some lovely gowns; you will put us all in the shade.'

If Anne had hoped to be thanked for her care, she was to be disappointed. Even the flattery did no more than raise an irritated twitch of Arabella's shoulders.

'Why do you not ring for the maid? I shall freeze to death standing here like this.'

'The maids are busy at this time of day. There is hot water in the jug on the wash stand.'

'But how am I to dress? At home in London, Eliza and I have our own maid to help us. I cannot dress myself.'

'Then I shall have to help you,' said Anne cheerfully, repressing the urge to remark that a girl of seventeen who could not dress unaided was scarcely old enough to embark on matrimony, and undertake the running of a great house in Sussex. She helped her sister to wash and dress, picking out the simplest of the many morning gowns and draping a shawl of Norwich silk over it. Arabella sat before the looking-glass while Anne brushed her dark, curling hair, and arranged it in a stylish knot so that a few curls hung gracefully against the pink and white cheeks.

'There, now, you look very pretty,' said Anne. 'How fortunate you are to have curling hair, and no need of uncomfortable curl papers! Shall we go downstairs?'

Arabella was soon installed on the sofa in the sitting-room. Hearing the bustle of her descent, James allowed Henry to leave his lesson books and greet his sister. Henry, who scarcely remembered her, was impressed by Arabella's fashionable appearance and pretty face, and said so. Charles, who had followed his friend, simply gazed in wide-eyed admiration. Anne was relieved to see that the admiration of the two boys was balm to Arabella's sore heart.

'You will stay and keep me company, won't you, Henry? And Charles too, of course. They may, mayn't they, James? My own brother, after all, and I scarcely know him!' Arabella begged prettily, and James was quick to give his agreement.

'Just for this morning, mind. And tomorrow I shall expect great things from you, and perfection in those irregular verbs, if you please!'

Anne judged that the 'invalid' would do better without her inhibiting presence, and withdrew. She felt tired after a sleepless night spent worrying about her sister, and thought that she would have liked nothing better than to be tucked up, also, on a comfortable sofa. However, the house would not run itself, and it was already obvious that Arabella's presence was going to make a deal of extra work for the servants. Anne went down to the kitchen, prepared to spend half an hour in cajoling, persuading and pacifying.

That done, she put on bonnet and pelisse, and sallied forth into the village. A practical girl, she was by no means too proud to do her own marketing when necessary, and she intended to give her weekly order at the little grocer's shop, and inform the butcher in no uncertain terms that the piece of beef she had set before the rector two days earlier had been decidedly underhung, and tough as an old boot.

Minterne Abbas was quite large, as country villages went, boasting a fine old church, a pretty high street with a stream running down one side of it, and the ruined remains of an old abbey that gave the village its name. The rectory was a commodious house, built during the last century and set in its own three acres of walled garden. Anne walked down the gravelled drive to where the wide gateway gave on to one end of the main street. It was a relief to be out in the fresh clean air of a bright October day, to leave the house and its problems behind her for a moment. Anne stepped briskly out, a small basket on one arm and her mind full of housewifely cares. The drive was shaded by trees and shrubs, and she paused in the gateway, dazzled for a moment by the sunshine as she left their shelter. The large man, leaning nonchalantly against the gatepost, loomed huge and shadowy as he stood upright and stepped towards her, and she recoiled instinctively.

Then his hat was off, and he bowed. At once she knew him. His size alone should have been enough, she thought, without that unwillingly remembered graceful inclination. She tightened her lips, and put her chin in the air. He was directly in front of her, looking as wide as a barn and about as immovable. She ignored him and continued to walk forward, assuming that he must move out of her way.

She was mistaken. She was forced to come to a halt before she cannoned into him. Swiftly she thought. She could swerve round him, of course, but she knew with horrid certainty that he would either move into her path again, or—worse still, and not to be contemplated—would put out one powerful arm, and seize her as she passed. So she stood still, and waited.

There was a short, charged silence. Anne knew only too well that however empty the village street might appear there would in reality be several pairs of eyes trained upon them. She took a step to the right, and at once he stepped in the same direction.

'You are impeding my progress,' she said in a soft, furious voice. 'Kindly move out of my path.'

'No,' he said.

Startled, she raised her eyes to his face. It was a long way, and she was forced to tilt her head back to do so. His grey eyes smiled lazily down at her.

'How fortunate that your bonnet is so out of fashion,' he remarked conversationally. 'If it had not been, you must have made yourself quite uncomfortable in order to look up at me.'

Anne seethed. It was very true, as she was all too well aware, that her bonnet was several years old, and that its shallow brim was far removed from the high-crowned, wide-spreading shape of the fashionable headgear that her sister had

arrived in yesterday. That this should be a matter
for congratulation, however, was intolerable.

'The fashion of my bonnet is nothing to do with
you, my lord,' she said icily.

'No, of course not. Though as a matter of fact it
becomes you very well. A little battered, of
course. The brim is a trifle bent, did you know?'
Before she could move, he reached out large
hands and straightened it, bending the soft straw
carefully. 'There, that's better. Now you look
much more the thing. Quite pretty, in fact, in a
shrewish sort of way.'

'How dare you?' She was quivering with rage.
'I could. . . Oh, I could kill you!'

'Oh, I don't think you could. Not unless you
have a weapon hidden in that basket of yours.
Perhaps I'd better take it from you, just to be on
the safe side. Only polite, in any case. A gentleman always carries a lady's parcels, or her basket,'
he informed her kindly.

'A gentleman! You're no gentleman. Give me
back my basket this instant, or I shall call for
assistance.'

'Really? That would give the villagers a nice
morning's entertainment, wouldn't it? Even better
than the spectacle of us playing tug of war with
the basket. Come now, Miss Winterborne. You
have no one but yourself to blame, you know.'

'To blame for what? You are punishing me, I
suppose, for daring to criticise you yesterday.
Well, you have done so. I hope you are satisfied.'

'Punishing you? My dear young woman, nothing

could be further from the truth. I meant only that you told me that I was not welcome beneath your roof. That being the case, I could not go against your express wishes by calling on you and your brother this morning, so I was forced to wait for you at the gate.'

'And how long have you been standing there?' Anne was horrified.

'Oh, not above two hours. But do not worry, I am not in the least tired. I am very strong, you know, and the gatepost is quite comfortable to lean against. I could have sat on the gate, I suppose, but I am rather heavy, and I didn't know whether it was up to my weight. Besides, a little undignified, don't you think, at my age?'

'Standing at the gate for two hours? I must indeed have offended you more than I thought, and I am glad of it. Now you have had your revenge, by making us conspicuous like that. I do not care for my own sake, but you might have respected my brother's position, at least. He, after all, has done nothing to deserve such treatment.'

He sighed. 'I am sorry that you should speak so bitterly. If I have done wrong to tease you, I beg your pardon. Will you now forgive me?'

'It is not for me to forgive, but my brother, and my sister. Is your apology for them also?'

'For everyone, if you wish it. I apologise unreservedly. I apologise to your cook, your church-wardens, your housemaid, your gardener, your kitchen maid, your relatives, your friends, your. . .'

With a little sob of rage she whirled around, and walked back through the gateway. She heard his heavy footsteps coming after her, and walked faster, willing herself not to break into a run. It felt like a nightmare: her petticoats and skirts twisted round her legs and impeded her, and she felt as though she was wading through deep mud, or sand. He was in front of her now, standing in the middle of the drive.

'Miss Winterborne.' His voice had changed. It was no longer hard and sarcastic, but low and resonant with true apology. 'I am sorry, that was intolerable. It is true that you made me angry yesterday, but you did not deserve to be treated like this. Forgive me.'

Her anger melted like ice in the sun. She strove to keep it alive, but the kindness in his voice disarmed her.

'I forgive you, of course. Now, will you let me pass?'

'If you wish. And here is your basket.' He held it out, and her hand trembled a little with the aftermath of emotion as she reached for it. Her eyes were blurred with tears. As she took the basket from him he put a gentle finger beneath her chin, and lifted her face. She looked straight forward, knowing that if she were to blink the tears would brim over her eyelids and run down her cheeks. Her eyes ached from the strain, but he was not deceived. He took out a linen handkerchief, and, with her chin still held by the strong fingers of one hand, wiped her eyes with its clean folds as if she had been a child. Then, in the most natural way possible, he leaned over and kissed her gently. It was done before she could move out of his grasp, and though she felt the quick colour flooding her face she thought it best to ignore what had happened. No good could be achieved by a hysterical show of prudery, she thought.

'There now,' he said. 'Dragons must not cry, you know.'

'Or shrews?' she said tremulously.

'Or shrews. But you are not a shrew, little Miss Winterborne. A mouse, perhaps. A brave little mouse, protecting her nest from a marauding cat. But I am not marauding, Miss Mouse. I was afraid that Miss Arabella had been — shall we say? — somewhat harshly treated by her uncle and aunt. I wanted to be sure that she had reached her home in safety. She is, if you will pardon me, somewhat headstrong, as you may have noticed.'

Anne sighed.

'I have noticed it. And your presence, though doubtless kindly meant, will scarcely improve that. To be blunt, Lord Delamere, she fancies herself in love with you. That is no doubt flattering to your self-esteem, but I beg you to consider what harm you might do to her by your presence in the village. She is only seventeen, after all, and has been very much indulged, I am sorry to say.'

He was silent for a moment.

'What do you want me to do?' he asked as last.

'Go back to London, leave us in peace.'

Even as she spoke, a pang went through her.

He was arrogant, teasing, almost the epitome of what she did not like in a man, but the thought of never seeing him again was unbearable.

'If you insist. But I think that you are wrong.'

'Wrong? How wrong?'

'To send me away. I have a certain amount of experience with the ways of young girls. Rather more than you, perhaps.'

'I do not doubt it. But do not forget that I, too, was once a young girl.'

He laughed, an open, cheerful sound.

'You still are, my dear Miss Mouse! And, as such, the worst possible judge! Do you not know that absence makes the heart grow fonder? If you want your sister to fall out of love with me, the best thing you can do is to implore me to stay in Dorset for several months! She would soon learn that I am by no means the romantic hero that she thinks me!'

'I do not doubt that,' Anne snapped. 'Nevertheless, I have no intention of imploring you to stay. Or of imploring you to do anything, come to that.'

'But you do not forbid me to stay?'

'Would it make any difference if I did?' Anne felt suddenly exhausted, as if she had run a long race.

'Honesty compels me to admit that it would not. I shall leave you now to do your shopping, but I am afraid this is not the last that you will see of me, Miss Winterborne.'

He bowed, turned, and strode away. Anne stood gazing after him. She felt as though she had been lifted up and twisted round in a whirlwind. Words and ideas spun about in her head, refusing to settle into any kind of coherent pattern. He was, without doubt, the most infuriating man she had ever met. And the most attractive. She wished she knew what he was about. Undoubtedly, he was intending to stay in the area. Perhaps, after all, he really was in love with Arabella. There was nothing very unlikely in that. Anne wished that she could return to the house, take refuge in her bedroom, and spend the rest of the day puzzling over the things he had said. That, however, was no more than an idle dream. She and her family had provided the village with quite enough gossip for one day, and now she must try to undo some of the damage.

With the basket once more firmly on her arm, she set out back to the village. She had no doubt whatever that she would meet, as if by chance, with almost every able-bodied inhabitant who was not out working in the fields, and so it proved. She parried enquiries, both direct and subtle, with the ease of long practice. Yes, her sister was home, a little tired from London life. Lord Delamere? An old friend of Miss Arabella's uncle. A fatherly interest, as one might say. Yes, most kind of him. A stay in the country? She really could not say, she scarcely knew the gentleman. By the time she reached the rectory again it was time for luncheon, and she felt as if she had been in the ring and done ten rounds with Jackson, or Cribb.

Her silence at luncheon went largely unremarked, since Arabella talked enough for two. With Henry and Charles as an eager audience, she recounted the glories of Mayfair, and the delights of the London season. If her youthful auditors cared little for the intricate rules of Almack's, or for the latest play or opera, they were more than happy to drink in the famous names of those she had — so she said — known so well. Certainly she was perfectly *au fait* with all the society gossip, and if some of the tales she recounted made James frown Anne was too thankful to see her sister cheerful to remonstrate with her.

After the meal the boys were sent, protesting volubly, back to their books, and Arabella, with the same amount of complaint, was told to go upstairs and lie down on her bed.

'I know you have not really been ill, but you had a tiring journey yesterday, and it will do you no harm. I do not ask that you sleep; you may read, if you wish, or sew. Just so long as you stay in your room. If anyone should call, I want to be able honestly to say that you are lying down on your bed.'

'But if anyone should call, I want to be there! Supposing Delamere should come?'

'Highly unlikely, but if he does I promise to send for you at once. Will that content you?'

'I suppose it must. But I have nothing to read!'

Anne pointed silently to the shelves full of books that covered almost every available wall in the downstairs rooms. James's only extravagance was books, and she herself had been guilty on more than one occasion of buying a new novel, or a book of poems, when she would have done better to invest in some new silk stockings, or a more fashionable bonnet. Arabella wrinkled her nose, and pronounced the books 'fusty stuff'. When Anne assured her that *The Castle of Otranto* and its like were not to be found within the walls of the rectory she stared, and could not believe it. At last Anne persuaded her to take *Pride and Prejudice*, which favourite of hers she hoped would beguile her flighty sister for a few hours, and even impart a few useful ideas.

Down in the sitting-room Anne took out her sewing again, and was forcibly reminded of how she had sat with it the previous day. How different everything seemed now! If only. . . She abandoned this train of thought, and resolutely set herself to hemming a seam.

Half an hour later, Lady Sudbury was announced.

'My dearest Anne! You will forgive the intrusion, I hope, and grant me leave to show a little vulgar curiosity? I could not stay away, I am afraid.'

'I am very glad that you did not,' said Anne, rising to greet her friend with a kiss. 'You cannot know how glad I am to see you, or how much I am in need of your advice.'

Mary, Lady Sudbury, was Anne's particular friend. Though five years older than Anne, she was still very youthful in her interests and ideas, in spite of her happy marriage to a man considerably older than herself. Her only foible, and a very pardonable one, was her anxiety over Charles, her only child, whose childhood illnesses had several times threatened to carry him off. Though he had in fact outgrown his weakness she was still inclined to think of him as delicate, and Anne often thought how fortunate it was that the sweetness of his nature had prevented him from turning into the spoiled mother's pet he could so easily have become.

Now she was happy to tell her friend the whole story of her sister's return, secure in the knowledge that her confidences would go no further. Her description of Lord Delamere was limited to a few condemning phrases. Nor was she particularly forthcoming about her well observed meeting with him earlier that morning, a meeting about which Lady Sudbury was already well informed, village life being what it was. Apart from that she spared her hearer nothing, and she derived much comfort from the telling.

'Forgive me for burdening you with my tale of woe,' she said at the end. 'I feel I cannot worry James with it. He is so very good that any flaw in the behaviour of others makes him quite dreadfully unhappy, and I do not want him to be upset! But Arabella, I am afraid, is going to be a problem, and I confess I am at a loss to know what to do with her!'

'My dear Anne, I can understand it only too well. They are much at fault, as you do not say but I know you think, and both Arabella and the rest of you have been badly treated.'

'She is not accustomed to our quiet kind of life,' said Anne sadly. 'She will be bored, and miserable, and where will that lead? To no good, I am afraid.'

'Well, we must try to see that she does not get too bored,' said Mary Sudbury robustly. 'I have been thinking for some time that we are by far too rustic in our ways. Nothing but tabbies and tea parties! We must make a little stir. After all, Charles is growing up, as you never cease to tell me. It is time that I increased our circle of friends, enlarged our horizons. We shall have — what? A party? Yes, certainly that. And perhaps a dance. Why not? I am sure we can find at least twelve couples, probably more, and only think how the young people will bless us! And when there is one party, you know, another always follows. I have often observed it. They are contagious, you know, like the measles.'

'Oh, Mary!' Anne could not help laughing at her friend's flow of high spirits. 'Charles is far too young for dancing just yet! And you should not be going to so much trouble just for Arabella.'

'Nonsense, I am doing it for myself. I am not yet so old that I cannot enjoy a waltz with the best of them. Besides, you have not yet heard my own news. What do you think? The manor is let, at last!'

'The manor? To whom?' Minterne Manor, about three miles outside the village, was the other

great house in the area, and had been standing
empty for more than two years, to the great
impoverishment of local society.

'To a gentleman!' Lady Sudbury paused impres-
sively. 'A *single* gentleman,' she added in triumph.
She looked speculatively at her younger friend,
her head on one side like a bird.

'I know what you're thinking,' said Anne austerely, 'but you can put any such idea out of your
head at once. Matrimony holds no charms for me,
I can assure you.' She was quite sure that she
meant it.

CHAPTER THREE

GREATLY to Anne's relief, the rest of the week passed comparatively easily. As a new arrival in the village, Arabella was naturally of the greatest interest to everyone. Lady Sudbury, who stayed to meet and talk with her on Tuesday, was quick to spread word of her charm and beauty, and the rest of what passed for high society in Minterne Abbas and its environs was not slow to follow where she led. Morning callers arrived almost in crowds, and every afternoon Arabella was to be found holding court on her sofa, the centre of a lively group of young and not so young.

A certain Miss Dewlish, daughter of a local lawyer, found herself ousted from the position of the local beauty. Things could have been awkward, but by the greatest good fortune she was blessed with silvery blonde hair. Anne dropped a few airy remarks about how well each set off the other's looks, and after a thoughtful pause Arabella set herself to make a friend of her rival. Several hours spent in the delightful activity of trying on all the fashionable clothes that Arabella had brought from London, and the judicious gift of two gowns that did little for Arabella's dusky beauty, but set off Celia's golden hair to perfection, cemented the friendship.

By the end of the week, the little household had begun to settle down into its new routine. Arabella had been wide-eyed with astonishment when she had learned how few servants were kept, and that her sister did not even have a maid of her own and was, moreover, not above lending a hand in the kitchen from time to time, as well as doing much of the household mending. Her own needlework was confined to delicate pieces of embroidery, and the nearest she came to making anything useful was in decorating a flounce for a dress.

'Are we so very poor, then?' she had enquired childishly, eyeing the tablecloth that Anne was darning with tiny, neat stitches. She looked around her, as though expecting the bailiffs to come in at any moment and carry away the furniture. Anne laughed.

'By no means! We are not rich, of course, but we are able to command the comforts of life, if not all its elegancies. It is my nature, I am afraid, to be of a saving disposition, and I cannot abide waste. James believes that the rectory should set an example in this, for otherwise how can I visit the homes of poorer people and exhort them to thrift and industry? There is, besides, the matter of Henry's schooling. We hope very much that he will go to Harrow when Charles does. They are such good friends, and nothing is more important for a boy in his position than a good education.'

Arabella looked solemn.

'I shall still have my allowance from Uncle John. He told me that he did not think it right to deprive

me of it. Do. . .do you want me to give it to you?
I have plenty of new gowns, for the moment at
least.'

Anne kissed her sister, pleased with this evidence of the good heart that evidently beat
beneath the flighty exterior.

'There is no need for such a sacrifice! By all
means save it up, if you do not need any clothes.
Who knows? In a year or so we may contrive some
kind of come-out for you — not as grand as you
might have had in London, perhaps, but still
something.'

'Or for my bride clothes?'

'Your bride clothes? Well, yes, for that also, if
necessary.'

Anne saw that her sister had by no means
forgotten Lord Delamere. Indeed, his name was
constantly on her lips, and Anne was heartily sick
of the sound of it. Nothing more had been seen of
his lordship in the village, however, and she
hoped — she was quite sure that she hoped — that
he had returned to London.

On Saturday afternoon, Anne and Arabella
were sitting together towards the end of the afternoon, alone for once since the weather had settled
into heavy, blustery rain that kept any possible
callers indoors. The sound of the front door, and
of a manly voice in the hall, made them look at
one another in surmise.

'It is him!' said Arabella ungrammatically. She
jumped to her feet and ran to the looking-glass
over the mantelpiece, anxious fingers tweaking at

her hair, biting her lips to redden them. Anne frowned.

'It doesn't sound like his voice. . .' Fortunately Arabella was too preoccupied with her appearance to question her sister's familiarity with Delamere's voice. The door opened and she whirled round, her mouth opening in an O of astonishment and disappointment. Anne, however, jumped up and ran to the newcomer.

'William! Oh, my dear, what a delight to see you!'

He bent to kiss her.

'Hello, Nan. My word, I do believe you're shrinking.'

She laughed at his familiar teasing.

'And you could not possibly have grown some more, could you? But you have not greeted Arabella.'

'My little sister! And so very grand, I hardly dare speak to you!'

Such speeches were just what Arabella liked. She held out her hands.

'My big brother William! I declare you are very fine yourself; I should not have known you. Is this really the old Will, who pulled my hair, and hid my doll at the top of a tree? I tore my pinafore to ribbons, I remember, trying to get her down again!'

'Shame on you, to remember only my sins. I am sure I must have been kind to you some of the time. And are you well again? I heard that you had been ill.'

'Oh, yes, I am very well. Did you come all the way from Cambridge because of that? How very kind of you.'

He accepted her praises with becoming humility, but Anne, who knew him rather better, eyed him sharply.

'Oh, William! You knew very well that Arabella's indisposition was only slight, for I saw James's letter to you.'

'Yes, but. . .my own sister, after all! I did not want to miss the chance of seeing her. . .'

'William, have you been rusticated?'

He grinned ruefully at her.

'Well, only slightly. I mean, just for a few weeks. . .'

She sighed.

'Oh, dear, James will be so disappointed. What was it this time? Or is it not fit to sully our maidenly ears?'

'Now, Nan, as if I would! No, it was nothing so dreadful, just high spirits, you know. There were some travelling entertainers, you see, and there was a monkey. . .'

'Yes, I see. Nothing could be more natural, of course.'

'It was quite a small monkey. . .'

She could not help laughing.

'You are incorrigible! Oh, well, since you are home we must make the best of it. You had better make your peace with James, and then go and change out of these wet clothes before you catch cold.'

Sitting in the rectory pew the following morning, Anne allowed her eyes to rest with satisfied pleasure on the united presence of her family. They were, she thought, an attractive sight as they sat in a row waiting for James to enter and begin the service. Beside her Henry, scrubbed to angelic cleanliness, wriggled in the stiff discomfort of his Sunday suit. Beyond him was Arabella, equally angelic in her blue velvet pelisse and bonnet. Her lovely eyes were raised to the monument on the wall above her head, and her face bore an expression of piety that probably meant she was planning the trimmings for a new bonnet. At her far side William, slightly chastened by James's sorrow at his indiscretion, was staring straight before him, since the height of his collar precluded any movement of his head. The folds of his snowy cravat had cost him much anguish, but his reward had been Arabella's admiration of his careful Osbaldeston.

In all three of them Anne could see traces of their mother's dark beauty. She thought sadly that even Henry was already nearly as tall as she was, and soon she would be dwarfed by all of them. She tried not to envy their good looks, but it was sometimes hard to be so little that even her twelve-year-old brother could pick her up with ease.

She heard a little mutter of voices, and the bustle of an arrival. Arabella was uninhibitedly craning forward to look, and from the corner of her eye Anne was aware that one of the church-wardens was leading some people into the pew opposite. Arabella's face was vivid with excitement; it was impossible not to look. She turned her head and gave a swift glance.

The tall figure of Lord Delamere was instantly recognisable, though he was turned away from her and was politely handing a young woman through the open door of the pew. Beside him was another man, looking small by comparison but probably of more than average height. The pair of them were correctly and impeccably dressed in sombre Sunday attire, and the young woman with them wore a pelisse of Levantine twill in sage-green, cut in the military fashion and decorated with darker green braid. The few curls that were to be seen within the brim of her silk-lined bonnet were glowing auburn. Anne, seeing the look on her sister's face, concluded with a sinking heart that here must be another candidate for his lordship's fickle affections.

The entry of James and the start of the service recalled all eyes to the front of the church, and it was not until the last prayers were over and the last hymn had been sung that Anne was again able to glance towards the opposite pew. Though her eyes had remained steadfastly forward, she had been aware of a strong tenor voice joining her own contralto as she sang, and it had taken every ounce of her will-power not to look across the aisle and see which of the gentlemen was singing so tunefully. Now she turned her head, and was instantly aware of Lord Delamere, who at once smiled and bowed. She accorded him a modest inclination of her head, and wished she might chivvy her family out through the vestry. A glint of laughter in his dark eyes told her that he was aware of the thought.

As she stepped out of the pew, they were face to face. Or rather, since she was so diminutive, face to chest. She fixed her eyes on the plain silver buttons of his striped silk waistcoat, revealed within the open front of his dark blue coat. Once again it was impossible to get past him: his large figure blocked the aisle.

'I do hope my waistcoat meets with your approval, Miss Winterborne,' he murmured. 'I feared it was perhaps a little brash. What do you think?'

'I know nothing of such matters,' she snapped back. 'Fashion, as you have already pointed out to me, is not my strong suit.'

'Then I had best consult your sister. Good morning, Miss Arabella! I am glad to see you so well recovered! You are in fine looks, I see!'

Arabella blushed prettily, smiled, and dis-claimed. Gracefully she introduced her two brothers, while Anne stood by, gritting her teeth on her annoyance. After a few minutes, Delamere turned back to her.

'May I beg leave to present my friends to you, Miss Winterborne? Miss Lydford, and her brother, Thomas Lydford. Emily, Thomas, this is Miss Winterborne, Miss Arabella Winterborne, Mr William Winterborne, and young mas-ter Henry.'

It was impossible, without discourtesy, to refuse the introduction. Anne smiled, shook hands, and saw that Miss Lydford was just as pretty as she had thought she might be, and probably not a great deal older than Arabella. Her brother was pleasant-faced, older than she though looking younger then his friend, and seemed an amiable man. Anne found herself walking out of the church with him, resigned to hearing Arabella's voice chattering vivaciously to Lord Delamere, while William talked with shy admiration to Miss Lydford.

'You are staying in the neighbourhood, Mr Lydford?' she asked.

'Indeed, we are to be neighbours, if such a word may be applied to a distance of two miles,' he smiled at her.

'Oh, I had not thought! Is it you who have taken Minterne Manor, then?'

'Yes. My sister and I being alone in the world, we have been looking for a place in the country where we might settle. We are so delighted with the manor, and today is our first opportunity to meet our new neighbours. Sir Robert Sudbury was kind enough to visit us the day before yesterday, and we hope soon to make many new acquaintances.'

Anne smiled, thinking of her friend Mary Sudbury's plans with regard to this gentleman. She peeped up at him again. Yes, certainly a pleasant, open face, though not one to cause any serious palpitations.

'I am sure my oldest brother, the rector, will call on you very shortly, and then perhaps we may look forward to seeing you and your sister at the rectory? We have a pleasant set in Minterne, though I am afraid you will think us sadly quiet and countrified.'

'Quiet and countrified is just what we prefer, Miss Winterborne. And may I hope that my friend Delamere is included in your kind invitation? He has been so good as to accompany our move, and stay on to cheer our solitary existence in our new home.'

'Oh, of course,' said Anne hollowly. 'You are all most welcome.'

'Excellent,' said a deep voice in her ear. 'I knew you could not refuse my friend Lydford. Now, Thomas, I know you are aching to make the acquaintance of Miss Arabella, so I will escort Miss Winterborne home.'

'I am in no need of escorting,' she said crossly, as with a smiling word Thomas Lydford left her side. 'It is only a few steps to the rectory.'

'Ah, but I am bent on proving you wrong. When you said I was not a gentleman,' he explained kindly in answer to her enquiring look.

'Oh, dear, is *every* ill advised word I have ever spoken going to be thrown back in my face?' she said. 'Am I to be punished again?'

'Is it such a punishment to walk with me?'

'Yes, it is,' she snapped. 'For one thing, our relative sizes must make us appear quite ridiculous.'

'You should not be so sensitive about your appearance. I never am.'

'Or about anything else, I suppose. How did you contrive to drag your poor friends down to the manor, I wonder. You certainly moved very fast. Would it not have been easier simply to take the place yourself, for as long as it amuses you to plague us with your presence?'

'My dear girl, acquit me at least of such Machiavellian contrivances! I have by no means so much influence over Lydford, nor would I care to have! Believe it or not, it is the purest coincidence that they are here. I do not deny that it suits me admirably, having them to stay with, but they have been planning to come here for several weeks, I can assure you!'

'I beg your pardon,' she said stiffly. 'I allowed myself too much licence in my speech.'

'Do not guard your tongue on my account,' he begged her earnestly. 'It is one of the many pleasures of your company, my dear Miss Winterborne. You cannot imagine how refreshing it is to be with someone who says exactly what she thinks.'

'It is not a habit I normally indulge.'

'Do you not? I generally do. It saves time in the long run.'

'In your position, you may of course do as you please. But what is forgivable in Lord Delamere would be counted very ill bred in plain Miss Winterborne, the rector's sister.'

'Not plain, my dear. Several things, but not that.'

She lifted her head to frown up at him. They were at the door of the rectory.

'You will not get round me with flattery, my lord, particularly when it is so ill founded. Kind words butter no parsnips,' she quoted at him. He smiled lazily.

'But then, I do not care for parsnips, buttered or otherwise,' he said. 'And remember, little Miss Winterborne, I have just told you that I speak my mind.'

The arrival of the rest of the group made it impossible for her to answer, which was just as well since she could think of nothing to say. Farewells were spoken, and promises of visits exchanged. James arrived, and more introductions were made. By the time they were safely indoors and alone again, Anne could feel the beginning of a headache tightening her brow and throbbing behind her eyes. Arabella was in tearing spirits, seizing Henry's hands and performing an impromptu dance round the hall.

'Did I not say that he would come here to be near me? Now do you believe me, Anne?'

'He is simply here to accompany his friends,' said Anne weakly.

'Oh, pooh to that! If he wanted to stay in the country, he has many more friends than the Lydfords with whom he might stay! He would have gone north for the shooting, if he had cared to. What did he talk about? Did he mention me?'

'Not at all,' said Anne dampeningly.

'Well, there you are, then,' was the maddening reply. 'His love is too deep for words, I dare say.'

Henry groaned theatrically, and even William grimaced at this.

'A nice girl does not think of a gentleman being in love with her until he has declared himself,' said James gently. Arabella stared at him.

'Most girls never think of anything else,' she said candidly.

'But they do not speak of it,' said Anne firmly. 'Come and take off your bonnet. It is time for luncheon, and I don't care to keep the servants waiting on Sunday.'

It was generally agreed, during the next few days, that the new inhabitants of Minterne Manor were an excellent addition to the society of the village. Formal calls had been made and returned, and if the addition of another pretty girl did not please every young lady it was admitted that Miss Lydford was well mannered, if surprisingly shy in view of her startling colouring, and her wealth.

'She will have twenty thousand pounds, you know,' said Mary Sudbury to Anne. 'A very pretty little fortune. And I believe that Mr Lydford has no less than ten thousand a year. He really would do very well for you, my dear Anne.'

'He is hardly likely to notice me, with Arabella here,' said Anne.

'Nonsense, my dear! You should not so belittle yourself!' Anne burst out laughing, and her friend was forced to join her. 'Not the happiest of words, perhaps, but you know what I mean! You have many good qualities, dearest Anne, that your sister lacks.'

'That may be, but do gentlemen look for good qualities, when they may have beauty? I think not. Besides, I have told you before, I am perfectly happy here with James.'

'And if James should marry?'

Anne looked rather blankly at her.

'Then I should have to go, of course. Not that he would expect me to, but still. . . I could house-keep for William, I suppose, or Henry. . .'

Her friend said nothing, allowing this new picture of her future to sink into Anne's mind. She had thought, though she had not voiced her suspicions to anyone, that the rector's eyes strayed rather frequently to the glowing auburn head of Miss Lydford, when she was present. And Miss Lydford, who was undoubtedly very shy, seemed to enjoy his quiet company.

The days passed swiftly, and to Anne seemed filled with unusual activity. For Arabella, however, the simple pleasures of calls, little family dinners and country walks were beginning to pall. Much though she regretted the cause of it, Anne was deeply thankful for the presence of William. He, when his sister pouted and complained of their quiet life, was often able to laugh her out of her dismals. He took her on walks and visits, and even talked of hiring horses so that they might ride.

'I do not know how it is that you do not keep a

carriage, James,' Arabella frequently complained. 'Country living is quite intolerable without!'

'My dear, it is quite beyond my means,' said her brother candidly. His stables contained no more than an elderly cob, on which he rode to visit his more far-flung parishioners. 'I could hire the gig for you, if you wish,' he suggested kindly.

'That old thing? I would rather walk,' she answered him crossly, and Anne could have slapped her. She knew very well what was on Arabella's mind. Since Sunday, although the rector had ridden out to Minterne Manor and paid a formal call of welcome in his capacity as both priest and neighbour, it had been impossible for Arabella to go there. Of course, she had met with the Lydfords and Lord Delamere at Minterne Grange, the home of the Sudburys, and when they called at the rectory, but she was longing to visit the manor in style. Lord Delamere had been charming, of course, and full of compliments whenever they met, but he no longer seemed to single her out for special notice. Arabella felt sure that if she could be with him in a smaller group, with the chance of getting him to herself, she would be able to entrance him once more.

On Wednesday afternoon, she was visited by what seemed to her a wonderful plan. Rather against her will, because she could find nothing else to read, she had been continuing with the novel *Pride and Prejudice* that Anne had lent her. Now, quite suddenly, it occurred to her that Mrs Bennet's plan of sending her daughter Jane to visit

on a wet day, in the hope that she would be invited
to remain for the night, might very well be adapted
to her own purposes. Anne, she knew, would be
busy at her sewing circle, which met every week
on that day to make garments for the children of
the poor. Arabella, who was bored by plain
sewing, had already excused herself from
accompanying her.

The weather, too, was very promising. Not
raining as yet — she could not quite bring herself
to contemplate walking two miles in a down-
pour — but with enough heavy dark clouds moving
in from the west to make a later rainfall almost
inevitable. William, whose conscience had been
activated by James's pained expression, had shut
himself in his room with a pile of books and given
orders that he was not to be disturbed until five
o'clock, and Henry was at the grange with
Charles. As Anne left for her meeting, Arabella
kissed her affectionately and murmured that she
might make some calls during the afternoon.
Anne, thinking no more than that she meant to
spend a few hours discussing fashions with Celia,
nodded abstractedly.

If Anne had seen her sister, half an hour later
when she left the rectory, she might not have been
so calm. Arabella had dressed with the greatest of
care in an afternoon gown of delicate sprigged
muslin. Her pelisse was of fine wool in a daring
shade of cherry-red, with matching kid half-boots
and ruched silk lining to her bonnet, which cast a
becoming glow on her face. She hesitated over a

fur muff — it was very beautiful, certainly, but she recollected that she would need her hands free to hold her skirts clear of the mud. They would not say of *her* that her petticoats were inches deep in mud. Thus arrayed, she slipped from the house.

Anne, returning home at half-past four, was rather surprised to find the sitting-room, and Arabella's bedroom, empty. When, by five o'clock, her sister had not returned home, her surprise began to change to anxiety. Whether they dined alone or with friends, Arabella always insisted on spending a good hour on her evening toilette, and it was unheard of that she should not be back by this time. Anne rang for the housemaid.

'Oh, yes, miss, I saw her go,' said the maid in answer to her query. 'Like a picture, she was, in her red pelisse. She asked me the way to the manor.'

'To the manor!' exclaimed Anne. 'But that is all of two miles!'

'Oh, no, miss, not if you takes the short cut. You know, miss, that path as goes through the woods. Cuts the whole corner off, that does. I told her to be sure to take that way, miss, and she thanked me that nicely.'

'But the rain!'

'Oh, it wasn't raining then, miss. She'll have got there long since, you can be sure of that.'

The maid left the room, and Anne looked around her for inspiration. The book that Arabella had been reading was lying open on a little table.

Anne picked it up, glanced at the page, and gave a little groan, cursing herself for ever giving it to her sister. James was out attending a dying farmer, and might not be home for hours. Should she fetch William? She was reluctant to interrupt his studying. No, she thought, angry with herself, she was to blame for this ridiculous escapade. She must go after Arabella. Without giving herself time even to think, she ran upstairs for a thick cloak that she hoped would keep off most of the wet, scribbled a note for her brothers, and left the house.

She was familiar with the path through the woods. In late spring and early summer it was a favourite walk of hers, the ground thick with bluebells. At this time of year, however, it was slippery and treacherous with mud. Nor was it as clearly marked, to eyes not accustomed to country walks, as it might have been. Trying not to imagine her sister lost, or worse still lying injured somewhere, Anne hurried down the lane and climbed over the stile.

She fixed her mind on the thought that Arabella must have reached the manor safely. Anne knew that the Lydfords would have offered the use of their carriage to convey her safely home in the rain, and she could imagine only too well how prettily Arabella would thank them, and how she would refuse to allow them to have their horses put to for such a purpose. She would declare her intention of walking home, a thing which they would naturally not allow, and so would achieve her object of spending the evening, and the night, at the manor. Anne, however, would not scruple to make use of their carriage, and intended to carry her sister off forthwith.

Though there was still at least an hour of daylight left, the thick clouds and the added shadow of the trees made it dark on the woodland path. Anne hurried along as fast as she could, but the ground was uneven, and twice she slipped in the mud and only saved herself by grabbing at a branch. She was wet and dirty, and within the hood of her cloak she could feel her hair slipping from the restraint of its neatly pinned bands. In considerable discomfort, she tried again to hurry.

Her speed was her undoing. The path was steep, curving its way down the side of a hill. She felt her feet beginning to slide, and reached out, but there was nothing but slender twigs, which broke when she grasped them. She fell awkwardly, with one foot twisting beneath her. When she tried to rise, she fell back with a gasp, her ankle sending pain that made her head buzz and nasty little spots of light shimmer in front of her eyes. She sat still, then when the pain dwindled to a dull throb tried again. This time she cried out.

To her amazement and relief, her cry was answered. She called again, hearing the sound of her rescuer approaching, and closed her eyes against the sick feeling of faintness. Heavy footsteps came nearer, and she opened her eyes.

'You,' she said bitterly. 'It would be.'

'Whom else?' said Lord Delamere.

CHAPTER FOUR

IN SPITE of her words, Anne was inexpressibly relieved to see him. Already the rain and mud were soaking through her cloak, and her body was shaken by violent shivers. To remain where she was for much longer would have been to risk a severe chill, at the very least. Now the sight of that strong masculine figure gave her a feeling of safety. She tried to sit up, and at once his arm supported her.

'Don't try to move yet,' he said. 'How badly did you hurt yourself?'

'It's my ankle,' she said, resting her head thankfully against his broad shoulder. 'I can't put any weight on it. I don't think it's broken,' she added hopefully.

'Good. It's probably just a sprain. I must look at it, though. Can you bear it?'

'Yes' she said, hoping that it was true. His arm squeezed her shoulder for a moment, and when he moved it away from her she felt suddenly cold and lost. Then his hands were touching her legs, feeling gently down towards her feet. She jumped as he touched her damaged ankle, then clenched her fists and gritted her teeth as his fingers probed and manipulated.

'Not broken, thank heaven. But it is swelling

already. I must take off your boot, my dear, before it gets any worse. I will try not to hurt you any more than I must. Are you ready?'

'Yes.' His throat felt dry; her voice came out as no more than a whisper.

'Good girl.' His deep voice was calm. Carefully he unlaced her boot, then with the utmost gentleness began to ease it off. The wet leather clung tightly to her swollen foot, and he was forced to pull harder. She made no sound, but tears of pain ran down to mingle with the rain on her face, and the sharpness of her nails digging into her palm was something she scarcely felt. At last the boot came off with one last pull, and she could not help giving a little whimper. The grey buzzing was back in her head, and for a dreadful moment she feared that she would be sick. She closed her eyes and her mouth as tightly as she could, and concentrated on breathing deeply.

'That's my brave little mouse.' He was holding her again, his strong arm supporting her. Once again he was wiping her face with his handkerchief; the fresh smell of the clean linen was wonderful, a reminder of comfort and civilisation. 'I am going to carry you back to the manor.'

'No,' she whispered, shaking her head. 'Too far. Too heavy.'

She felt his laughter quiver through her.

'Too heavy? There's nothing of you. I could carry you all day and not notice it. Besides, how else are we to get you back? If you stay here you will soon be beyond human aid. And it is far nearer than your home, or I would gladly take you there.' She knew that he was right. He lifted her carefully in his arms, cradling her against his chest, and she could do no more than let herself lie there as he stood up. Not since her distant childhood had she been held like this. The wool of his coat was soft against her cheek. He set his feet down with care, both to avoid slipping and to keep from jarring her ankle as he walked, and she felt herself being lulled into warm, dark sleep.

'Anne!' His voice was sharp in her ear. 'Anne! Open your eyes!'

'Hmm?' She drifted up from the velvet depths. 'Sleepy,' she murmured, turning her face into his shoulder.

'I know, but you must not sleep. Open your eyes, Anne.' He stopped walking, and looked anxiously down at her pale face, which gleamed white in the darkness. 'Wake up, my dear.'

It was an enormous effort, but she opened eyelids that felt as if they were weighted with lead.

'Good girl. Now, stay awake, if you please. Tell me, for a start, what ridiculous maggot got into your head, that you must rush headlong through the woods in such weather when you have two able-bodied brothers at home. Ridiculous, my dear Miss Mouse, and quite unnecessary. Explain yourself, if you please.'

His brusque tone fanned a little flame of anger within her. She frowned.

'Arabella. I had to fetch Arabella. Bring her back.'

'Your sister is perfectly safe at the manor, as you might easily have found out by sending a servant with a message.'

'That is easily said, my lord,' she said, annoyance giving fluency to her tongue. 'We do not have unlimited servants, however, and certainly not one I could send on such an errand. My brother James is out, and has taken his horse with him, and William was studying. Perhaps I should have sent him, but I did not care to disturb him. Nor did I choose to advertise my sister's foolish behaviour by asking anyone else.'

'That's better,' he said with approval. 'Now you sound like yourself again. So, you came to save Arabella from my evil wiles? Or was it to save me from her?'

'Neither. Both. I don't know. If only you had sent her back in the carriage. . .'

'We tried, you know, but she was too polite for us.'

Anne bit her lip.

'She is so young,' she made excuse for her sister.

'Of course she is. This is not the first time she has played such a trick, you know. I am becoming quite accustomed. There is something so endearing about her single-minded pursuit.'

'What do you mean?'

'The night she came to Vauxhall. Did you really think, my dear Miss Mouse, that I am so lost to all senses of propriety that I would invite a young girl, without the consent of her guardians, to visit

such a place? Even though I had thought her older
than seventeen?'

'I. . .I don't know. I suppose I did.'

'Thank you. I thought as much. As a matter of
fact, it is not my habit to ruin the reputations of
young girls, of whatever age. I had mentioned the
party, of course—I may even have said what a
pity it was that she was unable to attend it—but
there was never any expectation that she would be
there. As a matter of fact, I scarcely saw the poor
child. She must have wandered around the gar-
dens for quite a while, looking for my box. That
was when she was seen by her uncle's friends.
When she did find me, I gave her a thundering
scold, and took her straight back to the house.
She slipped back in without anyone being any the
wiser—the rest of the family were at the opera—
and if it had not been for that meddling woman
tattling to Mrs Littleton no harm would have come
of it.'

'I see.' Anne spoke in a very small voice. She
should have known, she thought. A week and a
half of Arabella's company should have taught her
that this was just the kind of silly trick that the
poor child would play. She had no idea of the
danger she could have been in, of course.

'I would not have mentioned it,' he said kindly,
'Only since you insist on treating me like
Bluebeard. . .'

'I did not! But you were so. . . And besides, I
knew only what the Littletons had told us!'

'And I can imagine only too well what that

would have been. It is not for me to criticise, but I do think that they reacted with undue harshness. Arabella did not deserve such a punishment. And I feel sure that if it had been their own daughter who had played such a trick they would not have been so angry with her. In fact, they would probably have attempted to turn it to their advantage, to encourage us into a betrothal.' He was silent, feeling perhaps that he had said too much.

'Did you ever. . .had you intended to marry Eliza?' Anne knew she should not ask, but the words slipped out. 'I beg your pardon, that is nothing to do with me.'

'Is it not? Since you have asked, I do not mind telling you. Unlike Bluebeard, I have nothing to hide. Did you know that my grandmother has been friendly, since childhood, with old Mrs Littleton? Eliza's grandmother? And Arabella's too, of course.'

'Yes. Yes, I did know.'

'So, when my grandmother asked me to be kind to the girl, during her first season, I thought nothing of it. Nothing, that is, until I met Arabella. Then, of course, the idea of marriage was put into my head.'

'Oh.'

'Yes. You are doubtless surprised, Miss Mouse, to learn that I am so biddable. But I had no idea of encouraging any hopes in Miss Eliza's maiden breast. In fact, if anything, I would have said that she was terrified of me. She certainly evinced no pleasure in my company. If I was mistaken, then I was at fault, but I think that any hopes her parents might have cherished were built on decidedly shaky foundations. I had not, until recently, given the idea of matrimony a great deal of serious thought. But when I did come to consider it, I realised that, for me, any hope of lasting happiness must be built not merely on suitability and the approval of my relatives, but on a strong and mutual attachment.'

'Oh.'

'Yes. In short, Miss Mouse, I will marry for love, and where love is. Deplorably common-place, you will say. But there it is.'

She spoke through dry lips.

'Not at all. It sounds. . .delightful. I wish you every happiness.'

'Thank you.'

'We are nearly there.' His voice was matter-of-fact, as if they had been discussing the weather. 'You will be glad to be indoors.'

'Very glad.' Her voice sounded hollow, and she made an effort. 'I hope you are not too tired,' she said brightly.

'Not at all. Only relieved to have you safe. They are on the watch, I see. Someone is opening the door.'

The lamplight seemed brilliantly dazzling as they entered the hall. Anne closed her eyes for a moment, aware of surprised, anxious voices.

'Good heavens! It is Miss Winterborne! What has happened, Edward?'

Edward, thought Anne hazily. I never knew his name was Edward.

'Oh!' A long scream from Arabella. 'Oh, she is dead, she is dead! Oh, Anne!'

Anne opened her eyes and turned her head, embarrassed to find that she was still being held in Edward Delamere's arms.

'Of course I am not dead! For goodness' sake put me down, my lord.'

Arabella, already beyond the reach of reassurance, was crying hysterically, and being comforted by Miss Lydford.

'Put you down? Don't be ridiculous, I can't put you down here. I intend to carry you upstairs. Is that all right, Miss Lydford?'

She looked up from where she sat with her arms round a weeping Arabella, now mercifully quieter but still quite overwrought.

'Yes, of course. The housekeeper will go with you. The room that was being prepared for Miss Arabella, if you please, Mrs Carne. Send a man for the doctor, and with a message to the rectory also.' Her voice was calm and sensible, and Anne smiled at her with relief and approval.

'You are very good. I am sorry to be the cause of so much trouble. If you will only send me back to the rectory. . .'

'No, it is no trouble, and you must get out of your wet clothes and warm again as soon as may be. I shall bring your sister up presently, when she is calmer.'

Lord Delamere was already walking to the

stairs. It was a strange feeling for Anne, who was used to looking after and thinking for others, to find herself so helpless. She would have liked to insist on being taken straight home, but was sensible enough to know that if she was to escape the very real dangers of cold and wet she must submit for the time being to allowing others to do what was best for her. She tried to relax. It was difficult not to be conscious of Delamere's close embrace. In the cold and darkness of outside, it had not seemed so very embarrassing, but in the warm, lighted house and under the eyes of others she felt herself trying to shrink from his touch.

'Lie still,' he said brusquely. 'I don't want to slip on the stairs and take a fall myself.'

She schooled her body into stillness.

'I am afraid I am very heavy for you,' she said. If she had expected a polite denial, she was to be disappointed.

'Well, anything begins to feel heavy when one carries it in one position for a while. I shall soon be able to put you down, however, and I am sure I shall be none the worse for it.'

Indebted as she was, it was impossible to give the sharp answer that rose to her lips. She pressed them together, therefore, and was silent. She felt a tremor of laughter shake his large frame, and glanced up to see that he was smiling.

'I know, it is most unfair,' he said, kindly. 'You are not used to being helpless in the care of others, are you, Miss Winterborne? Well, the experience may be a salutary one. You may learn how it feels to be on the receiving end, for once.'

In the warm bedroom he set her down carefully by the fire, and at once the housekeeper and maid set to work to remove her muddy pelisse and bonnet. Anne looked up at him.

'I do not believe I have thanked you for rescuing me,' she said stiffly. 'It was a lucky chance that made you take that path.'

'It was no such thing,' he said enigmatically, and left the room.

Jugs of steaming water were being carried up, and very soon Anne was revelling in the comfort of a hot bath next to the fire, within sheltering screens that excluded every draught. By the time the doctor arrived she was lying in bed, sleepily revelling in the luxury of a fine lawn nightgown, and smooth, lavender-scented sheets that had neither darn nor patch. The improvised support of a small stool kept the weight of the bedclothes off her swollen, bruised ankle. He examined it, nodding at the housekeeper's recital of cold compresses and arnica.

'Very good. You have done everything necessary. You must expect some swelling and pain for a few days, Miss Winterborne, and naturally you must not attempt to walk on it. My main concern is from the shock you sustained, and the effects of the damp and chill.'

'I never take cold,' said Anne with an attempt at her old forceful manner.

'Maybe not, as a general rule. But you leave

this bed at your peril, Miss Winterborne. Is that quite clearly understood? I expressly forbid you to get up.'

'But surely I can go home tomorrow? I am needed there.'

'Ah, they said you would say that. No, Miss Winterborne. Let them manage without you for a few days. It will do them no harm, you may be sure. And only think how much they will appreciate you when you do return.'

There was no point in arguing with him. It was true that the rectory household, well organised and with a clearly established routine, could quite well run without her for a little while. Anne closed her eyes, and accepted defeat.

Her next visitor was Arabella, very tearful but mercifully in command of herself once more. At the sight of her sister's pale face her lovely eyes brimmed over once again. She ran to the bedside and threw herself, rather dramatically, on to her knees beside it.

'Oh, Anne, dearest Anne, I am so dreadfully sorry! Do, pray, say that you forgive me! I never thought it would turn out like this!'

'No, I know you didn't,' said Anne, rather wearily. Her head was beginning to ache almost as badly as her ankle, and she longed to be left in peace and allowed to sleep. 'It's all right, you foolish child. Of course I forgive you. Only do, I beg of you, cease modelling your actions on those of the people you read about in books!'

'How did you know?' Arabella was astonished.

'My dear girl, it was only too obvious. You had been prosing on for days, complaining that we had no carriage to bring you here, and you left the book lying with the bookmark just at the place where Jane was sent to the Bingleys'. I wish I had never thought to lend you the book, if you intend to model yourself on such exploits. Jane, at least, had the merit of being the unwilling victim of her mother's vulgar machinations. For you, there is no such excuse.'

Arabella pouted.

'Now you are cross with me again, when you told me you had forgiven me. And you must admit. . .' She stopped, biting her lip with little white teeth and eyeing Anne with nervous triumph.

'That it has worked? Wretched girl, you deserve that I should send you straight back to the rectory to care for your brothers in my absence.'

'Oh, you would not, would you?' Arabella was horrified. 'But I do not know how to run a household! And besides,' she added piously, 'I feel that my place is at your side, my dearest sister.'

Anne could not help but be amused.

'No, you do not! You feel that your place is downstairs with the gentlemen! Much good it would do me, I dare say, if I should ask you to spend the rest of the evening with me, and all of tomorrow too!'

'I would do it! Of course I would! Only. . .only you are tired now, are you not? And the doctor said that you should sleep. I know he told Miss Lydford so, and left instructions that you were to be given some laudanum if your poor ankle should keep you awake. But I mean to stay with you until then, and of course I shall be sleeping in here too. There is a couch set up for me, so that I will not disturb you, or hurt your poor foot.'

It was as Delamere had said, thought Anne miserably. One could not help enjoying her naïve single-mindedness. He, at least, was obviously charmed by it, and who could blame him? Much could be forgiven of youth and beauty. She sighed.

'There, you are tired. Shall I read to you, or bathe your head?'

Anne suppressed a shudder.

'No, thank you. I will sleep, and I am sure I shall feel better in the morning. Go back downstairs, my dear.' For the first time she noticed the evening gown, of fine silk gauze over an underdress of blossom-pink satin, that her sister was wearing. 'Did you have some clothes sent up? I do not know that gown, do I?'

'No, Miss Lydford has kindly lent it to me. Of course, she should not wear pink anyway, with her hair. It is sadly red, is it not? But she is very kind, and much less shy at home than when she is out. In fact I did wonder. . .but she assures me that her brother and Lord Delamere are such old friends that she views him in the light of a brother. So that is all right.'

'Very satisfactory,' said Anne drily.

'Yes, isn't it?' was the insouciant reply. 'Well, if you are sure you do not want me to stay. . .'

'No, be off with you. Only do, for my sake, behave with decorum, I beg of you!'

'Oh, of course,' assured her flighty sister. Anne contented herself with the thought that there was no need for Arabella to behave otherwise. She closed her eyes as Arabella left the room, and willed her aching body to sleep.

She woke in the morning with a dry, tickling throat, a heavy head and a running nose, presaging at best a heavy cold. Strong and healthy, in spite of her diminutive size and pale complexion, Anne was seldom ill, and was heartily annoyed with her body for betraying her. Nevertheless, the very real danger of serious illness made her unusually biddable to the decrees of the doctor, who prescribed inhalations, the rubbing of throat and chest with strong-smelling ointment, and all manner of unpleasant draughts and potions that she swallowed with as good a grace as she could.

Arabella was banished from the room, for fear of infection, but Miss Lydford spent much of the day with Anne. Under her shy exterior she was, Anne found, a young woman of strong character and quiet goodness, blessed with a sense of humour that made her a pleasant companion. She was sitting and sewing by the window when the rector arrived to visit his sister. At once she rose to her feet and made to leave the room.

'Do not go,' said Anne. 'James and I have nothing in the least private to discuss, unless you count such things as the laundering of his shirts and neckties as personal!'

'There are things that I should attend to downstairs,' was the quiet reply as she slipped out of the door.

'What a very kind girl she is,' said Anne appreciatively. James gave a little start, and turned back to her.

'Yes, indeed. My poor Anne, this is a sad state I find you in! Poor William is quite angry with you, that you did not send him instead of risking yourself!'

'It was foolish, I know. I had hoped to manage everything quietly, you see. I guessed at Arabella's little plan — she was hoping to be invited to stay here, of course — and wanted to make sure she came back. Instead, I have ensured her a stay of several days, at least!'

'Well, that is not so terrible, is it? She is very young, of course, to be thinking of matrimony, but there is no denying that it would be a great match for her, if Delamere is serious in his intentions. As he seems to be.'

'Oh, do you think so?' Anne asked hollowly. He looked at her in surprise.

'But of course! To follow her down at all, though that might have been no more than a feeling of responsibility for her safe arrival and welcome at home. And he returned, very correctly, to London the following day. But to come back again, and to this very village, argues a strong attraction, surely. Unless you think that it is Miss Lydford who engages his interest?'

'No. Arabella tells me she considers him as a brother, and from what she has said I believe that to be true.'

'I am very glad of it,' he said. 'For Arabella's sake, of course,' he added hastily. 'Dear me, I sound just like a matchmaking mama, don't I? But one cannot deny that in the circumstances it would be a happy outcome for her, would it not?'

'Very happy.'

'My dear, you are unwell. I am afraid all my chatter is making your head ache.'

'No. No, you are quite right. As Arabella's guardians, we should be pleased to have her so well settled in the world. If only I could be sure. . .she is so very young, and I am afraid she is more interested in his money and his position than in the man that he is.'

'Maybe so. But he is old enough to know his own mind. And while she may love him for what he has, will she not soon learn to love what he is as well? It seems to me that he is a man very well able to make a young woman love him.'

Anne found that she could think of no suitable reply to this remark. It occurred to her that she could not imagine that any woman could resist the attractions of Lord Delamere. Forthright, arrogant and maddening he might be, but there was something about him that could insinuate him into one's mind, one's heart. . . She frowned. Her own heart, she thought, had better remain proof against those charms. A man who could take his pick of all the elegant beauties that society could offer was scarcely likely to be interested in a mouse of a girl from a country rectory.

Towards evening Anne grew a little feverish, and she was not sorry to drink the paregoric draught that the doctor had sent up to the manor for her. Alternately shivering and burning, she felt miserable and irritable, and petulantly refused any company other than that of an elderly maid. She said, with some truth, that it would be of no possible benefit to have either her sister or Miss Lydford sitting with her, and that she would very much rather they kept out of the way of infection. She then spent the evening feeling decidedly sorry for herself, imagining the rest of the household enjoying themselves downstairs, heedless of her discomfort.

She passed an indifferent night, filled with muddled dreams, but towards morning fell into a deeper sleep. She awoke late, and was pleased to find herself substantially better. Her headache was gone, and though her voice when she spoke came out husky and deep her throat was no longer so sore. Best of all, she had stopped sneezing and her nose was no longer running and blocked.

During the afternoon she felt well enough to leave her bed for a little while and with the support of the maid and Miss Lydford to hop to a chair near the fire. Several messages and letters had come from friends in the village, and by the time she had read them all, and written little notes in answer, the evening had come and Arabella had come upstairs to change for the dinner. By now some of her own clothes had arrived from the rectory, and Anne tried to enter with suitable enthusiasm into the choice of gown.

'The muslin is very pretty,' she suggested.

'But so schoolgirlish! I cannot think what they were doing, to send it! I was thinking of the jonquil crape with the white satin slip, or perhaps the embroidered gauze with the blonde trimming. The blue satin underneath exactly matches my eyes, you know.'

'Yes, that is certainly very becoming. But for a family dinner, in the country. . .?'

'But one would not wish them to think that one had not made an effort,' said Arabella earnestly. 'Last evening, of course, we were very quiet, because everyone was anxious for you, but tonight you are so much better that we need not consider that! We shall have some music, I expect — there is an excellent pianoforte — and Miss Lydford plays charmingly on the harp. What a pity you cannot be there to sing to us!'

'At present I am afraid I should be singing tenor rather than alto,' said Anne. 'But we have not settled what you will wear.'

'Oh, the jonquil crape, since you think the gauze unsuitable,' said Arabella, with the air of one making a generous concession. 'Are you sure you will not be lonely?'

Anne looked at her sister. Her cheeks glowed becomingly pink, from the delightful walk that she had enjoyed that afternoon in the garden. Anne had been told how very attentive Lord Delamere had been; how he had actually lifted her over a damp place in the path so that she should not muddy her boots, and how he had complimented her on the cheerful manner beneath which she was concealing her natural anxiety for her sister. The guileless blue eyes looked into hers, and she could not resist the appeal in them.

'Not at all lonely,' she said. 'Enjoy your evening, and tell me all about it in the morning. Perhaps tomorrow I shall be well enough to come downstairs.'

'Perhaps, but you must be careful. One should not rush these things, should one? You must not risk a relapse.'

'Your solicitude,' said Anne carefully, 'is most affectionate. But make the most of your stay. I warn you that as soon as I am well enough we shall be returning to the rectory.'

'Of course, dearest Anne! But not until you are quite, quite recovered!'

CHAPTER FIVE

IT WAS with some surprise that Anne awoke two mornings later and realised that it was Sunday. It was the first time for many years that she would be absent from James's services at the church, and she found herself worrying about the state of his surplice, and whether he had been able to complete his sermon properly. It was strange to watch Arabella dressing to go to the morning service without her, and she found herself repeating her messages to the rest of the family several times.

When Arabella returned later in the morning, she found her sister out of bed and sitting in a dressing-gown.

'You are feeling better today? Do you think you will be well enough to come downstairs for dinner this evening? Miss Lydford has said that, if so, our brothers must come here for the evening. She means to invite the Sudburys also, and Celia, and some of our other friends if they will come. Will it not be fun? Practically a party, you know, but delightfully informal. Oh, do say that you are well enough, dearest Anne!'

'Only yesterday you were imploring me not to recover too fast,' said Anne jokingly.

'Oh, you may recover — indeed you may — but not *completely*,' said Arabella ingenuously. 'What do you think? Miss Lydford will be coming up presently to ask you. Shall it be yes, or no?'

'Oh, decidedly yes,' said Anne. 'I long to leave these four walls, delightful though they are. I think that as long as I do not over-exert myself I shall do very well.'

'You are the best of sisters!' Arabella ran to kiss her, and Anne could not help smiling as she returned the embrace.

During the afternoon she rested, and at four o'clock rose to begin making her simple toilette. Out of deference to her, the hour of dining had been set at the unfashionably early time of five o'clock. In spite of herself, she could not help feeling a little excited. In her quiet life, such an evening constituted a great event. Of course, she told herself, she was looking forward to seeing her brothers, and her friend Lady Sudbury. She found herself anxiously examining her evening gowns, and did not pause to wonder why it should matter which one she chose, since family and friends were well acquainted with all of them, and had been for two or three years.

Arabella flitted in, and found her sister in contemplation of three garments laid out upon the bed.

'The muslin is the newest,' said Anne. 'I think perhaps I should wear that.'

'Oh, Anne, you cannot!' wailed Arabella. 'Muslin, and so very plain! It will look so very particular if you are in muslin and I in silk when I am not yet properly out—though I might as well be, for the matter of that. If you wear muslin, then so must I, and I particularly wanted to wear the embroidered gauze that you said was too fine before.'

'Then it must be the lilac silk, though it is sadly old-fashioned.'

'It is more than that, it is positively dowdy,' said Arabella in forthright tones. 'Why do you not wear one of my gowns? You know I have plenty. Then I need not feel that I am dressing too fine.'

'My dear child,' said Anne in some exasperation, 'you are all of three inches taller than I am. Your gowns would look ridiculous on me, and I should undoubtedly trip over.'

'Well, so you would, if you were walking, but surely you will not attempt to do that? Your cold is better, I know, but not your ankle. And since you will be sitting down all evening, it cannot matter if your skirts are too long.'

Anne was much struck by the good sense of this, and looked at her sister with new respect.

'I declare I have been so long in bed, I had almost forgotten that I could not walk! And you are so slender, we are much of a size apart from the height. Very well, then, which one shall it be?'

It was impossible not to be excited at the prospect. It had been so long since Anne had bought herself a new evening gown, and when she did it was always of the simplest and most practical type. She had never possessed anything half so pretty as the selection that Arabella laid out before her. In the end she chose the simplest, a cream satin slip under a dress of net that was embroidered with sprays of leaves which were repeated as garlands in a decorated band along the hem, and across the wide neckline.

'It is cut very low. I do not think I have ever worn one so low. Perhaps a gauze scarf, or a fichu. . .'

'Nonsense, it would ruin the line! If one has pretty shoulders and neck, why hide them?' retorted her sister robustly. It was true that the white skin on the curves of her breast and shoulder rose very becomingly from the embroidered neckline, the rich cream colour of the satin suiting her pale colouring better than the more usual white. As a final touch Anne consented to borrow the gold chain set with citrines that Arabella had received as a birthday gift not many months earlier.

As the clock on the landing outside struck five, there came a knock at the door. Anne had not given much thought to how she was to get downstairs—she had assumed that a manservant, or possibly two, would be sent to carry her. Now, however, Lord Delamere walked boldly into the room.

'Are you ready? Though I do not need to ask, since I have the evidence of my eyes to tell me that you are, and most becomingly so. One of Miss Arabella's gowns, I collect?'

'Oh, Delamere! To think that you remember it! That was what I was wearing the very first time that we met!' Arabella, radiant in the embroidered gauze, ran lightly across the room, and dropped him a mock-curtsy. 'I remember you remarked on how well it suited me. I hope that you like this one just as well?'

He studied her appearance carefully, as she revolved before him.

'Even more delightful, if such a thing could be possible,' he said, with consideration. 'Now, shall we go down?'

He advanced on Anne, who shrank back in her chair.

'But surely. . . I thought one of the servants. . .'

'You did not think I would let the servants carry you down, while I was here to perform that office? I regard it as peculiarly my own, you know, since I carried you here in the first place.'

'But that was different; a case of necessity. I cannot allow you to. . .'

It was too late. With a complete disregard for her protests he had stooped and lifted her into his arms. She was aware of the warmth of his hands and body through the thin silk of her gown, and could feel a blush of embarrassment spreading from her face to neck and breast, and was even more conscious of her bare skin that must be turning pink. With an effort of will she resisted the urge to lift her kid-gloved hands to cover her neck and the soft swell of her breasts: to do so would only call more attention to that part of her.

'Put me down,' she whispered urgently.

'What, here?' They were already on the stairs. 'You could, I suppose, slide down the banisters.

But are you not a little grown up for such tricks? I think everyone would be surprised. However, if that is what you wish. . .'

He made as if to sit her on the broad wooden rail of the banister, and Anne clutched at the lapels of his black evening coat.

'You know quite well that I did not mean that! Why you must tease me so, every time we meet, I do not know!'

'It is quite irresistible,' he answered candidly. 'Now, are you ready for your reception committee? They are all gathered to greet you, as you see. Shall you be pale and interestingly languid, or do you mean to be cheerfully brave? What effect do you strive for?'

'I do not want any effect that must be striven for. I shall be myself.'

'Ah, but that is the most difficult effect of all, for most of us. I applaud your temerity, Miss Mouse.'

'I wish you will not call me that.' They were almost in the hall, and already those waiting for her were gathering round.

'You dislike mice? I am fond of them myself. Quick, resourceful, bright-eyed. . .'

'Small but troublesome pests,' she finished for him, and felt the shake of laughter he gave as he went down the last step into the waiting throng.

Awkward though it was to greet her friends and family while being clasped warmly in a gentleman's arms, Anne was so pleased to see them all that she managed to forget her embarrassment.

With some pride, William displayed the comfortable chair that he had fixed on to a wheeled platform, so that she might easily be moved about the rooms.

'James was going to bring out the old Bath chair that was in the stables, but I said that you could not possibly go about in anything so antiquated! Do you like it? Are you comfortable?' To her relief Lord Delamere had deposited her without ceremony in the chair, scarcely waiting for her words of thanks before moving away to speak to Arabella. She, used to being the centre of attraction in most small gatherings, was rather cross at finding how much attention was being paid to her sister, but she brightened when he spoke to her, and was soon involved in a low-voiced, laughing conversation with him.

They were a cheerful group as they sat down to dine. Anne found herself between Mr Lydford and her old friend Sir Robert Sudbury, where she was very comfortable. Mr Lydford she found to be a kindly, serious man, much concerned with the duties that his position in life entailed. At the other end of the table, Arabella kept up a lively three-cornered conversation with Lord Delamere and his other neighbour Miss Lydford. There was a great deal of laughter, and Anne had to make a severe effort not to attempt to listen to them.

When the ladies left the table, Arabella volunteering with great enthusiasm to push her sister in her wheeled chair, a kind of natural gravitational pull divided the group of ladies into two parts.

The younger ones clustered round the piano with much chatter and giggling. Lady Sudbury, as the unacknowledged leader of the older set, made her way to a chair near the fire. Arabella eyed the two groups, and without hesitation propelled Anne towards the fireplace, then flitted off to join her younger friends, who received her with acclaim.

Anne was neither surprised nor hurt by this relegation to the ranks of the middle-aged and dowagers. The responsibilities of caring for her family made her more fitted, she thought, for such company than for that of the young girls who were now playing spirited duets with more feeling than accuracy. She was perfectly happy to join in the endless exchange of recipes, complaints about servants and anecdotes about children, and it did not cross her mind that she was far too young to behave like a matron.

'Are you quite comfortable? Should you like to be nearer to the fire?' The soft voice was Miss Lydford's; as the hostess she was moving from one group to the other, finding chairs and settling her guests. Since most of them were old friends and acquaintances to each other, her task was not onerous, but she performed it with a graceful care that was pretty to watch, Anne thought. She smiled up at her.

'I am delightfully warm, thank you. And enjoying myself so very much; this is quite an occasion for us country dwellers, you know! You cannot imagine how thrilling it is for us to have such happy additions to our circle as your brother and yourself!'

'You have made us both so welcome! It is precisely what we had hoped for, to find such pleasant society. I do not care for town life, and nor does my brother.'

'So we may hope that you will make a long stay among us? I am very glad to hear it, and I am sure that James will be also.'

Anne spoke without intent, meaning no more than a polite remark, but she was startled when she saw a quick flush of colour on Emily Lydford's cheeks, and with no more than a hurried and inarticulate excuse the younger girl left her and almost ran away. Anne looked after thoughtfully. That her brother should admire this pretty new arrival in the village was not surprising; that his interest was returned — that was a matter of more moment. As a young woman of independent fortune she might look where she chose for a husband, and it might well be expected that her friends would look with disapproval on her throwing herself away on a country parson with no prospects of advancement. Anne's brow wrinkled a little, and she could only hope that Mr Lydford would be less exacting in his wishes than an ambitious parent might have been for the heiress.

It was not long before the gentlemen joined them. The atmosphere, which even among the older set had been expectant, alert for the sound of a masculine footstep at the door, brightened at once. The girls abandoned their playing, with much laughter and exclamation, and fluttered into a defensive cluster that positively demanded to be invaded and broken apart. Older ladies sat up straighter, brightening at the prospect of a hand of cards, with perhaps a little discreet gambling of pin-money. Anne, with no option but to remain where she was, remained an observer, amused and entertained by the spectacle.

'You look very Olympian. Do the antics of these mortals please you?' The voice, from just behind her, made her jump, and Anne wondered how a man as large as Lord Delamere could approach her so quietly that she did not notice him.

'Do I? How horrid. I have little to feel superior about, and I can assure you I do not. My stature, in every sense of the word, is too small to allow of it, in any case.'

'Not superior, merely detached. Well, perhaps a little aloof. Or is your ankle paining you?'

'Not at all, thank you. Though I suppose I am in a fashion isolated from my friends, until I can once again move unaided. It is a strange feeling, and I am not sure that I care for it.'

'It will not be for long, however. In a week or two you will be laughing with the rest of them again.' A lift of his eyebrow indicated the group of girls who were being importuned for some music, and standing back in favour of one another with real or assumed modesty.

'I?' She laughed. 'I do not include myself among them, my lord. I leave that for my sister. No, my place is here by the fire, where I am most content to talk to my good friends.'

'Don't be ridiculous.' His voice was lazy, but there was a spark in his eyes that she recognised, with surprise that probably equalled his own, as anger. The breath caught a little in her throat, and she drew it down into her lungs, breathing out slowly and calmly.

'Ridiculous, Lord Delamere?' She was pleased by the steadiness of her voice, but when she met his eyes again there was no more than a glint of teasing amusement in their glass-grey depths.

'Fishing for compliments, Miss Winterborne?'

'Certainly not! And if I had been, I might have been quite sure of failing, mightn't I? You are not precisely effusive in your praise of my person, are you, my lord? It is a good thing that I attach little importance to my appearance, else I should have been quite dismayed by your strictures.'

'Dismayed? I find it hard to imagine you in so enfeebled a state, Miss Winterborne. But what can I possibly have said to you, to merit such a criticism? On the contrary, I find your whole appearance most pleasing: neat, womanly, and on this occasion at least quite delightful. Fine feathers, of course, make a fine bird.'

'Well, if praise for borrowed plumage is a compliment, then I must thank you, if only on my sister's behalf. I doubt if I would be a fine bird, in your eyes, without her generosity.'

His dark eyebrows shot upwards.

'That would, indeed, be something quite new in

evening wear,' he said, his eyes travelling slowly over her and returning to her face, which was flushed pink with embarrassment. 'And, I am sure, even more delightful,' he added politely.

Crimson, she would not drop her eyes before his challenging look.

'That was not at all what I meant, as you very well know, Lord Delamere! And that you should say such a thing to me only goes to prove my point!'

'Really? Which point was that?'

'That I am no longer a young girl, of course. You would not have said such a thing to any of them.' Her glance flickered towards the group round the piano.

'Certainly not, if only for fear that they might take me at my word. But if I had, they would not have understood me, or at least would have pretended they did not. And of all the paralysingly boring conversational gambits I know, I do think that "Oh, what can you mean, Lord Delamere?" is one of the most stultifying, do not you?'

'So you compliment me on the quickness of my wits, if not my appearance? Thank you, sir.'

'On the contrary. I am trying, in the face of some opposition, to compliment you on both, if you would but let me. To be fair in outward semblance but echoingly empty within is sadly common among your sex, I fear — and, before you rise up and slay me, allow me to accept that the fault for that lies largely in the inclinations and expectations of my own gender. Given the choice, however, I prefer a well appointed and tended mind, in whatever housing.'

'Then you must allow me to tell you, my lord, that you are so rare that you would almost qualify for a freak-show.'

He made a little inclination, his eyes glowing with laughter.

'A compliment, at last! At least, I mean to take it as such. And its rarity gives it value, as I must hope that mine does to you.'

She scarcely knew how to reply, and was relieved to see that the tea tray had been brought in. During the general movement that followed its arrival he left her side, and she hardly knew whether she was glad or sorry to see him go.

Most of the young ladies had taken their turn at entertaining the company with playing or song, and while the older ladies were happy with their card game the rest were casting about for some new entertainment. Arabella, with a look of innocence that was enough to warn her sister that she had some plot afoot, looked over at Anne.

'My sister has not yet sung for us! And you know she has the loveliest voice of all of us, better by far than mine!'

This modest claim received its full due of polite disclaimers from the dazzled gentlemen around her, but it was in fact true that Anne's rich alto, though untutored, had a beauty that far surpassed the carefully trained thin soprano of her sister. Anne, who had not expected to be asked, said that she had not brought her music, but since most

of those present knew that she had no need of a
score for her songs she was overborne.

During her second song, she was somewhat
surprised to find herself joined, after a few bars,
by a fine tenor voice that chimed in, softly at first
but with increasing confidence when it was appar-
ent that she was not put out. Since the ballad she
was singing was one she knew very well, she was
able to take advantage of a break in the song to
glance around, while her fingers continued the
accompaniment. Not greatly to her surprise, it was
Lord Delamere who stood at her shoulder, and
she remembered the voice she had heard in
church. In the third verse, she ventured to impro-
vise a little, and he followed her without difficulty,
harmonising with her and taking, at times, the
tune while she chimed in below it. Piqued, she
modulated the key to a minor for the following
verse, and subtly changed the rhythm, but still he
kept effortlessly with her, singing with as much
confidence as if they had agreed the changes
beforehand, and practised them. With the last
verse she returned to the original key and time,
and was forced to react quickly when, as if in
retaliation, he slipped in a few variations of his
own. They finished triumphantly, to applause and
laughter, and she looked up at him and smiled for
the first time with uncomplicated pleasure.

'You are a musician, sir!'

'No more than you are,' was the careless reply.
'An amateur, in the true sense of the word.' She

bit her lip in mortification. 'Our voices blend well together.'

'Yes. It is a pity that all else between us should be so very inharmonious,' she snapped.

'If you think it a pity, the remedy is in your own hands, my dear Miss Winterborne. I have no wish for discord between us, I can assure you. In fact, it is very much the reverse.'

'The discord is not of my making, Lord Delamere. It comes, I believe, from a dissimilarity in our natures, which makes it impossible that we should ever find pleasure in one another's company.' She was playing all the while, her fingers running unheeded over the keys to cover the sound of their low-voiced conversation.

'Chalk and cheese? Oil and water? Yet one may always, of course, pour oil on troubled waters and by their very disharmony create peace. No, I would see us more as flint and steel, striking sparks from one another.'

'Then you must be careful, my lord, not to burn your fingers,' she said austerely.

'And you, Miss Winterborne, should beware of starting a conflagration.'

'I? I will never set the world alight, sir. I make only hearth-fires, nicely contained and neatly tended, to warm and feed my family.'

'Such fires, Miss Mouse, can be the most dangerous of all.' He was silent for a moment, unsmiling. Anne gave a little shiver, and her reaching fingers slipped so that the chord she had intended was sour as vinegar, and she gave an involuntary grimace, and took her hands from the keys.

'Oh, do not stop!' cried out Arabella, running over to her. 'You do not object to playing for us, do you?'

'I thought we had had enough music. Will you not find some other entertainment, a charade or a round game?'

'Oh, no, those are for children! No, we are hoping to dance. Was not that why you were playing? We thought it was your idea, and everyone is so pleased!'

Belatedly, Anne realised that while she conversed her fingers had betrayed her by slipping into a country dance, and when she looked across the room she saw that the carpet in the hallway next door had already been rolled back. She frowned.

'Dancing? But it is Sunday, dearest. Do you think that is quite proper? What does James say?'

'Why, only that he will not dance himself, but he sees no harm in it for the rest of us! Do play for us, Anne, please! You know all the best tunes, and you cannot dance yourself, after all, can you? Lord Delamere, can you not persuade her?'

'If you cannot do so, I do not believe it can be within my power.'

'But you will dance with us! Oh, I should not have said that, I suppose! You will think that I am being forward and fast, and asking you for myself!'

'Well, I hope that you are, since I have every intention of begging you to partner me, if Miss

Winterborne will be so obliging as to honour us. . .?'

It was quite impossible for Anne for refuse, nor did she wish to. If James saw no harm in it, then an impromptu dance with a few friends could not be frowned on. Certainly Lady Sudbury was quite happy, and was actually overseeing the moving of furniture by the servants.

'Very well, then, I am happy to play for you. Shall it be country dances only, or do you mean to waltz?'

'Oh, I leave that for you to decide, dearest,' said Arabella, unwontedly meek. 'Though the waltz is danced everywhere in London now. . .'

Anne laughed.

'Then do not let us be laggard. It will not do for our visitors to think us country bumpkins!'

'Best of sisters! I knew that I could rely on you!'

Arabella was gone in a flutter of gauze and a waft of orris and violet, with Lord Delamere drawn behind her by the hand to join the excited couples already forming a set in the hall. Anne dropped her fingers back on to the keyboard with a resounding chord, signifying that they must take their places for a country dance.

So she played for them, and even the devoted card players tapped their feet and applauded the end of each dance. It was scarcely Almack's, Anne supposed, but at least her sister was radiantly happy. She had danced twice with Lord Delamere, and twice with Thomas Lydford, and Anne could only regret that respect for his cloth made it impossible for her brother to dance with Miss Emily. She had noticed, when she had glanced round, how his eyes followed her, and she was more than ever determined to keep Mary Sudbury to her idea of giving a dance — and not on a Sunday, either. Almost as if her thought had summoned him, James stood up and came over to her.

'I think you must be tired, by dear. You have been playing for nearly an hour.'

'Oh, no, I assure you. And they are enjoying it so much, it would be a pity to stop yet.'

'It would, but I cannot permit you to continue. Do not think I did not notice how you rubbed your fingers and stretched them after the last dance! In any case, I have you in my power — I have only to wheel you away from the instrument. . .thus!' He acted even as he spoke, and there was an outcry from the young people in the hall. 'Yes, I know, but my sister has been unwell, do not forget. However, if you will permit me to take her place? I cannot do as well as she, but I think I know enough tunes for two or three more sets, if that will content you, and even a waltz or two.'

He pulled up the piano stool, and took his sister's place. Miss Lydford, who had been dancing with William, came hurrying over.

'My dear Miss Winterborne, how very selfish we have been, to trespass so on your good nature! Are you very tired?'

'Not at all, only my brother is so insistent! I

believe he merely wants to prove that he can play, even if he will not dance on this occasion!'

'Oh, yes, he plays very well. What a pity you may not have the pleasure of a dance also. We have had such fun.'

'Well, and why not?' said William. 'If you will permit me to leave you here, Miss Lydford?' He placed a chair for her next to the piano, and bowed low in front of Anne. 'If I might have the honour of this dance, madam?'

'Foolish boy!' laughed Anne. 'You know very well that I cannot set a foot to the ground, and if I did I should trip over our sister's skirts! Find someone else to tease, if you please.'

'Not at all; I mean that you shall have your dance. Come, you are such a little, light thing. . .'

Before Anne could realise what he meant, she found herself plucked from her chair and lifted into her brother's arms. He carried her as easily as if she had been a child, and without thinking she put her arms round his neck to support herself.

'Really, William, this is ridiculous!' she scolded him. 'Put me back in my chair; you are making me look quite foolish, or a hoyden, which is worse!'

'Nonsense. There can be no possible impropriety in being carried by your own little brother. And since your skirt is so long, even your feet are covered. Look, James is not shocked, he is laughing! And playing a waltz for us, the good fellow. I own I was a little puzzled to know how we could perform a country dance!'

Anne found herself whirled into the hallway, the centre of a laughing group of couples. After they had circled the floor once the rest of them joined in, and she gave herself up to enjoyment. It was certainly exhilarating, held up in her brother's strong arms and being twirled so that her long silk skirts fluttered and swung. Then, after a few moments, her old friend Sir Robert Sudbury was demanding that he should have a turn, and she found herself passed without ceremony into his care.

'Oh, be careful, my dear sir,' she said, as he carried her off. 'I am sure I am too heavy for you!'

'Not at all, foolish child. There's no weight to you at all. Unless you are implying that I am too old to be dancing with you?'

She cried out at that, and had to let him continue. As if his example had set them free of constraint, she found that all the other gentlemen were insisting on partnering her also.

'I feel a little like the baton in a relay race,' she said to Mr Lydford. 'I can assure you we do not usually behave like this in Minterne Abbas. Normally we are very staid, you know.'

'Are you? What a pity, this is much more fun. You do not object, I hope?'

'Object? I should not dare.'

'That is fortunate, for I see my old friend is waiting to take my place. He shall not do so just yet, however. I do not mean to part with you so soon.'

'Lord Delamere? Oh, do not part with me to

him, pray, Mr Lydford. I am sure he has had quite enough of carrying me already, and so have I.'

'And have him left the only man who has not had the pleasure of dancing with you? It is more than my life is worth, I assure you, Miss Winterborne.'

Nothing that she could say would move him, and she found herself passed into Lord Delamere's arms. She must, perforce, put her own round his neck, but she kept her touch as light as she could, and fixed her eyes on the blue-white shadowed folds of his intricately tied cravat. He was silent for a few bars, and then it seemed as though his grasp of her slackened so that she felt she was going to fall. At once, by instinct, she tightened her grip.

'That's better,' he said calmly.

'What a mean trick! I thought you meant to let me fall!'

'Why, whatever gave you that idea? As if I would! After all, I am quite accustomed to carry you now. You should feel perfectly safe with me, Miss Winterborne.'

'Oh, yes. Perfectly safe,' she answered hollowly.

'Good. Now there is nothing to stop us enjoying our dance, is there?'

He did not wait for an answer, but whirled her rapidly round a corner so that she was forced to cling once more to his neck. She thought the dance must be nearly over, but the music went on, and on, until she thought she could have screamed. At last, when she was breathless and dizzy, the quickened pace slackened, and James wound up the pieces with a thunderous chord. The couples around them, breathless and laughing, clapped.

'Thank you, Miss Winterborne,' said Lord Delamere punctiliously. 'Allow me to tell you that you dance delightfully.'

CHAPTER SIX

'Go HOME?' Arabella's voice was shrill. 'Already? But we cannot! When things are going so well, and we are having such fun! Besides, your ankle is not better yet.'

Anne, who had awakened from a night of unquiet sleep with a pounding headache, drew a deep breath and reached for patience.

'My cold, however, if quite gone, and I cannot use my ankle as a reason to stay. We are not, I should remind you, invited guests. Oh, yes, I know——' she held up her hand as her sister began an incoherent protest '—I know that we have been made most welcome, and I am quite prepared to believe her when Miss Lydford says that they are enjoying having us to stay, but it is not at all the same. It would be quite improper for us to prolong our visit. I have duties at home, after all, and you will find that Miss Lydford will quite understand my wish to return.'

'All very well for you, but what about me?' asked Arabella pettishly. 'I do not wish to go home.'

Anne was silent, but her look spoke volumes.

'Oh, I did not mean it to sound like that, you know I did not, Anne! Indeed, I am not unhappy at home with you, only. . .only this is such fun, and more like. . .more like. . .' Her lip wobbled, and the lovely eyes filled with tears.

'My dear, I do understand,' said Anne kindly. 'I know that the rectory is not what you have been used to, and it is quite natural that you should miss the gaiety and excitement of London. But we must all be governed, you know, by the common rules of behaviour. I cannot stay beyond another day, and though Miss Lydford will press me most politely to remain she will know that I cannot.'

'But I have no duties at home! May I not stay here, at least, just a few more days?'

'I would not insist on your return, but I am afraid that it would never occur to our kind hosts that you will not wish to return with me, and give me the assistance I fear I shall need. As a woman alone in a household of men and boys, I will be in want of feminine company.'

It was, of course, unarguable, but although Arabella could see that it must be so she was not inclined to accept it at all cheerfully. Anne did her best to cheer her, holding out promises of future delight in the dance that Lady Sudbury intended to give, and managed so well that Arabella was able to support, with tolerable equanimity, Miss Lydford's calm acceptance of their plans to leave the manor on the morrow. With Anne, however, she was still sulky, refusing in private to speak to her, and in public to accord her more than the coldest of civilities. It was very trying, but Anne did her best, continuing to address her sister as though nothing had happened, and hoping that she would not expose herself to censure by exhibiting her childish behaviour in front of others.

They passed a quiet day. Anne came downstairs to luncheon, carried this time by a manservant, and found that the gentlemen had both gone out riding, and were not expected to return until nightfall. Arabella pouted again, but the fortunate arrival of several friends, come to give their thanks for the previous evening, made her revive like a wilted flower in water. When Lady Sudbury was announced, Arabella scarcely gave her time to greet and thank Miss Lydford before rushing up to her.

'Oh, it is true, isn't it, dear Lady Sudbury? Do not tell me that it is not, for I declare I shall quite go into a decline!'

'My dear child, I have not the least idea what you are talking about,' said Mary Sudbury calmly. 'As for going into a decline, I am sure you are far too sensible to do anything so melodramatic and silly!'

'Oh, no! *I* am not sensible at all. It is my sister you are thinking of — she is the sensible one,' said Arabella, with an acid edge to her voice.

'Then it is just as well that you have come home,' was the placid answer. 'You may profit by her example. But what is it that you cannot live without, and which I presume I must provide? If it is a beau you must fend for yourself, for my poor Charles is far too young for you just yet.'

Arabella stared.

'Why, a dance, of course! My sister has been

telling me that you are going to give a dance very soon. But I dare say it was all a mistake, and you do not mean to do it after all.' She cast a scowling look at Anne, who blushed for her, but Lady Sudbury was too accustomed to the nursery tantrums that her own spoiled young son had treated her to in his infancy to be worried by such behaviour.

'Mean to do it? Of course I do! I had no idea that such a little thing could be of such importance to you. Yes, even before the happy example that we were given yesterday night I had been considering whether we might not get up a party of young people, and even the not so young ones, and have a dance. Not a formal ball, of course, merely a country hop among friends. I think, if we are lucky, we should be able to manage at least fifteen couples for the dancing, which is quite respectable for a small village, you know!'

'Oh, yes! It sounds delightful!' Arabella was all smiles again, the thunderclouds gone and nothing but gentle sunshine to be seen. 'When shall it be? I should be very happy to help you, Lady Sudbury!' she added ingenuously. 'I could. . .oh, I could write the cards for you, and things like that!'

'I shall be sure to ask you, if necessary,' said Anne's friend kindly, successfully hiding a smile. 'As for when it should be, I had scarcely got so far in making my plans. Fairly soon, I suppose, before the risk of severe weather. We cannot afford to have our guests benighted in snowy lanes. Soon, but not, of course, before your sister is well again.'

'But she is well! We are to go home tomorrow!'

'Well, perhaps, but not walking. We cannot have a dance until her ankle is quite better. You would not wish to deprive your sister of the pleasure of joining in the dancing, I am sure.'

'No. . .' Arabella's tone was doubtful. 'But I do not think she really cares for dancing, does she?'

'Not care for dancing! Surely every young girl must care for dancing. I am surprised to hear you say such a thing.'

Arabella looked surprised to hear her sister described in such a way. Anne, who was feeling every day of her twenty-five years old, and even rather older, smiled across at her friend.

'I am afraid that girls of seventeen view anyone over twenty as quite beyond the pleasures of youth! I am sure I did so at her age, did not you? And I can assure you that while I am not precisely antiquated yet I can do very well without dancing. Do not defer your party on my account, I beg you.'

'Well, if I thought you really meant that, I should really be worried about your health,' said Lady Sudbury. 'No, we shall wait. It is now the third week of October. What do you think of the second week in November?'

Arabella, looking less than thrilled, could do no more than assent.

Later, when they went upstairs to change for the evening, Arabella was more irritable than ever. Added to her annoyance at being forced to leave Minterne Manor, the blame for which she irrationally put on Anne, was the greater hardship of having to wait three weeks before the promised dance should take place.

'It is too bad!' she scolded, pacing up and down the room while her sister, confined as she was to a chair, could only watch her. 'You told me there was to be a dance, but not that it would be so long before it could happen! It is very selfish of you, Anne, to mind about dancing at your age! You, who are always preaching propriety to me! After all, you managed to join in the dancing last night, didn't you?'

'Yes, but if you think I am going to be carried about the room in every gentleman's arms at a public dance you must be quite about in your wits,' said Anne frankly. 'It is one thing to allow it in the privacy of a small family party, and quite another to behave so at a formal dance!'

'I suppose, because Delamere sang with you, and spent some time talking to you, you think you have made a conquest,' said Arabella viciously. 'I am afraid you are mistaken. Any attentions he pays to you are solely because you are my sister. He came here because of me, and he stays here because of me.'

'Now that,' said Anne crossly, 'is quite enough. The dance will be held in November, because that is when Lady Sudbury wishes to give it. I do not care if I dance or not, but she does, and that should be enough for both of us. As for Lord

Delamere, he may go or stay as he chooses. It makes no difference to me; in fact I had liefer he went. If you admire him, then I cannot say that I applaud your taste, but if he wants you you are welcome to him. Whether you would in fact have a moment's happiness with an arrogant, opinionated, bully I take leave to doubt. But I will not listen to any more of your complaints.'

'Very well, then! You shall not hear them! And you need not think that I am going to lend you another of my gowns, for I shall not!'

With that Arabella retreated into silent sulking. With a sigh Anne readied herself, as best she might, for the evening. Standing on one foot, she struggled into the simple muslin gown that she had always intended to wear, and draped her favourite Norwich silk shawl over it. Her hair she was accustomed to dealing with for herself, and she had already brushed it out and rearranged it in the simple style she favoured. Arabella, with much rattling of drawers and slamming of cupboard doors, put on her own silk gown, but was forced to accept her sister's help with fastening it, and with the arranging of her hair. Her thanks were grudgingly monosyllabic, however, and as soon as she was ready she ran downstairs, leaving Anne to follow as best she might.

Not greatly to Anne's surprise, the door opened a few minutes later to reveal Lord Delamere.

'Are you ready? May I carry you downstairs?'

'Thank you,' said Anne repressively.

'You do not seem very pleased to see me,' he

said, as he lifted her into his arms. 'Have I done something to offend you?'

'Offend me? Of course not, how could you? Only. . . I wish you had sent a servant to fetch me, instead of coming yourself.'

'It is no more than a polite attention, you know, to my friends' guest. I should do the same for anybody. Well, almost anybody. It would rather depend on their size. If it should be Prinny, now. . .'

Anne could not repress a giggle, at the vision of Lord Delamere struggling to lift the rotund Prince Regent in his arms.

'It would be a great responsibility,' she said gravely.

'It would be a great weight! I believe he would make about ten of you. Did you hear that they constructed a kind of lifting device at Brighton, when he expressed a wish to ride and was unable to mount his horse? One can only sympathise with the poor horse. An elephant would have been more to the point, and only think how well it would have agreed with his surroundings!'

'You have been to Brighton? How I envy you. I have seen pictures, of course, of His Highness's Pavilion there, but one can scarcely believe. . .I thought they must be exaggerated. Is it really as wonderful as they say?'

'Wonderful it is. One wonders, in particular, how anyone still in his right mind can manage to live in it, without suffering a brain fever.'

'Lord Delamere, what you are saying is tantamount to treason!'

'Yes, isn't it? I believe I could support a spell in the Tower, however, so long as it has not been done over by our Regent.'

'You are very severe on him.'

'It is one of the penalties of greatness: everyone gets to criticise the cut of your coat, and the style of your home, and the innermost secrets of your closet. But, to say truth, for all his foibles I believe there is a great deal of good in him, and would have been even more if his life had not been as it is. His love of art is genuine, if at times rather misdirected, and I believe future generations may live to thank him for a very fine collection of paintings, so long as it is not all sold up when he dies.'

They were at the bottom of the stairs. Anne, however, had quite forgotten the discomforts of the afternoon in her interest in the conversation.

'Oh, but surely Princess Charlotte would not do such a thing?'

'Perhaps not, if she inherits.'

'But surely the succession is secure now? It wants only a few weeks to her *accouchement*, and if as we all hope the child is a boy, then there need be nothing to fear. Or do you refer to the dangers of revolution? There is unrest, I know, from the high taxes, but that little incident in January was grossly exaggerated, surely? I believe things are much quieter now.'

'It is bound to appear so, with the magistrates

having a free hand to imprison anyone they think might be a danger to public order, and the Habeas Corpus suspended. But I agree, I do not think there is any likelihood of a general uprising such as occurred in France. No, I meant merely that a child's life, and that of its mother, hangs by a thread. And the Princess, I believe, has not been in good health.'

'But surely she has every possible care?'

'Oh, yes, Croft is a good man, and he is already settled at Claremont. I expect I am too gloomy. Only it is a pity, with all the Royal dukes, that none of them has provided us with a second string, as it were. Plenty of little FitzClarences, but no heirs. Well, here we are. And there is a chair ready for you near the fire, I see.'

He set her down, and at once Mr Lydford came with his usual punctilious good manners to pay his respects, to ask after her progress and to mourn the news that she was leaving them the following day. Arabella, pretending to look over some books of music on the piano, glowered.

After the gaieties of the previous evening, the room seemed empty with only five of them, the dining-table showing an expanse of empty white damask. When the ladies, correctly, withdrew at Miss Lydford's signal and returned to the drawing-room, a desultory conversation was carried on, hampered by the fact that Arabella was set on behaving as though her sister were invisible and inaudible. Miss Lydford, with her accustomed good manner, seemed not to notice, and refrained as far as possible from meeting Anne's eyes, though on one occasion their glances crossed and they exchanged a wordless look, apology on one side, understanding and sympathy on the other.

The return of the gentlemen, and the arrival of the tea tray, brightened them all. Lord Delamere, appearing oblivious to the currents of emotion eddying round the room, applied himself to amusing Arabella, and succeeded so well that he soon had her laughing and smiling with every appearance of complaisance. Anne could not but be grateful, though his attention would no doubt encourage her younger sister to think that he was serious in his intentions.

And after all, thought Anne firmly, why not? She was a very pretty girl, and charming when she wanted to be. It was true that he had told her that he disliked empty-headed women, but many otherwise intelligent men thought the same, until they encountered just such young and lovely girls as Arabella. And if her education had not been everything it might have been, she was young enough for that to be rectified. Many men preferred a wife out of the schoolroom, who could be taught and moulded to fit their requirements. And if Lord Delamere were such a man, well, good luck to him, thought Anne crossly.

Anne, sitting quietly by Emily Lydford and discussing village affairs with her, watched him as he lounged elegantly against the piano, encouraging Arabella to play and humming through tunes for her. Against the sober black of his evening coat and knee-breeches his shirt and cravat were crisply white, the folds in the muslin neckcloth as precise as a mathematical diagram. His dark hair was cut by a master, and brushed with an artistry that was seen only by its naturalness. As she looked at him, he raised his eyes and met hers as if he had felt her glance.

Their grey depths were unreadable, and she could only hope that her own were also. She would not be the first to look away, but held his gaze with a face that she kept so still that she had the impression her flesh had turned to marble. In that still moment the realisation came to her that she was far from indifferent, as she had claimed to Arabella, to him. What seemed also very clear to her was that she, the small, insignificant country mouse, was about as likely to attract his interest as she was to fly to the moon.

With that thought came something that was almost hatred for him. How dared he appear like this in their quiet village, like some shining being from a far distant land, and dazzle her against her better judgement? Yet the fault was her own, she told herself. She had thought herself safe from such bedazzlement, and in her own arrogance had looked upon him, and allowed her mind and heart to be drawn insensibly towards him, while her outward thoughts and words were hostile. So she would bear it, as she must, in secret. And if it transpired that he did indeed want Arabella for his wife, then she would dance at their wedding, she told herself grimly.

'You are very serious again. I could almost say cross. Is your ankle hurting?'

Lost in her own thoughts, she had not noticed his approach. Arabella had settled into a long sonata, and was working her way conscientiously through it. Anne looked up, and hoped that her smile looked more genuine than it felt. Her cheeks ached.

'Hurting? Not at all, and if I looked serious, which I do not believe, it must have been a trick of the light.'

'Of course. I should not like to think that anything I might have said earlier would have worried you.'

'Earlier?' Anne cast her mind back. 'You mean when you carried me downstairs? Oh, no, Lord Delamere, I am not afraid of revolution, or upheaval. I do not believe it is in our English nature to behave with such violence.'

'Yet we, too, have executed our King.'

'Yes, but. . .that having been done, and the effects known, I believe that the general revulsion against the act was sufficient to teach us that such a thing cannot bring anything but general misery. An act of violence, however well intentioned, will breed only more violence, surely?'

'So one would believe. So you think that the English have been inoculated, as it were, against the disease of insurrection? One small dose, like Jenner's vaccine, and we are immune? You may be right.'

Involuntarily, she sighed.

'If it were only so simple,' she said helplessly, then, aware of the sorrow in her face, she reconstructed her smile carefully. 'Still, we will not solve the problems of the world in one conversation, will we? I believe Arabella is coming to the end of her piece.'

He glanced across the room, and caught the icy glare with which Arabella was favouring her sister.

'Is she troubling you?' he asked abruptly.

'Troubling me? Oh, no, why should you think such a thing?' Her voice sounded false in her own ears, and she was not surprised when he raised his eyebrows and looked down at her quizzically.

'As I believe I have already told you, I am not quite without experience of young girls,' he said, and with a heroic effort Anne confined her reply to a speaking look. 'Yes. Well, I can see that she is. . .shall we say. . .put out? What have you done to vex her? And do not attempt to deny it, for I shall not believe you.'

'How ungallant of you.'

'You have already informed me, on a previous occasion, that I am no gentleman, so let us not beat about the bush. I suppose that she is not, precisely, enchanted with life in the country?'

'As you say. Poor child, she pines for the life to which she has become accustomed. A party last night and the prospect of a dance in three weeks' time are scarcely sufficient to resign her to our quiet ways, I am afraid.'

'Yes, it is unfortunate that her uncle reacted with such violence to something that was, if indiscreet, fundamentally very innocent. Do you want me to see whether I cannot mend matters?'

'You?'

He smiled at her tone.

'I am, of course, responsible in a sense for her banishment. It seems only right that I should be the one to put it right. I do not like to see. . . I do not like to see her unhappy.'

Anne's mouth was dry.

'What did you have in mind?'

'Oh, not I personally. Since I am not to be their son-in-law, I am scarcely welcome at their house. But I believe that my grandmother has sufficient influence to persuade them to take her back. Should you like that? Shall I see what I can do?'

Anne gazed up at him in astonishment.

'I do not know. No, I am not prevaricating. If what you suggest were possible. . .but I cannot tell. I do not believe that my brother would be pleased. He has always felt, I know, that, much as we appreciate Mr Littleton's kindness to our sister, her place is at home, with us. Now that they have treated her so unkindly, I am not sure that he would wish her to return to them, even if they wanted it.'

'Understandable. But I find it hard to believe that she could not persuade him, if she put her mind to it.'

Anne, knowing how firm her brother could be when faced with any kind of moral choice, doubted it. Delamere, of course, would naturally be soon influenced by Arabella's cozening ways, if as she supposed he was fond of her. She shook her head helplesly, and at the piano Arabella brought her sonata to a conclusion with a thunderous chord, with rather more violence than would seem strictly necessary.

'My summons, I believe,' murmured Delamere, and left her seething with conjecture and a kind of numb misery. For the rest of the evening he devoted himself to Arabella, and though his goodnight to Anne was spoken with great correctness it was entirely lacking in warmth. Nor, she noticed with sad relief, did he offer to carry her upstairs.

Much of Arabella's irritation had been induced by tiredness, and she awoke the following morning in a more cheerful mood. By mutual consent the disagreements of the previous day were forgotten, and, though inclined to be tearful as she watched the maid pack up their clothes ready for departure, she supported the anguish of the actual leave-taking with tolerable fortitude. Anne, more temperately, gave her thanks and her farewells, and with a sigh of relief leaned back against the cushions of the Lydfords' carriage, in which they were being carried home.

At the rectory her brothers formed a little reception committee, and carried her indoors with some ceremony. Anne could not help being touched to see that the little sitting-room had been decked, in her honour, with branches of autumn leaves and sprays of bright berries that would, she knew, fall and be squashed into the carpet with disastrous consequences. Fortunately they were still inclined to look upon Arabella as a visitor, and in consequence she received almost as big a welcome as her sister, so she was not inclined to be too put out.

It was a relief, to Anne, to settle into the familiar routine of home. It closed round her like the warm folds of an old, familiar garment, and she found herself able to forget, at least some of the time, the misery of her newly awakened emotions. At night, it was true, her thoughts were apt to rise up and gibber round her head like hobgoblins, but to the outward eye she was the same busy, cheerful Anne Winterborne, who was perhaps a little pale because she could not, as yet, take her accustomed walks.

She encouraged Arabella to go out as much as possible. Nearly every afternoon she took herself off to visit Lady Sudbury, to mull over endless plans for the dance, or to visit Emily Lydford or Celia Dewlish, who was as excited as she. The Lydfords called several times, and Lord Delamere once or twice, but Anne usually managed to find an excuse to be busy, and leave him with her brothers.

By the time they had been at home for ten days, Anne found that she could put some weight on her foot, providing she was careful. William, with much teasing, presented her with a handsome walking stick, saying that when she had no more use for it as an aid she might use it to terrify the schoolchildren into good behaviour.

'And not the schoolchildren only!' said Anne,

shaking it at him. 'You, sir, are worse behaved than any of them!'

'Ah, not any more. I am become a model of rectitude. I mean to study faithfully, and pass my examinations. The only thing is. . .' He looked at her, a slanting look which roused her forebodings.

'Yes?' she asked mildly.

'Well, the thing is, Nan, that I don't really know that I'm cut out to be a lawyer.' He looked at her sheepishly, and her heart went out to him.

'My poor boy, do you think I do not know it? Only, if you do not, how will you live? You know James and I will do what we can to help you, of course but it will not be a great deal.'

'Oh, I know. And I would not ask any more from you; you have both done more than enough. But if the chance should ever arise, you know that what I should really like would be to go into the army, like Edmund.'

'I thought as much. You were always so alike. And I would not stand in your way, but commissions are so very expensive. . .'

'Well, there may be a way out of that. I believe, from something he said, that Delamere would not be averse to helping me.'

'Delamere? Why should he do that? And we could not possibly accept so great a favour from him.'

'Could we not? But if he should become a member of the family, there could be no possible objection!'

William's young face was radiant with excitement at the prospect. Anne felt her heart thud, sickeningly, in her throat.

'A member of the family?' she said, surprised to find that her voice still worked.

'Yes, of course! I mean, he is going to marry Arabella, isn't he?'

'Is that what he told you?'

'Yes! Well, at least, not in so many words, but he hinted that he might, one day, be a brother to us, you know! And a fellow has got eyes in his head, after all. Anyone can see he's head over ears in love with her. It would be a great match for her, Nan, and I believe he would do something for young Henry, too. Isn't it splendid?'

'Oh, yes. Quite delightful,' said Anne through lips that felt frozen.

'I thought you would be pleased,' said her brother, kindly.

CHAPTER SEVEN

LIFE, rather to Anne's surprise, drifted on much as it had done before. Lord Delamere appeared to be quite settled at Minterne Manor, and the village enjoyed such a round of dinners, and afternoon calls, and even parties, as it had never experienced before. None of these, it was true, could rival the evening at the manor, since none of the other houses had rooms large enough to permit dancing, but it was all very convivial. It was generally agreed that Miss Arabella Winterborne was a delightful girl, and fully deserved any good fortune that might, in the near future, come her way.

The other new arrivals in the village were also agreed to be a decided asset to the social life of the village. They provided, above all else, a delicious fund of gossip and conjecture. Miss Lydford was noted to be showing, in her quiet, ladylike way, a strong preference for the company of the rector, and this was seen by all as both romantic and desirable. The poor of the village, in particular, felt a glow of warm satisfaction at the prospect of their generous-hearted priest marrying so well endowed a lady.

It was Lord Delamere, however, who provided the most fruitful source of speculation. Any mother with a marriageable daughter was bound to welcome his presence in the country with a little spring of hope, however ill-founded. He was the same to everyone — polite, urbane, and amusing — and it was quite impossible to detect in his face or his demeanour a predilection for any one lady in particular. But since Miss Lydford, most obviously his equal in birth and fortune, appeared to have put herself out of the running, the generally held opinion was that he must, surely, be in pursuit of the lovely Miss Arabella. His arrival in the village at the same time as her, though ostensibly to accompany his friends the Lydfords, was seen as certain proof.

Miss Arabella did nothing to deny these rumours, flirting with a pretty impartiality with all the gentlemen but displaying, from time to time, a proprietorial interest in his lordship. Her sister, Miss Winterborne, parried all the discreet enquiries with an air of polite indifference, and her careful efforts to avoid Delamere's company went unnoticed by all but the gentleman himself, who derived a certain amount of quiet amusement from her antics but otherwise treated her, as he treated all the young ladies, as a friend.

At the beginning of November, with the Sudburys' dance beginning to occupy all minds to the exclusion of practically everything else, a letter arrived for Arabella. The family were seated round the breakfast table, and she made haste to tear it open.

'Oh! It is from my dearest Eliza! How wonderful! I thought that Uncle had forbidden her to write to me!'

'If that is the case, I cannot permit you to carry on a clandestine correspondence with your cousin against her parent's wishes,' said James firmly. Anne was glad that he, and not she, gave the reproof. Though Arabella had forgiven her for taking her away from the manor, and for being the cause of postponing the dance, she still did not take kindly to being corrected by her sister.

'Well, I must read it to find out,' pointed out Arabella pertly, undoing the seal before her brother could say anything to prevent her. 'Oh, it is all right! She has permission to write to me, and such news! What do you think? She is engaged to be married!'

'Engaged? I am very happy for her, and delighted to hear it. To whom? Is it anyone you know.'

Arabella's eyes ran swiftly down the page, pausing from time to time as she frowned over the close-packed writing.

'It is so difficult to read, she has written so small, and crossed it as well. His name is Anthony. . . Anthony Spendthrift, it looks like, but it cannot be! Oh, no, I have it now. Anthony Spendler. No, I do not recall. . .ah, she says here they met only a few weeks ago. Well! And he is the most delightful creature in the world, and adores her, and has a tremendous deal of money besides! A house in town, and a country estate. . . no title, of course, but even so. . .he has given her a diamond necklace, to go with her ring, and has promised her a pair of match greys and her own carrot. . .whatever can she mean? Oh, chariot, of course. Lucky Eliza! When I think. . .but anyway, all is now quite forgotten about Delamere. I always knew she did not care for him, and I am sure this Anthony sounds the very person to make her happy. So, I am to be forgiven, and she hopes that I will return very soon and help with her bride clothes and all the arrangements. There! You see, I always said that I had done nothing really wrong, and that one day they would come to see it, and send for me again! Now I shall be presented, as they always said, and have a proper season after all! Oh, I am so happy!'

Anne, her mind working furiously, was silent. Delamere, of course, could have had nothing to do with Elizabeth's betrothal, but the rest? This sudden forgiveness and welcoming back into the fold seemed to come too pat to be natural. Beside her James, too, was silent. Arabella, still puzzling over the details of her letter, did not notice at once.

'She has a new ballgown, in rice satin? No, of course, that must be rose. . .and one of white tarlatan, with knots of pearl — goodness — and she has found a shop selling glows. . .gloves. . .in the most delicious shades, she cannot wait to take me there, she bought six pairs at her last visit. . . Aunt is happy, and never tires of telling her friends about the marriage settlements. . . He is an only son, and an orphan as well, brought up by his grandmother. So Eliza will not have to worry about having a difficult mama-in-law, since the old lady is now quite bedridden. What a fortunate circumstance!'

'Not, perhaps, for the old lady?' suggested James drily.

'Oh, I expect she is happy enough,' was the careless response. 'And I am to write back at once, and say what day the carriage is to be sent for me!'

She looked up in triumph, and noticed for the first time the faces of her brothers and sister.

'What is the matter? Are you not pleased?'

'For Elizabeth, very pleased, if she is truly happy. Though it does sound rather as though she is wedding the young man's houses, and his bank balance, rather than the man himself,' said James. 'The letter is from Elizabeth alone? There is no word from her parents?'

'Oh, that is just her way. She is very sentimental, you know, and always told me she would never marry where she could not give her heart. So that must be all right! No, nothing from Aunt or Uncle, but I suppose there was no need, since she was writing.'

'Well, I think it's a shame,' said Henry, laying down his knife and fork and abandoning, with some reluctance, the dish of ham and eggs that lay before him. 'They send you away at a moment's notice, and then they want you back just as quickly, without a word of an apology or anything. If it were me, I'd stay here.'

'But then I am not a silly little boy, am I?'

'Well, neither am I. But you are a silly girl, if you let them push you around like that.'

'Oh, you nasty little beast! James, did you hear what he called me?'

'Yes, and I also heard what you called him, so let that be an end to your bickering. If you have finished your breakfast, Henry, you may leave the table.'

Henry cast a longing glance at the sideboard, where a dish of kidneys sizzled in a chafing dish in an enticing fashion, but he met his brother's commanding eye and slid, obediently, from his chair. James's glance moved round the table.

'Well, if you'll excuse me. . .' said William hastily, pushing aside his half-eaten plateful. 'Work to do, you know. Mustn't let the grass grow. . .' He slid from the room behind Henry, and closed the door behind him with exquisite care, as if it were made of porcelain. Arabella, frowning, watched him go, then turned her blue eyes on to her brother and sister.

'What is the matter? I cannot believe that you are not happy for me!'

James sighed.

'My dear child, we are glad to see you happy, of course we are. Naturally none of us cared to think that you had been so badly misjudged and treated by your aunt and uncle. But nothing can change the fact that they did, indeed, behave very unkindly towards you.'

'But it was all a mistake! And now they want me back again!'

'Yes, but. . . I cannot help wondering whether, as your legal guardian, I should be right in entrusting you to their care. To send you back, as they did, as if you had been a servant caught pilfering! To have so little care of you that you were sent here without the company even of a maid! And, worse than all that, the fact that under their charge you were able, without any difficulty, to behave with so little propriety. Forgive me, but it does not seem to me that they have given you. . .how shall I put it?. . .quite the tone of mind I would wish to see in a sister of mine.'

Arabella burst into tears.

'You hate me! I always knew it must be so! You are jealous, because I have had nice things, and a comfortable life, and you were left here in this nasty little house! And now you want to punish me, by keeping me here forever!'

James, hurt by her words and disarmed by her tears, would have clasped her in his arms and begged her not to cry, but Anne forestalled him.

'Arabella, I know you do not mean what you say. How could you be so unkind to poor James, who wishes for nothing but the best for you, always? There shall not be another word spoken until you have apologised.'

Her words, spoken in a firm if sympathetic voice, made Arabella stifle her sobs.

'Oh, I beg your pardon, James. *You*, I know, do not mean to make me unhappy. And I do not dislike it here so very much — indeed, I am looking forward to the Sudburys' party, and would not dream of leaving until that is over!'

As an apology this left much to be desired, but as ever James made allowances.

'Well, I am sure you did not mean what you said, and of course we all want what is best for you. I simply question whether that is to return to people who value you so little. I do not care to have my sister treated in such a way, as a chattel who may be cast aside, and then taken up again when the moment suits.'

'Oh, but surely that is no more than pride! And pride, as I have heard you say in your sermons more than once, is a dreadful sin!' countered Arabella ingenuously.

'That is very true, but there is pride, and pride. I believe this to be the proper variety, which does not hold cheap the duties that have been laid upon me.'

Arabella was silenced, and sat tearfully gazing at him. Anne, who was very sorry for her and blamed more than ever the upbringing she had been given by her relatives, went to embrace her. Arabella was stiff within her arms for a moment, then relaxed limply and wept into the folds of her shawl.

'We want you to be happy, darling,' said Anne. 'Only consider if they should send you away again! Once may be carried off as indisposition, as we did before, but if they reject you a second time. . .! I do not wish to puff you up in your own pride, dear, but you are so very pretty, far prettier than Elizabeth. Supposing. . .supposing her Mr Spendler should think so too? It is not impossible, you know. Then indeed they would turn against you, and would stop at nothing to blacken your name. You would be ruined.'

'But her engagement has been announced! He cannot break it off now! They could bring an action against him!'

'Yes, and think how much damage that might do! Besides, if you return to London, what of Lord Delamere? You would not want to go away from him, would you?'

There was a thoughtful pause.

'Oh, he would be sure to follow me,' responded Arabella thoughtfully. 'And if he did not. . . I don't know. He is very amusing, of course, and certainly very rich, but if I were to have a season in London I would go to so many balls, and I should meet a great number of men just as eligible as he is, shouldn't I?'

Anne could have slapped her. While she agreed that his lordship would almost certainly return to London if Arabella should do so, it was inconceivable to her that any girl should risk losing his love, and speak of him as if he were no more than one among many when anyone could see that, in the whole world, he was uniquely perfect.

'I thought you cared for him,' she said, very quietly.

'Well, so did I,' was the candid response. 'But we have been meeting nearly every day for all these weeks, and he has not yet spoken a word of love to me! I do not mean to waste my time on him if he will not come up to scratch!'

Anne winced at such plain speaking, and James frowned. Arabella, feeling that she had made a telling and sensible point, sat up and dried her eyes.

'Well, what is it to be?' she asked. 'What shall I do? I must answer Elizabeth's letter, after all. Am I to go, or not?'

Anne, unable to speak, firmed her lips together. James glanced at her with worried eyes, but seeing that he would get no assistance there he did not shirk his duty.

'You must, of course, write back at once, if only to express your pleasure at her happy news. You will say all that is proper on our behalf as well. As to your returning to London, you may say that you cannot do such a thing without a direct invitation from Mr and Mrs Littleton themselves, rather than through Elizabeth. It will do no harm to mention that you are committed to engagements for the next week or two in any case. Then it is up to them to write to you. If you really wish to go back to them, I will not prevent you, but I should like them to see that you are valued here. You deserve, at the very least, some words of apology from them, and even some reassurance that they will not act against you in haste again. Will you be satisfied with that?'

Arabella had heard no more than that James

would allow her to return. She jumped to her feet and ran to fling her arms extravagantly round him.

'Oh, thank you, dearest, dearest James! I knew you would not be so unkind as to keep me here, when I might be presented in London! I shall write at once! Oh, and to think that I was afraid that after the Sudburys' dance there would be nothing else to look forward to! How very happy I am!'

She danced from the room. Anne sat down in the chair her sister had left, and met her brother's worried eyes.

'Have I done wrong? Should I have insisted on keeping her here? She is a dear, loving, pretty little thing, but she has been sadly indulged, I am afraid.'

'Yes, she has. My dear James, I am afraid we could have done little to change that by keeping her here. I do not wish to say that it is too late, but I do not know how far one may undo the upbringing of many years. I am afraid that she is more fitted to the kind of London life that her relatives lead, and we can only hope that she will find happiness there. I am afraid that she would find very little here, with us.'

She carried the picture of her brother's sorrowful face with her as she went to find Arabella. That young lady was already writing her letter.

'I have told her about the dance, and the one at the manor — Eliza will not know that it was but an impromptu affair. I wonder what she will think when she hears that Delamere is here? She will be fit to scratch my eyes out! Or should I, perhaps, not tell her? For it might make Aunt angry with me again, to hear his name. What do you think?'

'I think that if he follows you to London you will scarcely be able to hide the fact that he has been staying here. But do, pray, use moderate language! It will do no good to make your cousin jealous of you.'

'No, you are quite right. I shall say that he is staying with the Lydfords — then they will be quite sure that it is Miss Lydford who interests him. Is that not clever?'

Anne felt a knot of pain tightening behind her forehead. She felt that she must, somehow, get out of the rectory for a few hours, and away from all her family.

'I think I shall walk up to Hill Farm this morning. There is a new baby there, and I have some little clothes ready to take them. You do not need me for anything?'

Arabella scarcely heard her.

'No. . .no, I don't need you at all. What a long way to go for a baby! Still, I know you like to walk.' She did not look up as Anne left the room.

It was indeed a long walk, almost five miles through the lanes and over the rounded hills. Anne walked fast, trying with exercise to drive out the thoughts that would not leave her. Why should she regret the thought of Delamere's leaving the village? It could do her no good to have him here, when every sense was attuned for the sound of his footstep, the timbre of his voice, even the merest glimpse of him in the distance making her heart race. The sooner he went the better. And if Arabella was what he wanted, then he should have her.

By the time she reached the farm she was ready enough to sit down and take the new baby, a squalling white bundle, into her arms. She admired the infant and offered her gifts, refusing with some tact the offer of elderberry wine but happy to accept a drink of fresh milk and a piece of cake. Thus fortified, she set out for home. A few clouds were massing in the west, but the morning sun still shone bravely on trees and hedgerows that were still bright with colour. She dawdled along, stopping to pick sprays of autumn leaves and refusing to admit to herself that she was putting off returning home. A kind of dismal melancholy filled her, and try as she might she could not prevent a few tears running down her cheeks from time to time. She ignored them, blinking hard and concentrating on her bouquet.

She was reaching high into a hedge for a cluster of glowing rose-hips when the sound of cantering hoofs smote her ear. The lane was very narrow, scarcely more than a footpath, and was bordered with steep banks on both sides. She shrank towards the hedge, feeling the hooked thorns of the wild rose catching at the wool of her pelisse, and stepped up on to a narrow ledge in the bank. With a sense of foreboding she turned her face away from the rider so that it was hidden by the sides of her bonnet, hoping that he would pass by.

It was, of course, to much to hope for. The

cantering hoofs slowed to a trot and a walk. Her face averted, she heard the creak of leather and the small thud of dismouting feet.

'Miss Winterborne! You are a long way from home.'

At the sound of Lord Delamere's voice she felt the muscles in her legs turn to jelly. She tugged at the spray of berries, not noticing the pain as the thorns ran through the fine kid of her gloves. It was her excuse for not turning her head.

'Good morning, Lord Delamere. I have been to visit Hill Farm, and am just now returning home with my trophies. Pray do not interrupt your ride on my account.'

'Allow me.' His arm came over her shoulder, and between his strong fingers the twig that had merely bent in her hand now broke off cleanly. 'Ah, you are entangled. Stand still, while I free you from the thorns.' In the most natural way in the world he unhooked, one by one, the briars that had by now established an octopus-like grasp on her pelisse. 'There, that is all, I think. Give me your hand.'

Reluctantly, she did so. She was encumbered by her basket in one hand, but he took the other in a firm clasp and helped her to step down from the side of the bank.

'Did you think I would ride you down? There was really no need to climb up into the hedgerow, you know.'

She looked down, carefully rearranging the twigs she had picked, which lay in the top of her basket. She was very conscious of his nearness; she was enveloped by the smell of horse and leather that came from his person, could feel a glow of warmth from his body. Her eyes felt hot; she knew they must be pink, and that there were snail tracks down her cheeks from the tears she had not bothered to wipe away. For almost the first time in her life she was glad of her small size. Her bonnet brim, the same unfashionably shallow one she had been wearing before, was sufficient to hide her face if she kept it slightly lowered.

He took hold of the hand that was fussing with the leaves, and turned it over. It looked very small within his large one, and there was a reddish stain on the kid.

'You are bleeding! Let me see.'

She tried to pull her hand away.

'It is nothing — a thorn merely.' He ignored her, unbuttoning the wrist and peeling off the glove.

'Your fingers are quite torn. For heaven's sake, what were you trying to do, climb up the rose bush? Keep still, there is a thorn still in the skin.' He bent over her hand, removing his own glove and pulling out the prickle. A new drop of blood beaded her skin, and he took out a handkerchief and bound it round her fingers.

'You are unhappy,' he said, in a low voice.

She had not seen him look at her, and had hoped he had been concentrating on her hand when he bent over it. Now her hands flew by instinct to her face, wiping her cheeks with his own handkerchief.

'Oh, no! That is. . .it is nothing. A slight head-ache, perhaps, no more.'

He put his fingers under her chin, and tilted her face up to his.

'A headache bad enough to make you cry would not allow you to go visiting so far from home,' he said. 'Will you not tell me what is troubling you? I should like to help you, if I can.'

The unexpected kindness of his voice made her eyes fill with tears again, and she firmed her lips to keep them from wobbling. She lowered her eyelids to hide from his gaze, and at once the hot tears brimmed over her lower lids and burned new tracks down her cheeks. With an exclamation of distress he wiped them away with his fingers, since she already had his handkerchief. Then he pulled her into his arms, holding her tightly against him. Her bonnet hid her face again. With a quick jerk he undid its ribbon bow, pulled it off her and flung it on to the bank. She struggled in his grasp.

'My bonnet! What have you done with my bonnet?'

'Confounded thing. You're better off without it.'

It was the last straw.

'But I have only one other, and that is for b-best! It was a very useful b-bonnet!' she wept.

'Forget the god-damned bonnet! I'll buy you another bonnet, I'll buy you ten more, only do not cry, Anne! Or at least tell me what has upset you so!'

'Oh!' She was speechless with tears and fury.

'You. . .you monster!' Her treacherous body longed to sink into his embrace, to cry luxuriously into that broad chest and be comforted. Her mind, however, recoiled from him and her anger, fuelled by self-despite, helped to drive away her tears. She set her hands flat against his chest and pushed him away with all her strength. It was nothing against his, but he slackened his arms.

'I? What have I done?'

'Everything! You come down here, so high-handed, upsetting everyone and throwing perfectly good bonnets into the dirt, and making everyone like you, when it is all your fault that my poor little sister is banished from the only home she has known for all these years, and for all I know you may have encouraged her to behave so shockingly! And, not content with that, you follow her down, and behave in a high-handed fashion and make yourself conspicuous hanging around at gateways, and make everyone think you are going to propose to her, though you don't do it, and then to crown it all you must needs interfere and have them invite her to go back again! It is too bad!'

He disentangled this remarkably garbled speech.

'Yes, it is! I can see that everything is my fault, though truly my intentions were good! I thought it would be for the best if Arabella should return to the Littletons.'

'*You* thought! And best for whom, might I ask?

For you, I suppose, since you have most to gain by it.'

'On the contrary. But for her, certainly. And, perhaps, for you.'

'Well, I do not believe you,' she said childishly.

'No, of course you do not,' he said soothingly, which had the effect of enraging her even more. She opened her mouth to answer, and as she did so several large fat raindrops splattered into the mud of the lane. The clouds which had been so far away not long ago had rolled over them, unnoticed by her though she had been vaguely aware of the sunshine's vanishing. A nasty little wind gusted through the trees and hedges, tugging gold and brown leaves free from their moorings and setting them whirling round them in a mad dance. She looked up at the sky, and as she did so the heavens opened in full earnest.

At once, in the high-handed manner she had complained of, Lord Delamere scooped Anne up in his arms and, pulling his horse's reins free from the branch where he had looped them, ran to the shelter of a large oak that canopied the lane a few yards away. He set her down with her back to its trunk, pulling the horse round to shelter them from some of the weather and interposing his large body so that she was protected so far as possible. The rain was torrential, however, and in spite of his efforts they were soaked to the skin within a few minutes. Looking back, Anne could see her mistreated bonnet lying abandoned by the side of the track, its crown rapidly filling with water.

'Oh, my bonnet! It is ruined now!'

'Yes, I'm afraid it is. And I suppose that the weather is probably to be laid at my door also, so I shall not try to shirk my responsibilities. But this is no time to be allocating blame. You will be sure to catch another cold if you stay here like this. We must ride back to the village at once.'

'Oh, no! I. . .'

She might as well have spoken to the rain. His hands were at her waist, and she found herself lifted up and deposited, sideways, on the front of the saddle. Speechless, she gasped for breath, and he put one foot in the stirrup and swung himself neatly up, keeping the reins in his left hand and holding her firmly with his right. Anne stiffened, but he pulled her into the shelter of his arm.

'Don't wriggle,' he said into her hair. 'You don't want to fall, do you?'

She tried for a dignified head shake, marred by the realisation that her neatly arranged hair was slipping down her back, and dripping nasty cold trickles down the inside of her collar. She shivered, and was thankful for the warmth of his embrace.

He urged the horse into a canter. There was a brief moment of trotting, when she thought she must have been jolted loose from his hold, then the stride went smoothly into the three-cornered rhythm. She found, to her shame, that she was clutching at the front of his coat with white knuckles, and at once she loosened her grasp. He was concentrating on the road ahead, watching for holes, but she was aware by some alchemy that he was smiling. As they reached the village she fought down an instinctive attempt to hide her face from public view and sat up very straight, cheeks flaming, as they clopped down the street. At least, she thought, the rain would be keeping everyone indoors.

At the door of the rectory he dismounted. She would have jumped down, but the height was considerable and she could not be sure of landing without hurting her ankle again, so she sat with what dignity she could muster while he shouted for a servant to take his horse, then reached up and lifted her down. She expected to be set on her feet, but instead he carried her as he had done before, right up to and through the front door, opened by a wide-eyed maid.

'Your mistress has had the misfortune to be caught in the rainstorm,' he said suavely.

'Put me down!' spat Anne.

'I shall put you into your brothers' care,' he informed her austerely. 'They, perhaps, may be able to see that you do yourself no more mischief.' As he spoke James, William, Henry and Charles Sudbury appeared in the hall.

'*Now* will you put me down?' begged Anne.

'Certainly. You really should not permit your sister to traipse round the countryside in this weather,' he said rather severely to James, who blinked.

'Oh, I know! But it is quite impossible to stop her, she is so very. . .so very decided,' said James.

'Pigheaded, you mean,' said Delamere brusquely, and strode back out of the house before anyone could say anything else. Anne stamped her way upstairs, leaving the men of her family exchanging glances of surmise, and amusement.

CHAPTER EIGHT

AT LEAST this time she had not caught a cold, thought Anne with would-be cheerfulness the following day. She had taken a hot bath at once, and changed into a dry gown. It had to be admitted that if it had not been for her chance meeting with Lord Delamere she would have been in a very different state. The rain continued for several hours, and if she had been obliged to walk all the miles home in the wind and wet she would have been lucky to escape with only a cold. She felt miserable and confused about her feelings, and wished uselessly that she had never even heard of the name Delamere.

Arabella, having sent off her letter to London and knowing that it was impossible that she should receive an answer for a few days, threw herself with even more enthusiasm into the plans for the Sudbury's dance. Though an afternoon spent quietly sewing and reading made her fidget, and declare that she was exhausted, she had boundless energy to expend on the party. Fired by her eagerness, Lady Sudbury allowed her own, more moderate expectations to grow and blossom, and she freely admitted to Anne that she hoped to have her little gathering declared the local event of the year by those fortunate enough to be invited.

Two days before the great event was due to take place, Arabella went to spend the day with Lady Sudbury, to go through the final preparations. With her, unwillingly, went Anne, who out of loyalty to her friend was forced to show an enthusiasm she was far from feeling. As they walked to Minterne Grange after breakfast, Arabella prattled cheerfully.

'Only two more days, and such a deal to see to! I do not know how it would have been if I had not been here to advise dear Lady Sudbury. She is so very old-fashioned in her habits—for of course she is not precisely young, is she? Though very charming and delightful, of course. Only think, she was to have served nothing but negus, and perhaps some wine for the gentlemen! Of course I told her at once that it must be champagne, for indeed to serve only negus would be decidedly shabby! Not that we must not have it, for the old tabbies.'

'I am quite fond of negus myself,' said Anne mildly. 'Champagne makes me sneeze.'

'Oh, Anne, you are so very. . .but there, you have not known the advantages of living in society. And as for the supper I am sure it will be perfectly adequate, though her cook makes her own ices and I cannot believe they will be as good. . . No, what particularly exercises my mind is the musicians. It is all very well to dance to a piano at an impromptu hop, but naturally we must have proper players, and in the country is such a thing to be had? Nothing could present a worse appearance than amateurish bucolics who do not keep to time, or to the tune! I declare I am quite hagridden with worrying about it!'

Anne glanced at her. Arabella's cheeks glowed with health and the exercise of walking in the cold air, and her eyes were a clear and brilliant blue.

'So I see,' she said. 'If they turn out to be so very bad, I shall be happy to play in their stead,' she said kindly.

'Oh, no, that would never do!'

'I do not mind, truly. I do not believe I really care to dance on this occasion.'

'Oh, it is not that!' responded her sister blithely. 'I am sure you need not dance if you do not want to! But with as many as fifteen couples, we cannot dance to a piano! So rustic, and besides, not nearly loud enough!'

They reached the gates to the grange. The drive was long, bordered by a fine avenue of lime trees. Arabella sighed.

'How you can manage to live like this, without a carriage, I cannot conceive,' she said irritably. 'Only think of the time it would save. We would have been there this twenty minutes, at least!'

'It would scarcely be far enough to warrant the trouble of having the horses put to. You know that nine times out of ten Mary walks rather than rides to the village.'

'At least she does so by choice.'

'Not so far now, and only look how beautiful

the trees are. In the early summer you can smell
the blossom almost in the middle of the village
itself. And the walk has given you a very becoming
colour,' said Anne cunningly.

'Well, there is that,' conceded her sister. 'Not
that there will be anyone to see, of course, except
Sir Robert, and ten to one he will be out riding
round his estates. The Lydfords may call this
afternoon with Delamere — I took care to tell them
I should be here all day — but the colour will
hardly last until then.'

'You must pinch your cheeks, then, as you
usually do,' responded Anne, with a little flare of
temper. Since her disastrous walk to Hill Farm
she had managed to avoid all sight of Lord
Delamere, finding duties with the cook or the
housekeeper when he called, and making excuses
for not making any calls at the manor. She had
hoped that on this occasion Lady Sudbury would
be too busy to encourage any visitors.

The morning passed by in a great bustle of
activity. Anne was required to pace out the great
hall, to determine precisely where the musicians
must be in relation to the dancers, and to relieve
a sudden apprehension on the part of Arabella
that it might not be possible to accommodate more
than fifteen couples, should any of the older guests
wish to join in the country dances. They decided
on the exact disposition of the tables in the supper-
room, the number of card tables to be set up in
the library, and exact arrangement of sofas and
chairs in the drawing-room so that groups might

form to converse, or couples sit out a dance in decorous semi-seclusion.

By the time luncheon was announced, Anne felt as though she had been pounded in a wash tub, and put through the wringer afterwards as well. Never had the sight of cold meat, fruit and bread been so welcome to her, and for once she did not refuse a glass of wine, which had the unfortunate effect of making her feel very sleepy.

Afterwards she would have preferred to slip away, but Mary Sudbury looked so hurt when she suggested it that she subsided meekly back into her chair in the drawing-room.

'It is so many years since I have given such a party, I really am quite nervous,' admitted her friend. 'Arabella is the greatest help, of course, but I rely on you to keep me as calm as possible, my dear!'

Anne could do no more than smile and agree, but when the Lydfords and Lord Delamere were announced half an hour later she wished more than ever that she had been able to make her escape. She sat stiffly in her seat beside Mary, hoping that the presence of her friend would protect her from the necessity to converse, but it was not long before Lady Sudbury left her, driven to demonstrate to Miss Lydford the excellence of the great hall for the purpose of dancing. Without even so much as a piece of work to occupy her hands and eyes she picked up a book of engravings, and tried to appear engrossed in its insipid beauties.

'I am glad to see that you have taken no harm
from your wetting the other day,' said a voice
firmly, and she was forced to look up. Edward
Delamere stood before her, directly between her
and the rest of the room as if blocking her retreat.

She gave one rapid glance up at his face, hoping
that it might somehow have changed, that it might
have lost whatever quality it possessed that made
her heart lurch within her. It had not, and she
fixed her eyes firmly on his middle waistcoat
button.

'No harm at all, thank you, my lord,' she said in
a wooden voice.

'Good. I beg your pardon, I believe I have not
yet wished you good afternoon. Good afternoon,
Miss Winterborne.'

His hand was held out to her, and she must
perforce take it. Impossible, in Mary Sudbury's
drawing-room, to insult him by refusing to shake
his hand! She touched it with the tips of her
fingers.

'Good afternoon, Lord Delamere.'

She would have withdrawn her hand at once,
but he grasped it, turning it over to examine her
fingers before letting go.

'Quite healed, I see.'

She thought of his handkerchief, which she had
carefully laundered and which she had hidden,
mawkishly, beneath her own in their case.

'Quite. Thank you, my lord.'

'Perhaps I may sit down? I have no burning

wish to anticipate the pleasures of two days' time
and view the dancing place in advance.'

Once again it was impossible, without extreme
discourtesy, to refuse. Anne folded her hands
primly in her lap, and sat ramrod-stiff, staring
straight ahead of her. He would not stay long, of
course. This was, she supposed, the merest polite-
ness to Arabella's sister, and perhaps an attempt
to win her consent to an early return to London of
the girl he so admired. She made no attempt to
inaugurate a conversation, but he seemed quite
undeterred.

'Have you heard the news?' he asked.

Her mind ran on village matters.

'Yes, triplets, and two of them living! It is quite
an event, is it not?'

'Triplets? Surely not! My correspondent said
nothing of that, and it must have been the most
significant of items.'

'Oh, yes, I assure you. I went to visit them
yesterday, and have seen them with my own eyes.
Poor little things, I wonder whether they can live,
though I did not say so. They seemed very small,
and weak.'

'Ah! You are referring, I believe, to the recent
confinement of the blacksmith's wife?'

'Yes, of course.'

'I beg your pardon. I was speaking of news from
the great world outside Minterne Abbas. It is
hard, I know, to believe that it exists, but I assure
you that it wags on quite merrily.'

Anne blushed painfully.

'We are inclined to be parochial in our interests, my lord. The village is my world, and I expect to know no other.'

He would not be deterred.

'Nevertheless, its events cannot quite be kept at bay. However, if you do not wish to hear about it I shall not tell you more than that the Queen is no longer in Bath.'

Her eyes flew to his face, as he had hoped they might.

'Not in Bath? You mean. . .she has gone to Claremont? The Princess's confinement is imminent?'

He nodded, pleased and amused by her instant attention. In spite of her attempt to uninterest, he knew her to be well informed on the events of the day, and he more than once had been surprised to find her so astute a judge of the currents and whirlpools of court and political life.

'So I am told. The Queen left yesterday, I hear, as soon as she learned that the Princess was in labour.'

'So, it may well be that the new heir is born already! How exciting! No wonder you were start-led when I spoke of triplets!'

He laughed.

'I was indeed.' He was delighted to see that her interest in his news had made her forget that she was angry with him. The hard set of her lips had relaxed, and the flecks of gold he had already noticed in the depths of her eyes glinted in the afternoon sunshine. The wine she had drunk with luncheon had brought a little flush to her usually pale cheeks, and the brown hair, which she had arranged with its usual neat severity that morning, had been loosened a little, and released a few soft wisps against her smooth brow, and on the ivory pale skin of her neck. His hand moved involuntarily with the urge to stroke them away, and set his fingers, and his lips, where they had been. He realised she had asked him a question.

'I beg your pardon? I'm afraid I did not hear you.'

She looked surprised, but repeated, 'Is the Prince Regent not at Claremont also?'

'No, I believe he has gone shooting in Suffolk, with the Hertfords.'

'And yet I have heard you speak of him as a fond father?'

'So he is. Surprisingly so, considering the aversion in which he holds his wife. No, like many men, I believe that he is terrified by the whole idea of childbirth, of the risk and suffering which the Princess must undergo. He may feel that there is no place for him in the midst of so strictly feminine an event. Or it may be that he is convincing himself that all will be well, that he must carry on as normal in order to make it so. He himself, of course, has but indifferent health, and was considerably weakened by his cupping in September, before Baillie treated him.'

'How strange and sad it is,' she mused, 'that the poor have so many children that it is a burden to them, yet our royal family, for all the doctors can do, is so small.'

'Small! You would not say that if you had seen Prinny last summer, when he left off his stays in the heat! Not for nothing do they call him the Prince of Whales!'

She laughed.

'Yet as a young man he was much admired, was he not?'

'You imply that I am old enough to remember. Should I be insulted?'

'By no means insulted, venerable lord. . .at least, I assume that your memory is as yet unimpaired by your great age?'

'Such flattery. Yes, by all accounts he was a veritable Adonis, which, translated from the kind of language used of Princes, means that he was not ill favoured.'

'What a pity he was not able to marry a beautiful Princess, like the Princess in the fairy-tales. Or, if not beautiful, at least someone he could love and be happy with.'

'It might not have made so much difference. The poor King, after all, was devoted to Queen Charlotte, and yet of all their many offspring can you pick one, in truth, who is fitted for rule?'

'Treason, Lord Delamere?'

'Not at all. I do not suggest that we do away with them, unsatisfactory or not. We are obliged, as in so many things, to accept what we have and make the best of it.'

'Well, it may be that even as we speak we have

a new little heir to make the best of. Let us hope that he will be the best that we could hope for.'

'And if he should prove to be a she?'

'Then,' she said with dignity, 'we are of course even more fortunate. It may be that a Queen, rather than a King, is what our country needs.'

He laughed aloud. Arabella, just then returning to the room with those who had been in the hall, came flitting over to his side.

'Well, Delamere, so you are here? And yet you did not choose to come and see how very well we have managed in arranging the great hall for dancing? You would be surprised, I believe, by its commodiousness.'

'Not at all surprised; I know it for a magnificent apartment, and yourself for a wonder at such contrivances. No, I prefer to wait and be dazzled.'

'Then dazzled I shall expect you to own youself. I declare you are every bit as provoking as Anne, who will not allow herself to be excited by anything! Of course, I make allowances for you, who are used to attending so many balls and parties in London.'

'On the contrary, you behold me agog. And one of my purposes in coming here today was to attempt to steal a march on the others by begging you to reserve a dance for me, and Miss Winterborne also, naturally. I know how great the competition will be, you see.'

'Oh, Delamere, how charming! Of course I shall dance with you — the first dance, if you like, and a waltz also. I should not consider dancing it in

London, of course, not being quite out yet, but for a country dance among friends there cannot be the least impediment!'

'You are too kind. I feel that as her guest of so long I must solicit Miss Lydford's hand for the first dance, but I shall hope for the second, and hold you to your promise to waltz.'

'Oh, I shall not let you forget it!' If Arabella was disappointed in being denied the first dance with the most eligible bachelor in the village, she was worldly enough to realise that he could not do otherwise. Nor, having seen how Emily Lydford's eyes followed James whenever he was present, did she feel concerned. She gave him a brilliant smile, and darted off to speak to Lady Sudbury. Anne assumed that he would follow her, but he sat down again beside her.

'And you, Miss Winterborne? I hope you mean to waltz also?'

'I believe I have arrived at an age when few eyebrows are likely to be raised at such a sight, though I have not been formally presented! Nevertheless, I must beg you to excuse me on this occasion.'

Assuming that his invitation had been no more than a polite form, she expected him to accept her dismissal with a few polite regrets, but he was frowning down at her, his dark eyebrows drawn together into a straight line above the uncompromising clarity of his grey eyes.

'Your ankle is not still paining you, is it?'

It would have been wonderfully simple to accept

the offered excuse, but after her long walk of a few days before she could scarcely claim still to be in pain. She returned his look as straightly as he.

'No, it does not hurt. I do not care to waltz, that is all.'

Impossible to tell him that the idea of being held in his arms in the close embrace that the dance necessitated was a thing so blissful that it would be painful.

'I did not realise. You seemed to enjoy it that time at the manor.'

The memory made her blush and drop her eyes.

'I do not know why you must always argue with me,' she said in a low voice.

'My dear girl, I did not mean to distress you! Now do not, pray, be angry with me again! You need not waltz if you do not wish to, but you will not deny me a country dance or two, at least?'

'I am sure you will have many claims on your attention,' she said.

'Very likely. But so will you, which is why I wished to make sure of a dance with you. I don't mind doing the polite and dancing with all the other girls, but I'm dashed if I'm going to forgo dancing with the people I want to!'

'There is no need. . .'

'Now who is arguing? I could wish that we understood one another better, Anne.'

She was so flustered by his remark that she scarcely noticed his use of her name.

'But I do! I understand you very well!' she exclaimed earnestly. 'If I seem to stand in your

way, it is only because James and I are so concerned about Arabella! But I do understand!'

'Do you?' He sat still for a few moments, his
eyes on her averted face. Then his friend Lydford
called across the room to him, and with a murmur
of apology he left her.

Anne prepared for the dance, when the day
came, with a troubled mind and heart. She had
not seen Lord Delamere again, and although she
had received a flattering number of requests for
dances she looked forward to the evening with
very mixed feelings. They had been invited to dine
at the manor, and the Lydford carriage had been
put at their disposal to convey them there as well
as to the grange and home again afterwards, which
greatly pleased Arabella since she was very
scathing about the shabby hired chaise which was
all that the village inn could offer.

Once again she had insisted on lending her sister
a gown, and rather against her will Anne was
arraying herself in an underdress of white satin,
with a floating gown of palest pink crape, orna-
mented, at the hem and on the little puffed
sleeves, with fine bands of pink satin ribbon. A
basket of hothouse flowers had been sent down
from the Lydfords, and from this she had taken a
few clustered buds of late roses, their white petals
just blushed with faintest pink, to set in her
carefully arranged hair.

Arabella, a vision in spangled gauze over white
satin, was pleased to approve her sister's appearance, while Henry, who as a great treat was

permitted to go to the grange and keep his friend Charles company, was almost dumbstruck at so much magnificence. Anne could only hope that he would stay that way.

The carriage was prompt, and the journey short. As she climbed down the steps from the conveyance, supported by James's arm, she told herself that it would not be so bad, that in only a few hours it would all be over and then, surely, Arabella would return to London and take his lordship with her. Then Anne might return, as best she could, to her old quiet life, and the simple pleasures that had once been so dear. Arabella, eager, ran ahead into the house, and she followed more sedately, arranging her face into an expression of anticipation and pleasure.

As soon as they reached the drawing-room, however, it became clear that all was not well. Emily came rustling towards them, her face pale and serious.

'Good evening! You must forgive me if I am not as welcoming as I should like to appear. We have just received news of the most serious nature. . .'

Her eyes filled with tears. James, unable to bear the sight of them, took her hands in his.

'I am so very sorry! Some trouble in the family, I apprehend. Not——' he glanced round the room '—not your brother, surely? You do not mean that he is ill, or hurt?'

'No! Oh, no, nothing of that nature! It is. . .oh, here is my brother, and Delamere, who will be

able to make all clear to you. It was he who
received the news. . . Delamere, here are the
Winterbornes just arrived, and who have not
heard the dreadful tidings!'

Anne, in the relief of seeing him come into the
room unhurt, felt that she scarcely cared what the
news might be, but the sight of Delamere's serious
face drove all such thoughts from her head. He
shook their hands, briefly.

'Oh, what is it? You are frightening me!' said
Arabella. 'Is someone dead?'

'Yes. I have but just this last few minutes
received news. . .the Princess Charlotte was deliv-
ered of a stillborn son yesterday, and died herself
in the early hours of this morning.'

The colour came back into Arabella's cheeks.

'Oh, is that all? How you frightened me,
Delamere! I thought it must be someone related
to us, or a member of your family!'

'The heir to the throne, Arabella,' said James
seriously. 'I must send to tell them to toll the
church bell, and inform my people.'

'Well, of course it is all very shocking, but it
does not affect us, does it?' Arabella looked from
one to the other of them as James left the room.

'Oh, hush,' said Anne, embarrassed for her
sister's want of conduct. 'The Princess was only
twenty-one. To lose her child, and then to die
herself so young, is a sad thing for anyone. But
for the Prince's only child, the King's only
grandchild. . .'

'Well, of course I am very sorry for her, poor

thing. But they will find someone else, you may be sure of that! Must we spoil our evening with long faces?'

'Have you sent word to the grange?' Anne asked in a low voice.

'Yes, straight away. I thought it right to do so. I only wonder that we did not hear news of this sooner, but my letter was delayed on the journey, and the weather must have held up any other messages also.'

James returned to the room, and soon they could distantly hear the sound of the bell, telling out its sonorous message of death. All were silent for a moment. Then a servant entered, and whispered to Miss Lydford, who glanced at her brother and received his nod.

'Dinner is served. There is no purpose to be gained by our starving ourselves, so I suggest that we go through and eat it.'

They processed through to the dining-room. Arabella, annoyed that the anticipated pleasures of her evening were being spoiled, sat silently sulking. The rest, however, could think of nothing but the momentous news. Lord Delamere repeated such details as he had been told.

'I believe there had already been some cause for concern, and Croft was keeping a close eye on the Princess. The Queen left Bath four days ago, as I told you before, and I think the Regent also left Suffolk as soon as he had news that the labour had begun. His own health is so very indifferent, however, that he was unable to travel fast, though he sent for news at every halt he made. He reached Carlton House in the night, was told that the baby was dead, and was roused from sleep soon after by the Duke of York to tell him of the death of the Princess.'

'Poor man. The most dreaded news for any father, Prince or not,' said Emily Lydford. James gave her an approving look.

'Did he go on to Claremont?' asked William.

'Yes, he was there by nine o'clock, and saw the bodies, then drove away with the coach blinds down. I imagine he must be prostrate with grief. It could be enough to kill him.'

'And after him, who? The Duke of York, of course, for a while, but he is not a young man, and the Duchess has never had any children. That leaves Clarence and Kent. I suppose they will both now be forced into marrying suitable foreign Princesses. It is going to be the most tremendous muddle, and very expensive. After all, they both have — people to provide for.'

'You mean all the little FitzClarences?' said Arabella brightly, entering into the conversation with disastrous accuracy. 'How many of them are there? Nine, or is it ten?'

'Ten, I believe,' replied Lord Delamere calmly. 'And if Miss Lydford will forgive me for mentioning the subject, the Duke of Kent has been living with Madame St Laurent for at least twenty-seven years also. It would be a farce, were it not so tragic, to see them making their dynastic marriages in such a hurry.'

A servant came in with a note for Miss Lydford. With a word of apology she opened and read it.

'It is as I thought,' she said. 'Lady Sudbury feels that it is quite impossible, in the circumstances, to continue with our plans for this evening.'

Arabella stared at her.

'Not continue? But. . .the dance! Everything is arranged! It cannot be put off now!'

'I am afraid that it must be. It would be quite unsuitable to be dancing at such a time, and of course none of us would wish to show such a want of respect to the royal family. Lady Sudbury has sent messages to all those invited, cancelling the party.'

'Cancelling. . .? But she cannot! This cannot be! Oh, no!' She burst into a storm of tears, and Anne hurried to comfort her.

'There will be other parties, my dear. Many other parties, even better than this one. You must not mind so much.'

'But it was this one I was looking forward to! Oh!' She rounded on Delamere. 'It is all your fault! Why could you not have kept the news to yourself for a few hours? Nobody need have known, and we could have all enjoyed ourselves!'

'I did consider it,' he admitted ruefully, 'but I could not think it right to do so. I am sorry for your disappointment. But your sister is right, and perhaps Lady Sudbury will rearrange things for another night, very soon.'

'I don't care! I don't care! It should have been tonight!' was all that Arabella would say. Mortified, Anne tried to quieten her, but Arabella quickly lost any control, and her sobs grew to cries and hysterical screams until her sister was forced to slap her.

'I am very sorry,' said Anne to the room at large. 'I think I must take my sister home. She is unwell, and must go to bed.'

'Of course,' said Emily Lydford with her usual calm kindness. 'Poor Arabella, she is very young, and it is a great disappointment to her. Indeed, we are all disappointed, I will ring for the carriage at once.'

The rectory party returned home in silence. Anne, stealing a glance at her brothers, thought that she had never seen James look so severe. On reaching the shelter of the house, he gave Arabella such a scolding that she dissolved into tears again and ran away up the stairs, slamming the door of her bedroom behind her.

'She behaved badly, but she *is* very young,' said Anne, hoping that the repetition of Emily Lydford's words would soften him. 'I know you did not mean it when you said that such conduct showed her to be unfitted to go back to London! She will be sorry tomorrow, I am sure.'

'I am afraid that London, and the Littletons, are all that she is fitted for,' was the stern response. Anne followed her sister upstairs and managed, with much cajolery, to get her undressed and into bed.

'James is so cruel to me,' sobbed Arabella into

her pillow. 'Everything goes awry for me! It isn't fair! It isn't fair!'

Eventually she cried herself to sleep, and Anne went wearily to her own bed. The flowers in her hair, which she had quite forgotten were wilted and drab, and she threw them away. She had wished she need not go to the dance, but such an answer to her prayers was terrible.

Exhausted, she slept late in the morning. Going downstairs, pale and heavy-eyed, she found that James had gone out and taken William with him. Henry was still at the grange, and the house was silent. Reluctantly she went up to Arabella's room.

It, too, was silent. Silent, and empty. Arabella had gone.

CHAPTER NINE

ANNE stood for a moment in the doorway, then, as quietly as if there were a sleeping figure in the bed that she feared to waken, stepped forward and closed the door behind her. She knew, straight away, that her sister had left the house. Before she laid a hand in the tossed bedding and found it cold, before the cupboards and drawers revealed their rifled and depleted state, something in the quality of the silence told her that only the servants, moving quietly through their allotted tasks, shared the rectory with her. A small sound made her jump and turn, but it was only the fire in the grate, relaid and lit by the housemaid at an early hour while the rest of the house slept, and now burned down to a bed of coals and soft, shifting ashes.

Was that when Arabella had gone? Would the housemaid, intent on her task and still sleepy herself, have noticed in the darkness of early morning whether the bed was empty or not? She could not believe that comfort-loving Arabella would leave the shelter of the house in the middle of the night, and risk the dangers of dark and cold. But by the time the housemaid came, she would have known that dawn would not be far off.

Anne brought her icy hands down from her

cheeks, and tried to be practical. A glance at the
dressing-table revealed no note pinned to the pin-
cushion, nor was there anything propped on the
mantelshelf above the fire. The trinket box that
usually held pride of place on the dressing-table
was gone, and so were the silver-backed brushes
that the Littletons had once given her as a birthday
gift. Most of the numerous gowns and bonnets
were still there, naturally, since Arabella would
have been restricted to what she could carry
herself, but the blue velvet pelisse with its matching bonnet was missing.

Anne left the empty room and ran downstairs
to the hall. The elderly maid, a trusted friend who
acted as housekeeper, looked at her mistress in
horror when summoned.

'Gone? Miss Arabella gone? But where to, Miss
Anne? All by herself, what will become of her?'

'What indeed,' said Anne grimly. 'She means, I
suppose, to take herself back to London. She will
be hoping to travel on the stage, I suppose.'

'But how would she get to Dorchester? It's
more'n ten miles, and she'd never walk half of
that, our fine young lady.'

'No, you are right. She will have tried to hire a
horse, or a conveyance of some kind. Oh, I must
go after her!'

'Shouldn't I send for Rector, madam, or at least
Mr William?'

'No. No, the rector was very vexed with my
sister, and I do not wish to make him more angry
with her. Mr William, I believe, has gone hunting

in another part of the country; I know he was invited to join some friends. Besides, there is no time to be lost; I must go at once.'

On the point of running upstairs, she was arrested by the sound of a knock at the front door. Impossible to run away, for she was clearly visible through the two windows that flanked the door and through which she could see Miss Lydford and her brother, and Lord Delamere.

'You had better let them in,' she said. 'I will tell them that my sister is unwell, and keeps to her bed. At all costs we must try to keep this a secret from the world.'

As the visitors entered she smiled wanly, and greeted them as calmly as she could. She did not know how pale she was, nor that her eyes had bruise-like shadows beneath them.

'We wished to enquire how Miss Arabella Winterborne is today,' said Emily Lydford, her eyes dragging themselves from the door of the rector's study. 'I hope she is recovered from her disappointment?'

'Oh, yes, quite recovered, thank you,' said Anne. 'That is to say,' she corrected herself hastily, 'she is still in bed. She is a little. . .a little feverish this morning. I was just going upstairs to sit with her. She will be so grateful for your kind enquiry.'

'May I perhaps perform that office for you, and sit with her for a while? Forgive me, Miss Winterborne, but you do not look quite well. I am afraid that you have not had a good night. Was your sister unwell?'

'No. . .well, yes, a little. It is so very kind of you, but I am afraid she will see no one but me. I am afraid that she did not behave well last evening, and she might be embarrassed. . .'

'Oh, there is no need! We all understood how disappointing it was for her; indeed, I was disappointed myself! And. . .the rector? He is not at home?'

Again her eyes flickered hopefully towards the study door.

'No, he has gone out. I believe,' said Anne with cunning mendacity, 'that he may be intending to call at the manor. What a pity if you are not there when he calls!'

'Oh, yes! But we may not miss him. I can see that you are much occupied, Miss Winterborne, so I will not stay any longer.'

They took their leave. Lord Delamere, who had done no more than utter a few words of greeting and farewell, looked carefully at Anne as he shook her hand. Her own trembled and was cold, and the pupils of her eyes were contracted with shock. Outside the door he spoke in a low, urgent voice to his friend Lydford, who looked at him in astonishment.

'Trouble? Do you think so? And do you think it right to interfere? I thought Miss Winterborne was in a hurry to be rid of us.' He was soon persuaded, however, and drove off with his sister, leaving Edward Delamere at the gate. He sauntered slowly up the high street of the village, pausing in the shelter of a recessed doorway and standing in its shadow, ostensibly lost in admiration at a display of dusty leather boots. He was soon rewarded by the sight of Anne, unmistakable to him although she was bundled up in an old cloak with the hood pulled up over her head and obscuring her face. When she had passed him on the other side of the road, he left his hiding place and followed her. When she went into the Minterne Arms he halted outside it, waiting until a smart phaeton drove up at a spanking trot. He spoke a few quick words to the groom driving it. Then, with a quick wave of his arm towards the inn's courtyard, he went inside.

Anne wished that she were on better terms with the innkeeper. An irregular church-goer, he regarded the rectory almost as he would have done a rival establishment, as a threat to his livelihood. While invariably polite to his face, he had been known to refer to the rector as 'too young, and a bit soft in the head'. His opinion of the rest of the family was unknown, and though she knew him well enough by sight Anne had never got beyond the formal courtesy of a greeting if they should pass one another in the street. Now she was in the awkward position of having to question him about her sister's flight, which was impossible to do without revealing the fact of it to a man who had the opportunity of spreading this juicy titbit of news round the entire countryside.

Her first halting requests met with blank, even

hostile silence. He denied all knowledge of a young lady, whether in a blue pelisse or not. He spoke with authority, but his eyes shifted a little, and she did not believe him.

'I beg you, sir, to help me!' she begged in a low voice. 'May I not go into a more private place, so that I may explain to you? It is a matter of. . .of great delicacy.'

The florid face did not soften.

'Don't seem to me to be much point in that, miss. Nothing to tell you, for one thing, and for another I'm busy. Very busy.'

'At this time of day?' Anne looked indignantly round the fortunately almost deserted taproom. She could not believe that her sister had not come here, for there could be no other way of obtaining some means of travelling, and she would certainly not have attempted to walk, even had she known the way to Dorchester. The conviction was growing in her that the man's silence had been bought. She rummaged in her reticule, wishing that she had been able to bring more money with her. 'If it is a question of money, I would be able to pay you for information.' She drew out half a sovereign, but the man looked at it with contempt.

''Ere! You trying to bribe me? There's no call for that, miss. No call at all. I got nothing to tell you, and that's flat. Now, I got me work to do, and I'll thank you to let me be.' He leaned his considerable bulk against the doorway that led from the taproom to the rest of the building, and watched her scrabble in her purse again.

'I don't mean to bribe you, merely to buy the information I need,' she said. 'I have not a great deal of money, but I could give you five guineas, and my brother the rector will give you more, if I ask him.'

'How much more?' For the first time he seemed slightly interested.

'That would depend on what you are able to tell me,' she said firmly. Lord Delamere, standing just outside the door, applauded her silently.

'And if I tell you nothing?'

'Then you get nothing,' she said, but her voice shook and she could not keep the note of pleading out of it.

'Not quite,' said a voice behind her. The innkeeper quickly abandoned his doorpost, and stood up straight. 'What you will get, my good man, is a taste of my fist.'

'Oh, Delamere!' exclaimed Anne in horrified relief.

'Assault, that's what that is! I'll have the law on you!' blustered the innkeeper.

'Not at all. I heard you threatening the young lady, and am merely protecting her, as any gentleman is bound to do.'

'Threatening? I did no such thing!'

'But it will be your word against mine, won't it? And I am afraid that a magistrate will be more inclined to believe a peer than an innkeeper. Come, Miss Winterborne. I believe our business here is quite done. Except, of course, that if I find that you have spoken of this conversation to anyone — anyone, mind! — I fear that you will very speedily find yourself regretting it. Good day.'

He offered his arm to Anne, who put her hand on it without thinking, then snatched it away.

'But I can't! I mean, I am very grateful, but I would be even more so if you would kindly go away, Lord Delamere!'

'There you are, see!' muttered the innkeeper. 'You ain't wanted, lord or no lord.'

'Nonsense,' said his lordship briskly. 'Come along, Anne. There is no need for this, you know. And I really do not think we should discuss anything in front of this. . .gentleman. Do you?'

Nervelessly, Anne allowed him to lead her outside and round to the yard.

'Ah, there is Toby. I wonder, Toby, have you picked up any gossip from the ostlers?'

'Yes, my lord. A young lady came along, very early, and said she must get to Dorchester at once, as someone was very ill and she must get the stage to London. The chaise was already booked, but she made such a fuss and offered them a deal of money, and in the end she went off in it. About half-past seven, that would have been.'

'Oh, dear! It is just as I thought, and she paid the wretched man to keep silent! Half-past seven, and it is now nearly eleven! What is to be done? I must go after her.'

'Of course you must. Here, climb up.' Anne felt herself caught round the waist, and lifted neatly into the phaeton.

'What are you doing?' She did not sit down, but

stood where he had put her on the wildly swaying vehicle. Delamere walked round the back of the phaeton and sprang up beside her.

'For heaven's sake sit down. You're frightening the horses, and making a spectacle of yourself besides. Do you not wish to catch your sister?'

'Yes, but. . .'

'Then sit down. Let 'em go, Toby!' He gathered the reins in his capable hands. Anne sat down abruptly as the horses stepped out. 'Pull the hood of your cloak right up, and keep your face down,' he ordered. 'We'll just have to hope you're not recognised. Goodness knows that garment is shapeless enough to house almost anything.' He shook up the horses into a trot, and Anne obediently hid her face and huddled down beside him.

'They will recognise you, at any rate,' she pointed out mutinously.

'Oh, everyone expects lords to behave like this, making off with innocent country girls, that sort of thing,' he informed her airily. 'I dare say they will all be very shocked, but nobody will be greatly surprised. I shall tell them it is an old maidservant, desperate to visit her dying brother, or some such tale. They won't believe a word of it, of course, but they won't dare to say so if the Lydfords back me up.'

They passed through the village, and he roused the horses to a canter. Anne had to clutch at her hood to keep it from being blown back from her head by the wind of their movement. It was very cold, and she was thankful she had put on two warm petticoats as well as an old pelisse under her cloak. He glanced down at her.

'Are you all right? Not too cold?'

'No, thank you. Please keep your eyes on the road!' she begged, as he took a corner so fast that the well sprung phaeton tipped wildly and she clutched at the side of it. He laughed.

'Don't be frightened! I'm accounted a tolerably good driver. We must go quickly or not at all, you know. She has a good start on us.'

'Yes.' She paused. 'How did you know?' she asked with difficulty. 'I didn't tell anyone. Or did she. . .did she confide in you?'

'Certainly not! Do you think I would have allowed her to go off on such a madcap scheme, if I had known of it? No, I guessed. You are not a very good liar, dear Miss Mouse. I am afraid your face gave you away. I sent the Lydfords home with instructions to have my groom bring the phaeton down to the village, and then I loitered in the street by the cobbler's, and followed you to the inn. You were so preoccupied that you did not see me.'

'Oh. I had hoped to hush it up somehow. . . William has gone off hunting, and James was so upset—I did not want to worry him further. I thought if I could get her back, quickly, he need never know.'

'And so you shall, if it is possible. If not. . . well, do not worry about that now. We shall do our best, at any rate.'

Anne, who knew that he was intent only on

saving his love from the consequences of her folly, was nevertheless comforted by his presence. She had no idea what she would have done if he had not intervened, but supposed that she must have confided in James and thereby lost still more time. As it was she had no idea of the time the stage-coach left Dorchester, and whether it was still possible to find her sister before she boarded it. If not. . .would Delamere be prepared to follow? His phaeton was certainly a great deal faster than the stage, but even so it might be a long drive. It came to her that she herself would be compromised if, as was possible, they were forced to travel into the evening and the night.

There was no profit in such thoughts, however, so she sat quietly and allowed her companion to concentrate on his driving. She knew little of the art, but it was soon obvious that his claim to be 'tolerably good' was over-modest. As fast as they went, he judged each twist and bend in the lanes to a nicety, and seemed to have a sixth sense about what might lie ahead. Once, meeting an oncoming trap, she thought that they must be overturned, but somehow he whisked the phaeton through the narrow gap without so much as a scrape, scarcely slackening their speed.

On the outskirts of Dorchester she again lowered her face, and pulled her hood half over it. She visited the town seldom enough, but was well aware of the risk of being seen and recognised. She gave directions in a low voice, and soon they were pulling up outside the White Hart. Anne looked around her in dismay. The coaching inn looked suspiciously quiet. No travellers waited, no piles of luggage and parcels stood in the empty yard.

'It is too late,' she said in distress.

'So it appears.' He summoned an ostler to hold the horses, jumped down, and came to assist her to descend. 'You had better come inside. You cannot sit out here while I ask.'

Inside the inn it was blessedly warm, and Anne found herself shivering with reaction.

'A private parlour for the young lady my cousin, if you please,' commanded Lord Delamere. 'You seem very quiet, landlord?'

'Yes, sir. But you should have seen us not an hour and a half since! Proper bustle, that was, sir, with so many people wishful to get on the stage.' Anne gripped her hands tightly together.

'There, you see, my dear,' said Delamere to Anne, with great kindness. 'Ten to one you would not have got a seat even if you had been in time! My cousin wished to take the stage to London,' he explained blandly to the landlord, 'and I have been trying to dissuade her. I am far from easy at the idea of a young lady travelling alone in a public conveyance.'

'Quite so, sir — not that many do not do so, in perfect safety. Why, only this very morning I put a young lady on the London stage, travelling all alone, the pretty dear, and with no more idea how to look after herself than a kitten! Just you leave it to me, miss, I said to her, and so she did, and I put her in the care of a nice, motherly woman that I know of, going to London with her little boy!'

'I am sure you did just as you ought, landlord. And I suppose, providing she was warmly and sensibly dressed, she would come to no harm, though a pretty young girl cannot be too careful, of course.'

'Very true, sir. Pretty as a picture, she was, with her hair all dark curls, and her blue eyes. And she was warmly dressed too, and sensibly, if you call blue velvet sensible!'

His hearty laughter boomed out, and Anne felt her senses swim. She sat down abruptly on a bench seat.

'Is the young lady poorly, sir? She looks very pale.'

'My cousin is cold, I believe. Perhaps you could bring us some coffee, or tea?'

The landlord bustled off. Anne bit her lip to keep it from trembling.

'Well, we have missed her, but at least we know that she is on the stage. Don't look so stricken, my dear. We should be able to catch up with her very soon.'

'You will continue, then?'

'Did I not say that I would? I will not abandon you, or her, so easily. But. . .are you yourself quite determined? You do not think it might be better simply to allow her to continue? Her aunt and uncle will scarcely turn her from the door, I imagine, and she will be very reluctant to return with us.'

'You may be right. But I must try. I do not think it right for her to go back to London in this fashion. Not running away, in a fit of pique! Such behaviour would cause a scandal if it became known. That would scarcely please Mr and Mrs Littleton, and suppose they should not accept her? Or, which is only too likely, they are away from home? She would be alone in London, with nowhere to turn. No, I must try to bring her home with me. If you will help me, I am sure that she will one day be grateful.'

'And you? Will you be grateful, Anne?'

'Yes, of course.' She looked up at him with troubled eyes, and he longed to hold her in his arms and kiss away that worried little frown that wrinkled her smooth brow. The entrance of the landlord with a tray of coffee, however, brought him back to his senses, and he became briskly practical again. They drank their coffee, which warmed and revived Anne more than she would have believed possible, and left as quickly as they could.

They made good speed, passing swiftly through Puddletown, Milborne St Andrew, and Winterborne. It was, in any other circumstances, a village Anne would have loved to visit since she bore its name, but now she hardly glanced at it as they went through at a brisk trot. At Blandford they learned that the coach was only half an hour ahead of them, and Delamere decided against changing horses, feeling that he preferred his own, though tired, to the doubtful reliability of hired beasts. Time enough to change horses when they had found, and passed, the stage-coach.

It was very cold. The warming effects of the coffee had long since passed away, and Anne's feet and hands were numb in spite of the rug that Delamere had produced and wrapped round her. Nevertheless, she continued to strain her eyes along the road ahead. When, at last, the lumbering and ungainly shape of the coach, with its burden of outside passengers, appeared as they rounded a bend, her exclamation was echoed by Delamere's grunt of satisfaction.

'There it is! Oh, thank God, we have come up with it!'

'Yes. We shall soon pass it, I hope. We cannot, as I hope you realise, hold it up like highwaymen and demand that they stand and deliver their passenger into our care.'

'No, of course. I had not thought. Where will the next stop be?'

'Salisbury, I suppose. We will be there first, and hope to meet with her quietly. It will not do to have her make a fuss. We do not want to be accused of kidnap.'

'Surely she would not be so naughty!'

'Let us hope not. Hide your face as we go by. It will be better that she should not see us and be warned.'

Anne was longing to peer in through the windows and strain her eyes for a hint of blue, but she saw that he was right. They swept past the coach in high style, watched somewhat enviously

by the outside passengers who huddled, shapeless
bundles of coats and shawls, on the roof.

At the King's Arms, in Salisbury, Delamere
once again demanded a private parlour, and a
meal.

'Food? I could not eat!' exclaimed Anne.

'Yes, you could. It will be half an hour at least
before the stage arrives, and you will need all your
strength. It will do Arabella no good if you are
fainting when you should be persuading her to
come back with you.' Anne could see the justice
of this. Grimly she chewed and swallowed, forcing
down mouthfuls of cold chicken and ham that
tasted like sawdust in her mouth. She refused
wine, but was thankful to drink several cups of
tea, and admitted that she felt better.

She had just set down her cup when, with a
blast on its long horn, the coach swept into the inn
yard. Ostlers and waiters, with the smoothness of
long practice, moved into instant and frenzied
action, and almost before the coach had stopped
they were handing passengers down, and urging
them into the warmth of the inn.

'Stay here,' said Delamere. 'She will, I am
afraid, be more pleased to see me than you.' He
left the room, leaving the door ajar. Through it
came the sound of bustling activity, voices calling
for food, hot punch, hot coffee, and everything as
quickly as possible, if not quicker. Above the
hubbub Delamere's voice rang effortlessly.

'Miss Arabella! You have arrived safely, then!'

'Delamere! How delightful to see you here. I

knew that you would follow me to London,' Arabella's voice said coyly, 'but I did not think that you would be so quick! How very flattering!'

'Yes, isn't it?' he agreed smoothly. 'I have already engaged a private parlour, and ordered something to eat. Perhaps you will join me. And your companion, Mrs. . .?'

'Oh, this is Mrs Hampton. Lord Delamere is a friend, Mrs Hampton, as you can see.'

'Yes, indeed, my lord. And I'm honoured, I'm sure, by your invitation, but my little boy is not at all well, and I mean to see whether I cannot take a room and stay here a day or two. I own I was far from happy to think of leaving miss to travel on her own, but now she will be quite all right, won't she?'

'I certainly hope so. Well, Miss Arabella, if you will come this way? It is just in here, and I have a delightful surprise for you.'

'Oh, really? What could it be?'

The door closed behind Delamere, and Anne stood up and held out her hands.

'Arabella! Oh, my dear Arabella, how could you do this? Thank heaven I have found you!'

'Oh!' Arabella whirled round to Delamere. 'You. . .you traitor! How could you do this to me? I suppose this is all your doing, Anne. You could not bear to think of me happy in London, could you, and enjoying all the fun while you are stuck in your dreary little village? Well, I don't mean to go back there, and you may say what you like, you will not persuade me. And you cannot make me, either.'

'Maybe not. But I, on the other hand, can,' said Delamere calmly. 'Come now Arabella. You cannot really wish to make a spectacle of yourself by obliging me to carry you bodily from the inn, do you?'

'Would you really do so, Delamere? I had thought you would be pleased if I were back in London. Surely you do not intend to stay in Dorset, do you?'

'Certainly, for a while. And without your presence the village will be so very quiet, I hardly know how I should support it. You would not wish to leave us all bereft, would you? Then, you know, London is likely to be very dull for some time to come. Do not forget that the court must be in mourning, and society with it. I think you will not find the metropolis the lively place it was last summer, at least for a while.'

'Oh.' Arabella thought. 'I had not considered that. Will there be no balls?'

'Not for a while, I would think. You. . .we. . . are better off in the country. And you would not wish all your work for Lady Sudbury's dance to go to waste, would you? I believe she means still to hold it, in two weeks' time, and without your presence it must be a sadly flat affair, you know.'

He smiled down at Arabella. Anne, watching, knew that her own bones would melt if he were to look at her like that. A pretty face, she thought sadly, would make a man forgive almost anything in the way of wilful, even downright bad behaviour. She wished that he did not care for Arabella as he obviously did, to go to so much trouble on her behalf. Indeed, his words had been tantamount to a declaration of love. It did not occur to Anne's bruised heart to wonder why he should be eager to have Arabella back at the rectory, when only a few days earlier he had been equally insistent that she should return to London. That it was her own worry and fear that he was bent on assuaging, rather than his own desires, never crossed her mind.

Arabella smiled back, her face lighting up so radiantly that Anne blinked at the sight of her.

'Oh, very well! I own it was perfectly horrid in the stage-coach. How anyone can bear to travel in them is quite beyond me! So slow, and so crowded, and so very uncomfortable. And Mrs Hampton would keep talking all the time, and her little boy coughed so much I could not sleep, though I was so tired. Is that chicken? And a pie? Oh, good, I am very hungry. Will you cut me some, Anne? And if that is tea I will have a cup, though I do not really care for it.'

Anne, in seething silence, obeyed, and then sat quietly by the fire while Arabella, in the best of humours, chattered to Delamere and made a very good meal.

'We must be going as soon as possible,' Delamere urged them. 'There are not so many hours of daylight left, and though the sky is clear and there is some moon I should prefer not to be travelling through the country lanes in the dark, behind hired horses.'

Anne was in a fever to be gone, though Arabella was wilful, refusing to hurry herself and ignoring her sister when she urged her to make ready with all speed.

'I will certainly not leave until I have changed my dress and put on more petticoats. It was cold enough inside the stage, crammed up against all those people, but how shall I survive the phaeton?'

'Borrow my cloak, darling. I have a warm pelisse, and there are rugs as well.'

'Wear a cloak, like a beggar or a servant girl? No, thank you. I shall put on two more flannel petticoats, and you may keep your horrid cloak.'

In the phaeton, by common consent, Arabella was placed in the middle between Anne and Delamere. She complained that she was so crushed she could scarcely breathe, but it was the warmest place and though she accepted a carriage rug Arabella was still firm in her refusal of a cloak. Anne, crammed right to the edge of the seat, edged a bit further over and looked at the ground rushing by below her, hoping that her numbing fingers would be able to keep their hold on the low side. She tried to feel pleased that she had safely rescued her sister. Things, she told herself, had turned out most fortunately. And the tears that kept filling her eyes were due solely to the cold wind in her face, nothing more.

CHAPTER TEN

ANNE thought that she had never before been so cold. Though she was warmly dressed and well wrapped up in carriage rugs, the chill of the rapidly darkening November day seemed to have crept right into the marrow of her bones. Beyond shivering, she felt her body heavy and dead as a lump of stone or iron, and knew it was the misery in her mind, rather than the cold of the day, that made her so. That Delamere should put himself to so much trouble for Arabella argued a deep attachment, and Anne no longer doubted that when Arabella finally returned to London he would follow her there. Then, in the sophisticated setting that was home to both of them, he would offer her his hand and heart, and be accepted.

By the time they reached Blandford the short winter day was drawing into dusk. Never had the golden gleam of lighted windows made so tempting an offer of warmth and shelter. Delamere, however, made no attempt to stop, and scarcely slackened the horses' pace as they went through the little town. Anne cast one longing glance at the open door of an inn, which spilled out a welcoming carpet of golden light over the muddy yard. The homely incense of wood fires, a waft of mouth-watering cooking from a well loaded oven, even the sour tang of spilled beer were like siren calls to Anne. She shut her lips firmly together, and set herself to endure.

Delamere, who had been watching her with swift, worried glances, made her start when he spoke.

'I am sorry, Anne. I should have liked to stop so that you could get warm, but it is getting so late. In another hour it will be full dark, and we must try to be past Dorchester by then, if possible.'

'It's all right,' said Anne through lips stiff with cold. 'I am all right.'

'Well, so am not I!' said Arabella crossly. 'It is all very well for you to say there is no need to stop, but I am sure if I shiver much more I shall have a seizure or something! Travelling in an open phaeton, at this time of year, it is enough to give me an inflammation of the lungs!'

'We must hope not,' said Delamere. 'I know how uncomfortable this must be for you, but we shall be home as soon as may be.'

Anne, being too cold for conversation, forbore to point out that none of them would have been out in the cold had it not been for her sister's wilful flight.

'I will need to change the horses at the White Hart: I don't like the look of the nearside beast; he's going short on his hind leg. I wish I had not been forced to change my own pair, but it was too far for them.'

They continued in silence for a few minutes,

until disaster struck. A hen pheasant, crouching in invisible stillness at the side of the muddy road, suddenly decided to take fright at their passing and lumbered into the air, screeching the unlovely cry of her kind. The horses, which had been plodding along with their heads down, both took fright and shied, then set off at a near gallop with the phaeton bucketing through the ruts behind them. Arabella shrieked.

'Oh, hush!' implored Anne, gripping the side of the phaeton with the numb fingers of one hand and putting her other arm to hold her sister still in her seat. 'Hush, or you will frighten them more!'

'Oh, we'll be killed, I know we'll be killed!' moaned Arabella, but even as she did so the horses faltered in their headlong rush. Anne saw the muscles bunch beneath the smooth surface of Delamere's driving coat as he hauled steadily on the reins, the tendons of his hands and wrists standing out through the leather of his gloves.

'Steady now, steady,' he repeated in a low voice, whether to the horses or to Arabella Anne could not tell. Then the horses were standing still, their heads hanging and thin sides heaving. Delamere glanced at Anne.

'Can I give you the reins for a moment, while I jump down? It will be quite safe; they will not run away again now.'

'Oh, no!' protested Arabella. 'You cannot leave us alone up here!'

Wordlessly, Anne nodded and held out her hands. He took them in his own firm grasp for a moment, and she could feel the warmth of his touch thawing her cold fingers.

'Good girl,' he said quietly. 'It is only while I descend; as soon as I am on the ground I shall take hold of their heads.' Once again she nodded, and gathered the reins into her hands while Arabella shivered and wept beside her. There was a lurch as he climbed from the seat, but the horses did not move. Delamere took hold of the reins again, then swiftly bent to run his hands down the hind leg of the nearside horse. He lifted the foot and looked at it, then came back to stand beside the phaeton.

'It is as I feared. The shoe was loose, and the sudden movement has made him cast it somewhere back there. Not only that, but the foot within the hoof is damaged and sore; I am afraid he will be quite lame. There is no hope of reaching even Dorchester with him in this state; we must go on slowly and hope to find some farmhouse or inn where we may get help.'

Anne nodded again, to show that she had understood. Her brain seemed numb; it scarcely mattered to her whether they reached Dorchester or not, but beside her Arabella wept in earnest.

'But I'm cold, and hungry, and I want to be home! Is there nothing we can do?'

'Nothing for the present.' He reached up to take hold of her hands. 'You are being very brave,' he assured her kindly. 'Only be brave a little longer, and things will soon be better, I am sure. I shall stay down here, and lead the horses. Do you watch out for a light—you can see further from up there. We cannot be far from a habitation. This is not Siberia, after all!'

Arabella huddled against her sister, and they clung together against the cold while the horses plodded slowly on. Anne tried to tell herself that it was not much darker, but strain her eyes though she might she had to admit that the surrounding countryside was disappearing into gloom. A mist, blue-white in the dusk, gathered over the ground, and now the horses and Delamere seemed to be wading through milk. She looked all around, even turning in case she might have missed seeing a light, but there was nothing.

Then, above the cold, flat smell of the mist and the warm tang of the horses she caught a scent. Smoke! Hardly daring to believe it, she breathed in, closing her eyes to concentrate the better. Yes, it was definitely the delicate scent of wood smoke. She opened her eyes and peered around her. The road was sunken beneath the level of the surrounding land, and bounded by thick hedges, and there was nothing to be seen.

'Smoke,' she said, her voice croaking a little. 'I can smell smoke.'

Delamere stopped, and tested the air.

'Are you sure?' he said doubtfully.

'Yes. I think so. Can you smell it, Arabella?' But Arabella had wept until her nose was blocked; she could smell nothing. They went on.

'There is a turning here!' exclaimed Delamere. 'Only a rough track, but still. . . Will you wait

here, while I go and see? If we take the phaeton
down there and it goes nowhere, we may have
trouble turning it again.' At this suggestion, however, Arabella became so distraught that he abandoned all thought of leaving them. It was a risk,
for it would soon be too dark to see their way in
so overgrown a track, but Anne had said she smelt
smoke, so. . .

'We will take the track,' he decided, and without more ado turned the horses on to it. The lame
horse jibbed, throwing up its head at the feel of
the rough, stony surface, but he soothed it and
urged it on. The track twisted and turned, and the
tree branches twined over their heads so that they
were in a dark tunnel. Anne sat in silent despair,
wondering if she had led them into a worse plight
than before. Then, to her relief, she smelt the
smoke again, and stronger this time.

'Oh, there!' she cried, and at the same moment
Delamere exclaimed aloud.

'Smoke! You were right. There must be a house
of some kind down here. Come on, old fellow!
Ah, you can smell a stable, can you?' For the
horse, now, had lifted its head, and was moving
forward more eagerly. They rounded another
corner and came out of the belt of woodland into
a group of houses, scarcely enough to merit the
title of hamlet, outside the largest of which stood
a long wooden bench beneath an ancient sign and
the tattered remains of a hanging branch, the age-
old symbol of an ale-house.

'Oh, thank heaven,' said Anne, feeling her eyes

fill with tears. Delamere shouted, and at once the
door was flung wide, and soon there were men
leading away the horses, and the sisters were able
to climb stiffly down from the phaeton. Anne
could scarcely stand, but with Delamere's help she
stumbled into the inn.

As a building, it scarcely merited the name,
being hardly more than the ale-house that the
hanging bush proclaimed. It was, however, warm,
and, doing her best to disregard the wide-eyed
stares of a group of local worthies clustering in the
taproom, Anne led her sister to the open fireplace,
where the best part of a small tree blazed across
ancient blackened firedogs. With the natural courtesy of countrymen, the men round the hearth
drew back to give them place, and one old gaffer
creaked to his feet and offered his place on a
wooden settle, nudging his neighbour with a bony
elbow to do likewise.

Anne thanked him with a smile and a low-
voiced word, and, sitting Arabella in the place,
drew off her gloves, and chafed at the small white
hands. Behind her she could hear Delamere's
voice, and, soothed by its sound, she abandoned
their future to him and gave herself up to enjoyment of the blessed warmth.

When at last he approached them, Delamere's
face was unreadable and Anne felt her heart sink
a little. He drew her a few steps away from
Arabella.

'I am afraid there are no horses to be had, for
any money,' he said. 'The farmer who owns them

is himself in Dorchester for the night, by a cursed mischance, and will not return before tomorrow. It seems that for tonight, at least, we must remain here. I am so very sorry.'

'You are sorry! If it had not been for your kindness to us, you would not find yourself in so uncomfortable a state! That I should have been so foolish as to run off after Arabella as I did, without leaving so much as a note for my brother, is beyond all belief! I am afraid you must be much regretting your generosity now!'

'Far from it — except that if I had not interfered you might be safe at home this very moment!'

'Safe, perhaps, but in what anxiety must I not have found myself, knowing that Arabella had travelled alone to London? However, that is the proverbial spilt milk, and there is no use in lamenting it. We must give thought to what is best to be done. My brother will be so very anxious! I only hope he may not have set out, in his turn, to find us!'

'Unlikely, I think. I confided my own anxieties to Lydford, and my groom knows very well that you and I came together in pursuit of your sister. He is a man in whom I repose complete trust, and you may be sure that since we have not returned he will have informed Lydford long since of our intentions. Your brother must, of course, be alarmed for you both, but he will at least have the comfort of knowing that I am with you. I had hoped it might have been possible to ride into Dorchester on the sound horse, but it is now so dark that I do not like to leave the two of you alone here, though the landlord seems a respectable enough fellow. Unfortunately, most of the able-bodied men of the place are absent, like the farmer. It seems that there is to be an auction tomorrow, of farm implements and beasts, and they have all made a holiday of it. There is no one to send but young lads or old men, and I do not care to ask them to make such a ride. At the most all that could be done would be to send a message to your brother, for it is too late now to hire another vehicle to convey us home.'

'Ride to Dorchester through these lanes, and bareback! I should hope you would not consider such a thing! We shall do very well here, I am sure, and it is only for one night, after all.'

'I had hoped you would say as much. There is no private parlour down here, I am afraid, but only this taproom, so I have desired the landlord to make ready a chamber upstairs for you. He is just now seeing to it, and I hope you may soon be more private. I have told him, by the by, that our name is Harris, and that I am your brother. I hope you do not object to such a pretence.'

'On the contrary, I am most grateful! And I am sure that no brother could have been kinder or more considerate than you have been to us today.'

He brushed aside her low-voiced thanks with a gesture, and glanced at Arabella, who was still hugging the rug round her and was leaning her head back with eyes closed in a white face.

'Is she all right? She is very pale.'

'I think so. I suspect she had very little sleep last night, and the exertions and emotions of today have worn her out. Once she is warm again, and I can persuade her to take some food, I am sure she will be very much more the thing.'

At that moment, as if on cue, the landlord approached them. A large, florid man, he seemed more anxious than pleased by the presence of his unexpected guests, and scrubbed his hands ceaselessly on his apron as if he feared they might not appear sufficiently clean.

'Fire be lit upstairs, sir, if the ladies want to come up. It 'on't be what they're used to, I'm feared, but we done what we can. Better than down here, anyways; no place for young ladies isn't this. Not a common taproom, no, not for the likes of them.'

'I am sure we are very grateful to be here,' said Anne simply. 'We were afraid, you know, that we would find nowhere before Dorchester, and that is many miles away.'

'So it is, miss, so it is, and nor you wouldn't have found nowhere, barring a few cottages! If you'll come this way, miss. . .can the young lady walk? She do look a shade particular, and that's a fact!'

Arabella opened her eyes and looked round her blankly for a moment, then fixed her eyes on Anne's face, the one familiar thing.

'Where are we? I must have fallen asleep, and I dreamed I was home again. Oh, Anne, where is this place?'

Her eyes filled with tears, and Anne took her hands in a comforting clasp.

'Why, we are quite safe, and lucky to have found so good a refuge! We are to stay the night here, in this inn, and tomorrow we shall have a carriage from Dorchester to take us home. Why, it will be quite an adventure! How we shall boast about it to our brothers. . .our other brothers!' Her cheerful tones encouraged Arabella to rise to her feet, and by dint of distracting her with a flow of commonplace chatter Anne was able to get her sister upstairs and into the room that had been prepared for them.

There, they found the landlord's wife, who curtsied to them with much more self-possession than her husband. The chamber was clean and surprisingly commodious, though the floor sloped up and down and the furniture was so massive and heavy that it must have been made where it stood, for it seemed impossible that it could ever have been moved. A bright fire crackled in the hearth, and cushions set in the carved wooden chairs beside it.

'There's hot water in the jug, miss, and you needn't have any fear of the sheets being aired, for I shall see to them myself. And no worries about the noise from the taproom keeping you awake either, for I shall see to it that they go home betimes.'

'Oh, pray do not disturb your customers on our account,' begged Anne. 'I am sure we shall do very well. How nicely you have prepared everything for us! Do you have many visitors?'

'Hardly ever, miss, but I was in good service before I was wed, and I know what's what! Anything you want, you just send for me. Now, you must be fairly starving, and here I am gossiping! There's no more than plain fare here, miss, and that's a fact, but there's a nice piece of beef and some ham, and I could make you a sweet omelette if you could fancy it?'

'That sounds excellent. I own I am not very hungry, but if we might have some tea? And perhaps a little bread and butter?'

'Of course you shall, miss, and cut nice and thin, too, like I was always taught! And could you perhaps fancy a nice fresh egg, boiled just so?'

'The very thing! How kind of you!'

'Though of course, a gentleman needs his meat. But I hope your brother won't turn his nose up at a nice round of beef, though there's no kickshaws to go with it barring some roasted onions and a batter pudding. Will your brother eat up here with you, miss?'

Arabella opened alarmed eyes.

'My brother? My brother is here?'

'Hush, dearest,' said Anne swiftly. 'You were asleep again, I think, and dreaming! My sister is very tired from all our travelling, and from the cold,' she confided to the landlady. That good woman subjected her to a careful scrutiny, frowning a little, then favoured her with a brisk nod.

'Well, that's as may be. You know your own

business best, I suppose, so I'll say no more.' To Anne's relief she left the room, and she turned back to her sister.

'Never tell me James is here! Oh, what shall I do? He will be so angry with me!'

'No, no, James is not here! And you should not fear him, even if he were! No, it is merely Delamere's discretion which led him to tell the landlord he is our brother. It looks so very particular otherwise, you know, now that we are obliged to spend the night here. And he told them, besides, that our name is Harris. Do, pray, strive to remember that, and not betray us! I fancy that the lady of the house is no fool, and more than half suspects that she is assisting in an elopement or some such thing! Though it must be a strange elopement where the gentleman runs off with two young ladies,' she joked.

'Oh, dear, yes, I see. I will try to remember. But my head does ache so, Anne, and I cannot seem to get warm, whatever I do.'

Her voice was that of a frightened child, and Anne could no more have scolded her for bringing them to this pass than she could fly.

'Come here to this chair, it is nearer the fire. Let me take off your bonnet and pelisse first. . . yes, I know that you think you will be colder, but it is not so! The pelisse is damp from the evening air, and is keeping the warmth of the fire from you. There, is that not better? And here is my shawl; I will warm it for a moment, and put it round you. In a moment you shall have some nice hot tea, and you will feel much more the thing, I am sure.'

For all her encouraging words, Anne could not help being alarmed by her sister's extreme pallor, and by the clammy, cold feel of her hands. She continued to prattle cheerfully, however, and was relieved when, after drinking two cups of tea, a little colour came back into Arabella's face. Her eyelids grew heavy, and by the time Delamere knocked for admittance she was fast asleep, curled up like a kitten among the cushions on the big chair. Anne opened the door, her finger to her lips in warning, and he walked quietly over to the hearth.

'Shall I lift her on to the bed?'

'No, let her stay as she is. It is warmer there, and the sleep will do her more good than anything, I believe.'

'And you? You are warm again, I hope?'

'Oh, yes, I am perfectly well, and thankful to see her so peacefully asleep. For a moment I feared. . .but it was no more than tiredness, I am sure. Arabella is never ill!'

'And you have had some tea, I see.'

'Yes, we were very glad of it. Will you have some? The pot is still hot.'

'No, thank you. The landlord mulled me some ale, which has warmed me. I am afraid that as your brother I am expected to keep you company up here. I am sorry to impose my presence on you, but not to do so might cause more talk and surmise.'

'Yes, indeed. I am afraid Arabella has already raised a few doubts by being surprised to hear that her brother was here. Her conscience made her fear that James had somehow found her out, of course! I hope I smoothed things over, and I believe she will remember our name is Harris.'

A knock at the door heralded the arrival of a meal, served with some ceremony by the landlord under his wife's critical eye. Arabella slumbered on as a table was set with a mountainous piece of beef and an equally generous ham, flanked by a fowl, the best part of two loaves of bread, and the 'kickshaws' as promised. For Anne there were no less than four eggs, a dish of pippin tarts, a plum cake that appeared as rich as it was indigestible, and a pot of quince conserve that was treated with much reverence, since the recipe for it had come from no less than a ladyship.

Anne expressed her pleasure as fulsomely as she knew how, albeit in almost a whisper, and when she had assured her host, no less than three times, that she was in no imminent danger of starving amid such plenty he and his spouse withdrew, leaving Delamere to join her at the table. She eyed the food anxiously.

'Oh, dear, I cannot eat more than two eggs at the most, and as for all the rest. . .but I would not for the world have them think that I am too proud to eat what they have brought! And indeed it looks very good, only I am not at all hungry.'

'Then it is fortunate that I am. Honour is at stake here, obviously! Do you make a start on your eggs, and I shall do my poor best to make a good meal.'

It seemed very strange to Anne to find herself thus dining tête-à-tête with Lord Delamere—for the sleeping Arabella could scarcely be said to constitute a third in their supper party. At first she was rendered silent by the awkwardness of their situation, but very soon the naturalness of his manner, which was a nice blend of formality and friendship, and the interest of his conversation, put her at her ease. By the time she had finished two eggs, eaten two tarts and buried two more in the glowing base of the fire, and drunk the glass of wine that Delamere insisted on pouring for her, she felt no trace of embarrassment at their peculiar situation.

'Well, I hope I may be said to have done my duty,' said Delamere at last, surveying the considerable inroads he had made on the dishes.

'Yes, I believe if there were a medal to be given for eating you would have earned it this evening,' she replied. 'I have half a mind to pin a pippin tart to your lapel, in lieu! Only think how becoming, and so novel! You might start a new fashion.'

'Yes, and practical too, if I should find myself overtaken by hunger in the night. Though at the moment I feel as though I shall never be able to eat again.'

'Yes, I must admit that after seeing William at the age of about fifteen I did not think that any gentleman's capacity for food would astonish me. But I think this evening he has met his match!'

'Well, there is a great deal of me to feed,' he pointed out. 'And when I was fifteen I ate even more than this!'

He spoke with simple pride, and she laughed.

'I believe you! And did you creep down to the kitchen at night, as William did, to fill up the corners with half a loaf of bread, and a pound of cheese, and a few slices of cake or so? I was forever finding the crumbs in his bed, and scolding him!'

'Yes, and the cook was in quite a puzzle, wondering where all the food disappeared to. I believe she blamed the boot boy, quite unjustly. . . though to be sure I met him, more than once. Indeed, I remember a game pie that we. . . Anyway, I owned up like a man, and just in time, for he was about to be turned out of the house.'

'Poor lad! A growing boy, of course, is hungry all the time, I believe. I know Henry is getting to be that way. I shall soon have to watch out for mice in his bedroom, and put the cat there as I used to in William's room.'

'You are well versed in the trials of bringing up a family. Young Henry does not realise how lucky he is that his brothers have paved the way for him. I was an only child, and my poor mother was forever at a loss to know what to expect from me next.'

'Did your father not remember his own youth? I know how Papa laughed at some of the scrapes that James and Edmund got into, and said that they reminded him of himself at their age!'

'My father died when I was still in short coats, and she never re-married. I know I sometimes wished that she would, for I should have liked nothing better than just such a tribe of brothers, and sisters as you have. My mother took her duties very seriously, however, and what with caring for my houses and estates, and overseeing my education, she never found time to look for another husband. And I believe she had loved my father too well to wish to replace him with one who could be no more than second best in her heart.'

'Does she still live?'

'Yes, though not with me. When I reached my majority, she insisted that she must have a home of her own. She would not consent to remain at my country seat, nor make her home in the London house, but took herself off to Bath. There she resides very happily with a companion and half a dozen little dogs. She goes to every concert and ball, promenades every day to take the waters, and is by way of being quite a landmark in the place.'

He spoke with pride and amusement, and Anne thought that he had been fortunate in his parent, who had brought up her wealthy boy without either spoiling or cosseting him, and had then set him loose on the world to make of it what he would.

'I wish I might meet her,' she said, without thinking.

'I intend that you shall. She is a lady of strong

character. I think you should deal extremely together.'

'I am not sure whether that is a compliment.'

'From me, it is.'

'But you called me a mouse, as I recollect.'

'And a dragon also. Does it still rankle? Shall I beg your pardon?' Before she was aware what he was doing, he went down on his knees before her.

'I beg your pardon, my dear Anne, for calling you after any denizen of the animal kingdom, real or imaginary. I give you my word that I shall never do so again. Am I forgiven?'

'Oh, get up, pray do! If someone should come in! Please, Lord Delamere!'

Unperturbed, he returned to his seat.

'What a pearl among women you are! Most of your sex want nothing more than to have men on their knees before them.'

She could not help laughing, but tried to frown at him.

'You wrong us, my lord! I should prefer you to call me after any creature at all rather than have you kneel to me.'

'I am sorry. I am afraid that I cannot resist teasing you from time to time. And at least I have made you smile a little, and forget your cares for a while.'

'Much is to be forgiven you for that. And in any case both Arabella and I owe you such a debt of gratitude as can scarcely be repaid. . .'

'We will not speak of that, if you please. I have an ample repayment in mind, but this is not the moment to speak of that. Listen, I think she is stirring.'

Arabella shifted on her chair, and murmured. Anne hurried to her side, and was in time to see her sister open her eyes.

'Oh, Anne, I have had the strangest dream,' she murmured. 'You will never believe how strange. . .and you were in it, and Lord Delamere. . . Oh!' She stopped as Delamere in his turn walked over to her. 'Oh, you are here! Oh, was it not a dream, then? Oh, dear, what is to become of me? James will be so angry with me, he will send me away, and if my aunt and uncle will not take me, what shall I do?' Her lovely eyes filled with tears that spilled over and coursed down her cheeks. 'Oh, I wish I were dead!'

'Hush, that is foolish talk! James to send you away, when you know how much he cares for you? And your uncle and aunt, who surely want you to return to them? You are tired and upset. Everything will seem much better in the morning, I assure you. I shall be with you, and I shall not let them scold you too much. No one can speak harm of you, when we are together. And besides, Lord Delamere is here. You know he will do and say whatever is necessary to protect us.'

A thoughtful look came over Arabella's face.

'Will you, Delamere? Will you really?'

'Of course. I give you my promise,' he said.

'Oh, good. Then I think I should like to go to bed now, Anne. I am tired, and my throat hurts.

But tomorrow everything will be all right, won't it?'

'Yes, my dear,' said Anne, stroking her hair. 'Everything will be all right tomorrow.'

CHAPTER ELEVEN

By the time she climbed into bed beside her sister, Anne felt so tired that her whole body ached as if it had been beaten. Exhausted beyond the ability to sleep, she stared up into the dark canopy of the old-fashioned bed that glowed dimly in the reddish gleam of the fire. For all her encouraging words to her sister, she was far from confident about the future. News of her sister's flight must, inevitably, have spread round the village by now, and the fact that neither of them had returned before nightfall would make the kind of gossip that could well drive her uncle to refuse to accept Arabella back under his roof.

When at last she fell asleep, her dreams were filled with nameless dread. Waking once from a restless sleep, she could remember nothing tangible, only something huge and shapeless that pursued her as she struggled to move with leaden limbs. Besides her Arabella slept, but she coughed fretfully and several times muttered incoherently. Anne lay as still as she could in the enormous nightgown that the landlady had lent her. Starched almost as stiff as a gentleman's high collar, it enveloped her in harsh, lavender-smelling folds that encased her as she sank into the stifling clutches of the thick feather mattress.

She woke the following morning with an aching head and heavy eyes. The clatter of fire irons had roused her from the deep sleep she had finally fallen into only two hours earlier, and she looked across the room. A round-faced girl was looking apprehensively towards the bed, and when she saw Anne open her eyes she gave an incoherent mumble and fled from the room. A few moments later the landlady surged in, quiet for all her bulk.

'I beg your pardon, miss, but that girl has no notion, no notion at all!' she said in a low voice. 'I'll do your fire myself, since I see the other young lady is still asleep.'

'Thank you,' said Anne, slipping carefully from the bed and reaching for her shawl. 'Pray do not scold her, though! I am accustomed to wake early, and in any case we must be on our way as soon as possible.'

'Not today you won't, miss,' was the chilling rejoinder. 'There's no hurry to get up, not the least in the world. You'd do better to go back to bed till the room's had time to warm up, 'stead of traipsing around in your bare feet like that.'

'What do you mean?' Anne ignored the cold wooden boards beneath her feet and stood by the bed, staring at the landlady. 'Of course we must leave today!'

'Can't be done, miss,' said the other, with rough kindness. 'It's that misty, nobody won't be going out today, not even them as knows their way around. Fog's thick enough to cut with a knife, and you can't see your hand before your face, and that's a fact. Can't you smell it, miss? I declare it gets into the house, though all the windows are shut fast.'

It was true, now that she came to think about it, that the air had a dank, numbing smell to it. Anne ran to the window and pulled aside the heavy old curtain. Outside the thick greenish glass there was nothing but greyish white. Low though the building was, she could not see the ground, nor the hanging sign that she knew should be only a few feet away. The mist, which had been no more than knee-high the evening before, had risen and curdled into a solid mass that sat, sullen as a broody hen, over all the landscape.

Anne felt her eyes aching, and found that she had been straining them, trying to pierce the cloud of white, so that they had become half unfocused. Her hand was gripping the musty fabric of the curtain so hard that her thumb had torn through the lining. Carefully she loosened her grip, and smoothed the place.

'Well, we must stay here, then,' she said blankly.

'That you must, miss, no mistake. There now, that's going well. Come and sit down here, miss, and warm your poor feet. And you with no luggage neither!'

The woman's eyes were bright with curiosity. Numbly Anne did as she was bid, and stretched out feet that she had not noticed were cold to the comforting warmth of the crocus-yellow flames.

'No, no luggage. I had not thought to need any,

you see! My brother and I had driven to Salisbury to meet my sister, who had come down from London on the stage. We should have been home well before dark, but were unexpectedly delayed and set off home later than we should have done.'

'What a shame, miss. And it's a pity you didn't think to meet your sister at Dorchester after all! Saved you a deal of trouble, that would, and once she was on the stage it would have been just as easy for her.'

'Yes, it would. But my brother likes to drive his phaeton and. . .and it was one of those impulses, you know!' Anne improvised hurriedly. 'Our sister has been living in London for some time, staying with her uncle, and we were so looking forward to seeing her again!' That part of her story at least was true. Heaven send, she thought, that Delamere hasn't told some quite different story already. The landlady, however, was perfectly ready to accept such foolish behaviour as no more than the vagaries of quality, who, having no proper work to do, must needs fill their days with pointless activity.

'Quite so, miss. Well, standing here gossiping won't buy the baby a new bonnet, will it? If you'll give me your gown, I'll iron it up for you, to freshen it a little. You'll want some hot water presently, and we'll see about breakfast when your sister wakes.'

'Thank you, that is so very kind! I am afraid we are making a deal of work for you, Mrs — oh, I beg your pardon, I do not recall hearing your name?'

'Carter, miss. Shall I take the other gown too, miss?'

'Yes, please, Mrs Carter. My sister's boxes have been sent on, and though she has a few gowns in her bag they will be very creased.'

'Well, first things first, and later on I'll see what is to be done with them.' She was gone with a competent whisk of her skirts, and Anne sat contemplating the fire with a kind of hopeless calm.

Arabella did not wake until Anne was already dressed, and when she did she complained hoarsely that her throat hurt and that she did not feel well. Though a little flushed she did not seem feverish, and after drinking two cups of tea she seemed better, and declined to stay in bed.

'No, no, I shall get up. After all, we must get ready to go, must we not?'

Anne, who had kept quiet about the state of the weather for as long as possible, cast a despairing glance at the window.

'What is the matter? Why do you look so strange?' Arabella leaned forward from the comfortable nest of pillows against which she was reclining, and looked at the window. 'Oh! What has happened? Is it snow?'

'Hardly, at this height. No, it is mist, or rather fog. I am afraid it is quite impossible that we should go out of doors until it lifts.'

'But we must! We must get home today!'

Her voice, though hoarse, was rising to a shriek. Anne hurried to her side and tried to comfort her.

'Come now, you must not worry! We are quite safe here, and it may be that the fog will clear in time for us to leave later today.'

'But James. . .and my uncle. . .oh, if only you had left me on the stage! Why did you have to interfere? Everything would have been all right, and I should have been in London by now!' She pulled herself clear of her sister's arms, and stood before the fire, her eyes glittering with tears and her cheeks patched with red. 'You have ruined everything, and done it to spite me, I do believe! Just because I am younger and prettier than you, and have had better fortune! You hate me, don't you? And I hate you, so there!'

The childish finish robbed the words of any sting they might have had, and Anne gave a little gasp of laughter, which she tried to hide.

'Oh, yes, that's very funny, isn't it? My life ruined, which is just what you wanted, and now you can laugh and gloat!'

'Oh, Arabella,' sighed Anne. 'I am sure you do not believe what you are saying, at least I hope so! Do think for just a moment, and stop enacting these tragedies! In London by now? Yes, you might have been, but where in London? At this time of year do not your uncle and his family frequently go on visits to their country house, and those of their friends? Have you not told me many times of the parties that gather for the shooting? Suppose you had arrived on their doorstep, with no more than a few shillings to your name after paying for the stage, to find the house closed up, as is only too probable? What would you have done? Where could you have gone? Then, indeed, you would have been ruined, and that is what I feared for you.'

Arabella, who had opened her mouth to argue, looked thoughtful and closed it again. While on the stage-coach, the unwelcome thought had crossed her mind that there might be no one at her uncle's house to receive her, since he preferred to take his servants with him to the country, but she had pushed it to the back of her mind and refused to contemplate it.

'Well. . .but you do envy me, don't you? You must, after all.'

'My dear, not one jot. I am accustomed to my life, and believe it or not it suits me very well! Strange though it may seem to you, I would not exchange my lot with yours for all the world. Some people, you know, are born to be old maids, and it may be that I am one of them. Certainly I view the prospect without dread. While I can be useful, and have my brothers to care for and love, my life can never be said to be empty. And some day I mean to be acclaimed as the best aunt in the world!'

Arabella gazed at her in some awe.

'But. . .an old maid! I don't know how you could!'

'Well, fortunately it is not likely that you will ever be faced with such a problem. Now, come away from that fire, do, before you set your nightgown on fire! Mrs Carter has freshened up your gown, and there is hot water for you to wash. Unless you want to return to bed?' Anne laid her hand on her sister's brow. 'You seem a little feverish. Or is that merely temper?'

She smiled to take the sting out of her words, but Arabella at once burst into tears and flung herself into her sister's arms.

'Oh! I'm sorry, I'm sorry, I didn't meant it!' she sobbed childishly.

'Of course you didn't! You don't have to tell me that,' soothed Anne. 'You are tired, and upset, and no wonder! You have been a little foolish, but no worse than that, and I am sure that everything will be all right. James is strict, I know, but he truly loves you and wants you to be happy. When he knows you are sorry, he will forgive you at once, I promise you. And even if your uncle should hear some rumour, as long as we tell him we were together he cannot say any harm.'

After a while Arabella calmed down, and was so meek and biddable that Anne wavered between worry that her sister might be ailing and the hope that the past two days might have taught her a valuable lesson. Anne told her of the story she had told Mrs Carter, and her sister regarded her with wonder and respect.

'Oh, Anne, I would never have believed you would be such a clever liar!' she exclaimed in admiration. Anne bit her lip.

'Not a liar, precisely, I hope,' she said. 'Much

of it was true, and as for the rest. . .well, I must hope to be forgiven. I own I was astonished at how easily the story came tripping off my tongue. I only hope that Delamere has not ruined all by making up something quite different! Oh, dear, I have never been so dishonest in my life before. How very uncomfortable it is, to be sure!'

'Oh, but white lies are quite different,' Arabella assured her blithely. 'Is that breakfast? I believe I am hungry after all.'

Breakfast it was, and hard on the heels of its servitors came Delamere knocking for admittance.

'Mrs Carter thought that we would like to breakfast together, if you have no objection, my dear Anne,' he said with the greatest aplomb. 'How do you find yourselves this morning, my dear sisters?' With much grace he bent and saluted each of them with a chaste kiss on the cheek, while Mrs Carter watched with approval. Arabella giggled.

'Quite well, thank you, Edward,' she replied pertly. 'My throat hurts, but I do not mean to make a fuss about it. I have been scolding Anne for being so foolish as to come to Salisbury to meet me, when I could quite well have travelled on to Dorchester from London! Then we would not have been in this pickle, you know! But she says it is your fault, because you wished to drive your phaeton! And there I was thinking that you were in a fever to see me, after I have been all this time in London! I declare I am quite put out!'

She gazed up at him with wide-open eyes. Anne

could cheerfully have slapped her, but Delamere smiled down at her.

'Of course it is all my fault! And how unkind of you to blame our sister, when she must remember how I pestered her to keep me company. There is no pleasure in trying out a new phaeton if one has no one to admire it and tell one how sweetly it goes! Of course, if I had known it would end like this. . .but still, we have found ourselves a refuge from the storm, so to speak, and at least we are not obliged to lie out in the woods, like the babes in the tale, and wait for the birds to cover us with leaves!'

'The very idea!' said Mrs Carter comfortably. 'Now, do you give over your bickering, sir and miss, and drink your tea while it's still hot. Anything you want, just give me a call.'

She withdrew with the air of a nurse leaving her charges on their honour to behave nicely. They listened to her footsteps receding down the passage, and Arabella giggled again.

'Well, I thought Anne was a good liar, but I must say you took me up *very* well, Delamere,' she said approvingly.

'Years of practice,' he said airily. 'And you yourself gave me the hint so cleverly! What a good team we make, don't we?'

Arabella smiled coquettishly through her eyelashes at him. Anne, who had been pouring the tea, put down the pot with a little more force than was necessary.

'Now, if you have finished congratulating one

another on your mutual duplicity, may we have some breakfast? You did say that you were hungry, Arabella,' she said in repressive tones.

'How disagreeable you are, Anne! I thought you would be pleased that I managed to warn Delamere so neatly before he had time to say anything!'

'And if he had already told a quite different story, before coming in here? That would have made you look foolish.'

'In that case we must all have looked foolish, whatever Arabella said,' pointed out Delamere peaceably. 'May I cut you some of this ham? I can vouch for it, having eaten it last night, and it is excellent. By the way, I think you had better get into the habit of calling me Edward, don't you? It would not do for you to refer to me as Delamere in front of the Carters.'

Anne saw the sense of this, and she took the plate that he held out to her and smiled her thanks.

'Very well, Edward. I am sorry if I spoke sharply.'

'Not at all. And if you had, then right was probably on your side. We should not be making a May-game of this.'

'Nor enacting tragedies,' put in Arabella, with a naughty look at her sister. Anne laughed.

'Very good, miss! Now perhaps you will eat the ham that Del — that Edward has so obligingly carved for you, and we may then all enjoy our breakfast.'

Edward and Anne made a tolerably good meal but Arabella, though hungry, complained that it hurt her to swallow, and she did not think she was so hungry after all. With much coaxing, Anne managed to get her to take a few mouthfuls of egg, but she soon pushed away her plate.

'I do not think this can be a fresh egg; it doesn't taste at all good.' Anne tasted it, and pronounced it new laid, but Arabella was not to be persuaded.

'No, I don't *want* it, I tell you!'

'Then come and sit by the fire, and let us plan how we are to amuse ourselves all day,' said Delamere. 'I am afraid that, since we may not go out, we would be best to keep to this room. The less we are seen the better, even by the few inhabitants still remaining here. Some of us, at least, are only too memorable, I fear.'

He cast a speaking glance at Arabella, who was much mollified by the compliment.

'Oh, I am sure we shall manage! I have a pencil in my reticule, and a little notebook for paper. Anne knows a great number of paper games, and then we may have charades, and tell stories; it will be the greatest fun! But what a pity I did not think to bring a pack of cards with me.'

'There may be some downstairs. I will ask Mrs Carter when she comes back. Meanwhile, I had better go out to the stable and see that those wretched horses are being properly cared for.'

Arabella looked alarmed at the idea.

'Oh, do not get lost, Edward! Must you really go?'

'Get lost, between here and the stables? I can assure you I shall not! And I shall be gone no more than a few minutes, just time for you to plan a charade for me.'

The morning passed cheerfully enough. A pack of cards was found, very greasy and bent, and they played games for ridiculous sums of money, recklessly pledging thousands of guineas on the turn of a card, and writing monstrous debts to one another on scraps of paper. As luck would have it, the flow of the cards was always in Delamere's favour, and he won time after time.

'Are you *truly* playing by the rules?' asked Arabella, after he had won yet again. 'You must be amazingly lucky, or else a skilful card-sharp. Which is it, sir? Be honest with me!'

'Oh, a card-sharp, of course! In fact, all my wealth has come from — er — plucking pigeons, as they say. Did you not know that I have a gaming hell of my own, very select of course, and that all my fortune is sunk in it?'

'No! Really?' Arabella gazed at him, round-eyed, 'Does Mr Lydford know?'

'Know? Of course he does! In fact, he is my partner. Well, one of my partners. The other —— ' He glanced around, and lowered his voice. 'The other is someone so exalted that I may not name him, but if I should say that he is connected with the crown. . .'

'Oh! How dreadful!' From the corner of her eye, Arabella saw Anne's shoulders shaking with suppressed mirth. 'Oh, how dreadful!' she exclaimed with a quite different intonation. 'You were roast-ing me! Of course, I didn't really believe you.'

'No, of course you did not,' he said, his lips twitching.

'Well, only for a moment. Though from the way you play it would not surprise me if it were true, would it you, Anne?'

'Not at all,' she returned promptly. 'In fact, I have pledged so much money I am now quite done up, and must retire on a preparing lease. There is nothing left for you to win, Edward.'

'Your heart?' His tone was playful, but there was a glow in his eyes that made her heart thud once and then seem to rise in her throat to suffocate her.

'I am sure you have already won plenty of those,' she said with attempted lightness.

'But they are not the ones I want,' he said, quite seriously.

'But Anne has no heart to give,' said Arabella, a little waspishly. 'She tells me she was born to be an old maid.'

'Well, I think we have had enough of that game,' said Anne firmly, though her hands shook a little as she gathered up the cards. 'What about a paper game? Or another charade?'

The awkward moment passed, and Anne told herself that she must put it out of her mind as no more than playfulness. Arabella, however, was very quiet for a while, and her answers when spoken to were disjointed. Mrs Carter brought them some luncheon, but none of them was hungry after their enforced incarceration, and it caused no comment that Arabella refused everything but a cupful of soup.

Afterwards they played at charades again, Arabella insisting that she should be first since she had thought of a good one. Tying a towel round her as an apron, she transformed herself into the very image of a pert housemaid, and performed a vigorous mime of taking something from the floor and carrying it outside to shake, while giving cheeky replies to imaginary remarks from passers-by.

'Maid?' hazarded Delamere. Arabella shook her head. 'No, too obvious. Rug? Door? Step?'

'Nearly,' said Arabella. 'Come on, it was so easy, I made sure you would guess it at once.'

'Carpet?' guessed Anne. 'No, too many syllables. I know, mat?'

'Yes, of course. Now, the next.'

This time she acted rather than mimed, a fierce old lady scolding a new and obviously inept maid, for chipping and cracking the edges of a complete tea set. Anne, who could see powerful echoes of Aunt Littleton in the portrayal, was helpless with laughter and could only gasp for breath and applaud at the end, leaving Delamere to guess that the syllable was 'rim'.

For the final syllable Arabella recklessly pulled the pins out of her hair and shook it out until it cascaded down her back. Opening her eyes wide, she stood with her hands behind her back and her toes turned in, the picture of a small girl caught in some childish crime.

'But Nursie,' she lisped, 'I on'y tore my pinafore a little, little bit. . .well, on'y a big little bit, then, and it was because Kitty was stuck up a tree, and crying so, poor Kitty, and I on'y climbed up a little way. . .on'y to that branch, you know! Yes, I know you said I shouldn't climb trees, but I on'y wanted to save Kitty! Yes, she did come down on her own, and I did get caught, but on'y for a while! The gardener's boy came when I called out, and helped me down. And I promised him something. . .no, not my shilling, Nursie! On'y a kiss! And I already gave it to him! Oh, Nursie, don't be so cross! It was on'y a little kiss!'

'Well, I think when Edward does open his gaming house you should certainly make a career on the stage,' said Anne admiringly. 'I had no idea you could act so well!'

'Yes, I am good, aren't I?' said Arabella with naïve pleasure. 'Shall I do the whole word, or have you both guessed it now? It should be an easy one, for it is something that is on everyone's mind—everyone that I know, that is! And I believe it should particularly be on yours, Lord Delamere! Matrimony, you know!'

He looked startled.

'I had no idea I was so transparent,' he said drily.

'Oh, you are not! But with the situation we find ourselves in. . .' she hinted coyly.

'I beg your pardon, I do not altogether understand you.'

Anne, who understood only too well, tried to turn the conversation, but Arabella was set too far on her course to be deflected.

'Why, I mean that we have spent — or we will have spent, if we go home tomorrow — two whole days and nights away in one another's company! As an honourable man, Lord Delamere, you would not wish to see a lady's reputation ruined, would you?'

'Arabella!' said Anne sharply. 'For heaven's sake, what are you at? You know quite well that since I have been with you no shred of dishonour attaches to your name. This is taking levity and playfulness too far, my dear. You should apologise at once.'

'Not at all. Miss Arabella has every right to speak out, if she so wishes. I own that I had not quite looked at matters in this light, but if you think yourself compromised. . .'

'Not at all. This is all ridiculous. Why, it is tantamount to blackmail, Arabella! I am ashamed of you.'

'Not at all.' Her sister did not spare her a glance. 'Blackmail is demanding money. But if one is merely suggesting something that is already wished for. . .it merely simplifies matters, that is all.'

'How very true.' Delamere's face was as unreadable as Anne's, while Arabella's was triumphant. 'I see that I have been remiss. I should have realised that my presence here, while it protected you, has also compromised you. I must make amends.'

'Oh, Edward!' Arabella held out her hands to him, but he had already turned away from her.

'I will not go on my knees, since you have already told me you dislike it,' he said, his voice low and warm. 'You see how attentive I am already to your lightest wish! My dear Miss Winterborne, will you do me the inestimable honour of accepting my hand in marriage?'

Anne sat frozen, her head lowered and her eyes fixed on her hands, which were tightly clasped in her lap. Arabella looked from Delamere to Anne, and back again.

'What do you mean? Is this another game? Edward, what are you at?'

'I am asking your sister to be my wife. She, after all, was the person seen leaving the village in my phaeton, with no other female to give her countenance. If anyone's reputation is at stake, it must be hers.'

'But. . .but that is ridiculous! You. . .and Anne. . . I never heard anything so foolish in my life!' Arabella's voice was shrill to the point of hysteria. She stamped her foot. 'Edward! Look at me, Edward! It is me you want to marry, not Anne!'

'Be quiet,' he said, without anger or even much interest. 'I am still waiting for my answer.'

'It is the same as my sister's.' Anne was surprised at how steadily her voice came out. 'You are being ridiculous, my lord. This is not a fit subject for games and mockery.'

'Games and mockery! I am serious, confound it! Do you think that I would allow you to feel even one moment's distress, even unease, without giving everything that I have to save you from it?'

Anne shook her head, her eyes full of tears. To be offered her heart's desire, and to know that it was no more than a sacrifice on the altar of convention, was more than she could bear. That he sounded sincere only made matters worse.

'There, you see!' Arabella's voice broke on a cough, and she paused to draw a hissing breath. 'She does not want you! I told you she was an old maid!'

He ignored her, but reached down to take Anne's hands into his own and draw her to her feet with a gentle insistence that she was unable to resist. She would have pulled her hands from his, but was paralysed by the feeling that the slightest movement at her own volition would break the thin shell of reserve that she managed to keep intact around her.

'Anne!' His deep voice sent shivers of actual pain down her spine, so that she quivered. 'Anne, my dear, I know this is not the moment, but. . . If you can look me in the eyes, and tell me honestly that you do not like me well enough, that you do not care for me, then I shall never disturb your peace again. But if not. . .look up, dear little Miss Mouse! Look up, and tell me if you cannot love me, just a little!'

'Oh!' Arabella gave a shriek, and ran at him, pummelling at his back with her fists. 'Oh, you. . .! Oh! Oh!' With rising fury she lashed out with hands and feet, succeeding only in hurting her toes since she was shod in light kid slippers and he, perforce, in his leather topboots. Her loosened hair flew around her in a cloud, she sobbed gustily, catching her breath on coughs as she did so. Forgetful of everything, Anne reached out to take hold of her, and received a buffet on the cheek that made her head ring for her pains.

'That is enough!' said Delamere sternly, taking Arabella's wrists in a firm grip and holding her away from him. 'If you do not stop, your sister will be obliged to slap you. And if she is too soft-hearted to do it, I shall take care of it myself!'

Shocked, Arabella raised tear-swollen eyes to his face. Then she wept in good earnest, but without the hysterical cries that had alarmed them before. She collapsed into a chair, and Anne leant over her, holding and rocking her as if she had been a small child. The door flew open, and Mrs Carter came in.

'Mercy on us, whatever is the matter?' she cried, looking round the room for evidences of fighting or bloodshed. Arabella was now quite speechless, crying and coughing at the same time, and Anne looked up and tried to summon her wits.

'I do beg your pardon, Mrs Carter, for disturbing the house! I am afraid that my sister and. . . and my brother fell to quarrelling, and. . .she became a little upset.'

'A little upset! I thought as she was being murdered!'

'My sister is of a very. . .very sensitive disposition,' said Anne with some truth. 'I am afraid she is liable to these attacks of hysteria. We had hoped she had grown out of them, but she is tired, and perhaps a little unwell. . .'

'Fine goings-on,' muttered Mrs Carter, but her darting eyes had been quick to perceive the glint of gold in the hand that Delamere was holding out to her, and after all it seemed that no harm had been done. 'Well, we'll say no more about it. Poor young lady, she does look a mite poorly. She should be lying on her bed, with a nice hot brick to her feet, and a nice hot posset to sip. That'll put her right in no time.'

'How *very* kind of you,' said Anne earnestly. 'I believe you are quite right. She shall lie down directly, and if you would be so kind as to bring a brick? And the posset? She has a very sore throat, as you may hear.'

'Poor little love.' Even dishevelled and tear-stained, Arabella's beauty shone like a lamp in the dingy room, and the landlady melted towards her. 'I'll be back directly, miss. A nice strong posset, with a drop of good brandy and some nutmeg — do her a treat, that will.'

Delamere stood silent by the fire while Anne coaxed her sister to the bed and laid her down. She took off the kid slippers and covered her with a quilt. Arabella alternately clung to her sister and pushed her away, but at last she was induced to lie down and close her eyes. Anne rummaged in her reticule for the little bottle of aromatic vinegar that she knew her sister always carried. She would have tipped some on to her own handkerchief, but a larger one, still crisply folded, appeared over her shoulder and she took it.

'Thank you,' she said quietly. 'I think — forgive me — but I think it would be best if you were to go away.'

'Yes, of course. I am sorry, my dear. I had no idea she would be so upset.'

'She is not used to being teased,' Anne made excuse for her sister. 'She is so young, and has been very much indulged.'

'As you say. Anne. . .'

'Please,' said Anne in desperation. 'Please, Lord Delamere, just go away. I cannot. . .oh, just go!'

She put out a hand as if to push him from the room. He took it, and raised it for a moment to his lips.

'I shall not be far away, if you need me,' he said, and left the room. Anne bit her lip fiercely, to hold back the tears, and concentrated on bathing Arabella's brow. Though still coughing her sister seemed drowsy, and by the time Mrs Carter returned she was fast asleep. Anne tucked the flannel-wrapped brick beneath the quilt, then drank the posset herself. She was, she thought sadly, in need of strengthening too.

CHAPTER TWELVE

ARABELLA slept for three hours, and while she slept the gloomy day faded almost imperceptibly into night. Anne remained sitting at the bedside all the while, her brow furrowed with worry. She had thought, at first, that her sister had merely caught cold, and had not been overly concerned. A cold, to be sure, was not something to be taken lightly, but she knew of Arabella's stout constitution and did not expect her to be very ill with it. The feverishness, the sore throat and the dry, painful cough presaged something worse, however, and Anne could not help remembering the coughing child who had sat next to her sister the previous day on the stage-coach.

Arabella continued to cough in her sleep, and from time to time she moaned a little, but without waking. Mrs Carter tiptoed in frequently, bringing sympathy and tea in equal measure. She stood over the bed, watching while Anne wiped the flushed, damp face and listening to the dry fretful cough

'She don't look too well, and that's a fact, miss,' she said at length.

'No, I know. I am so very sorry, Mrs Carter, if we have brought some sickness to your house! I would not for the worlds have had it happen so.'

'As for that, there's little harm to be done. For one thing you've seen no one but myself, to mention, and I've not known a day's illness for years, save the ones in the village I've nursed. My children are grown and gone long since, and there's none to take harm but that foolish Aggie in the kitchen, and she was in here only a minute. Don't you worry about that, miss. You'll have enough to worry about anyway 'fore long, if I have my guess.'

Anne sighed.

'I am afraid that you are right. It is too early to say what ails her, but. . .like you I have helped nurse many in my own village, and I know the signs. We won't speak of it yet, if you please, and never in front of her. She would be so frightened, and she is full of. . .of sensibility.'

'As you say, miss. I shouldn't wonder if sickening for this didn't add to her "sensibility", too. Though young girls of her age are prone to the vapours. Can I fetch you anything else, miss?'

'No, thank you. You are very kind. Will you tell my brother that she is still asleep?'

If anything, Anne was grateful for this period of quiet, and the possibility of recovering her usual serene self-control. It was, she found, preferable to worry about Arabella's health than the state of her own heart, and she concentrated on watching her sister, feeling her forehead for the mounting fever and laying careful fingers on the pulse that was beginning to race.

When, at last, Arabella opened bleary eyes she

looked about her vaguely. She licked lips that
were already dry and cracked, and took an eager
mouthful of cool, weak tea when Anne raised her
head and held the cup to her lips. Not knowing
the state of the local wells, Anne was unwilling to
give her sister plain water, and she greatly regretted the absence of lemons, which might have made
a more soothing drink for her sister. The single
mouthful of tea was only swallowed with an effort,
however, and Arabella turned aside her face from
the cup.

'Hurts,' she whispered. Her eyes wandered
round the room, and returned to cling almost
despairingly to Anne's face. 'Where. . .?' she
croaked.

'We are in an inn, dearest. You were on your
way to London, but the journey was interrupted.'

'Oh.' Her lips shaped the word but scarcely a
breath of sound came out. She seemed uninter-
ested, and it appeared that the events of the
previous twenty-four hours had vanished from her
memory. Anne could only be relieved. Nursing
her sister would be a hard enough task, without
dealing with her emotional storms as well.

Mrs Carter put her head round the door.

'Is she awake? I heard your voice.'

'Yes, she is awake, but a little confused.'

'I'll light the lamp, and the rest of the candles,
shall I? It's dark enough in here to confuse a bat,
when all's said and done. And there's Mr Harris,
wanting to know how this sister does, and whether
he may come in.'

'Oh, no!' The exclamation slipped from Anne's lips before she had even thought. 'No, he must not come in. There is no need for him to put himself in danger of taking any infection.'

'I'll tell him that, miss, but not what I don't think he'd take a blind bit of notice. A very headstrong gentleman, if you'll pardon my saying so.'

A tender smile curved Anne's lips.

'Yes, he is. Very headstrong.'

'So headstrong,' said a voice from the door, 'that only your direct command, or the possibility that my presence might upset Arabella, would keep me out.'

'Oh, Edward!' Anne turned a pale face towards him, and looked him in the eyes for the first time in what seemed like a lifetime. 'You must not come in! Indeed, you must not!'

Arabella, however, was smiling and holding out her hand, her lips framing 'Delamere', which was fortunately inaudible to all but Anne, who looked at him helplessly.

'She does not remember our — disagreement — at least. I am glad of that,' he said, coming to the bedside. Anne rose and stood blocking his way.

'You must not risk an illness to yourself, Edward,' she said harshly. He looked down at her.

'I think that is the kindest thing you have said to me today,' he said whimsically. 'It pains me to refuse you, but I will not leave you alone at such a time. As for infection, even if I feared it, the time for worrying is long past. If I have not already taken it, after spending half the day in her company, then I am not likely to now.'

'That's right, miss,' said Mrs Carter, 'you let your brother help. Proper worried he's been, all by himself in his room! It'll be a kindness to him to find something to occupy himself with, even if it's only keeping you company.'

Defeated, Anne moved aside.

'Very well, then. If you can persuade her to drink some more tea, I believe it will do her good.'

Edward cajoled her, with such success that Arabella drank two cups of tea, which seemed to refresh her, and made it easier for her to talk. When she had finished Anne brought the lamp to the bedside, and set it down where it shone over the pillows. She and Delamere looked at the sick girl.

Arabella's face was flushed, as if with anger. She coughed a little dry cough, and having started could not stop. When the fit passed she lay back in the bed, her cheeks a hectic pink and her eyes full of tears.

'Oh, my throat!' she moaned. 'It hurts so, Anne! It hurts!'

Anne put down the cup of tea that she had been holding for Arabella to drink from, and put her hand once again to her sister's forehead. This time the skin was perceptibly warm to the touch, and the hands that came up to clutch at her were cold. She took them in her own warm ones, and clasped them comfortingly.

'I know, dearest, I know. Poor little girl, I expect you have taken cold from yesterday.' She looked closely at the flushed face, then freed a hand to run gentle fingers along the line of jaw and neck. Arabella flinched from her touch.

'Oh, don't! That hurts too!'

'Could it be mumps?' suggested Delamere in a low voice.

'Mumps! Oh, no!' wailed Arabella. 'Not mumps, and my face all swelling up as it did last time! I looked hideous for weeks!'

'Last time? You have already had mumps? Then it is not that, thank goodness,' said Anne cheerfully. 'That's something you need not worry about, anyway. Will you open your mouth for me, darling, so I can look at your throat?'

Arabella turned her head away, screwing up her face and frowning.

'No, I don't want to. It will only hurt more.'

'I don't think so, and it is only for a moment. Please, darling?'

'Oh, very well.' Arabella tipped back her head and opened her mouth. Anne lifted the lamp, and felt it taken out of her hand and moved so that she might lean forward without casting a shadow. She examined throat and tongue carefully, noting the coated tongue and the inflamed throat, then drew back with a smile.

'There, that was not so bad, was it?' she asked cheerfully.

'Is it very bad?' asked Arabella fearfully. 'It's not. . .not diphtheria, is it?'

'No, of course not! Nothing of the kind!' said Anne encouragingly. It was true that there was no sign of the formation of the web that she had dreaded to see building up across the throat, which was indeed a relief. 'Now, if we ask Edward to leave us for a while, I think Mrs Carter and I had better get you undressed and into bed.'

'Oh, no! I don't want to move!' said Arabella weakly.

'I know you don't, dearest, but you cannot stay in your gown all night, and you will be much more comfortable afterwards, you know. Then, when you are all tucked up in bed, perhaps Edward will come back and sit with us, and we may all have a cosy evening together. Would you not like that?'

The ghost of a smile flitted across the pale lips.

'Improper!' she whispered.

'A little,' admitted Anne, smiling, 'but in the circumstances quite allowable, I think!'

'Perfectly allowable, for a brother,' said Delamere suavely. 'Now I shall go away, and you may summon me when you are ready, like old King Louis holding his *levée* or his *couchée*.' He sketched a bow, and was gone.

The undressing was a long business, for Arabella complained at every movement, and in the end they undressed her where she lay, like a huge baby, as Anne told her. As she removed petticoats and stockings Anne unobtrusively studied her sister. The skin of chest and stomach was white and unblemished, but on her feet. . . Anne bent closer, as she drew off the second stocking, and saw a faint pinkness, already marked here and there with little red spots. As she straightened up she met Mrs Carter's eyes, and they exchanged a wordless glance of understanding. Scarlet fever, thought Anne numbly. All the signs had pointed to it: the sore throat, swollen glands, and fever, and it was unmistakable now that the rash was coming. It was unlike other ailments in that it started in the extremities rather than the torso, and Anne had seen and nursed too many cases not to recognise it now.

Well, Arabella was not a frail, undernourished child but a strong adult, and with careful nursing there was every hope that she would survive. Anne sent up a short, heartfelt prayer of gratitude that they were thus isolated by a kind providence from the rest of the family, that young Henry and the precious only son, Charles, were in no danger from this infection. Mrs Carter, too, was a sensible woman, and by her own admission had some nursing experience. Together, they should do very well. Of the danger to herself she gave not a thought, since she had been in contact with the illness too many times to consider herself vulnerable. As for Edward. . .her blood ran cold at the thought of him in danger, but she knew that it would be well nigh impossible to protect him, and it was in any case by now too late.

Mrs Carter went to summon Delamere once Arabella was back in bed, swathed in the modesty of a shawl as well as her all-covering nightgown. When he came back into the room there was nothing in his manner to indicate that he knew the nature of the illness, but Anne was nevertheless sure that the landlady had told him of it. Between them they worked to keep Arabella both quiet and cheerful, and though at the end of the evening Anne felt as though she had been put through a wringer twice, once in each direction, she had had the satisfaction of seeing her sister smile several times, as well as of seeing her swallow most of Mrs Carter's posset, and several cups of weak tea besides.

He stayed with them until nearly eleven o'clock, for Arabella, having slept during the afternoon, was in no mood to settle too early.

'Well, it is time I said goodnight to you,' he said at last, rising to his feet. 'Here is Anne yawning as though she means to swallow an egg whole, and I am in not much better case!'

'You must keep fit for your gambling hell,' said Arabella in her harsh croak.

'Indeed I must! Why, my very livelihood depends on it, and that of my poor friend Lydford! I shall practise my skills upon you tomorrow, to keep my hand in.'

He took the hand she held out to him, and kissed it as though he had not noticed the beginnings of the scarlatina rash on it, then bent to kiss her forehead.

'Goodnight, my dear! And better health in the morning, I trust,' he said encouragingly. Anne, in response to his glance, walked to the door with him.

'Shall you be all right tonight? Will she sleep, do you think?'

'I hope so; it is hard to say. The fever is not too high; that is a mercy.'

'Promise me that you will call, at any time, if you have need of me. I have never nursed anyone, but I am a tolerably good farrier, and have frequently sat up with my horses. It cannot be so very different, after all!'

Anne was obliged to smile.

'Of course not! In fact, I should think horses would be more difficult, because they cannot tell one how they feel! Only, I beg you, do not tell Arabella that you put her on a level with a horse! She would be mortified!'

'Would she? But I am devoted to my horses. In fact, I could tell you the names of several men of my acquaintance who are far fonder of their horses than of their wives and children.'

'I do not doubt it. Arabella, however, is less used than I to being classed with the animal kingdom.'

'I see I am not to be allowed to forget that particular misdemeanour. But, seriously, I will do anything I can to help you.'

'I know. I wish I could have persuaded you to keep away. . .'

'Well, you will not. Though the moment the mist lifts you will not see me for dust, I promise you, for I shall be riding after a doctor as soon as may be. Now, remember your promise to call me. . .?'

'I will.'

'Good girl.' He bent and kissed her once, hard, on the lips, and was gone before she could catch her breath again.

Mrs Carter had set up a little bed in the corner of the room so that Arabella could have the big bed to herself. Anne was thankful to lie down, but tired though she was she did not expect a peaceful night. Keyed up to every sound from her sister, she woke at every cough, and left her bed many times during the following hours to add fuel to the fire, to make tea, warm posset, or simply to soothe the fretful girl who lay, half awake and half asleep.

At some time during the night Anne woke, conscious that some difference had roused her. At first, in panic, she listened for the sound of Arabella's breathing, but that was steady and not too harsh, so it was not any change in her condition that had alerted her. Something, though, had changed. Then she heard it, a sound so everyday that normally it would mean nothing: the gentle creak of the sign moving on its bracket outside the window. For a moment its significance did not strike her. Then she realised: the wind was blowing, and the fog would lift. She crept from her bed and peered out of the window, oblivious to the chill draughts that came through when she moved the curtain aside. The mist swirled past, but it was thinner already, and through it came the fitful gleam of moonlight. With relief she knew that they would no longer be isolated.

It was too late, of course, to get them home.

Even if Arabella had been well enough to move, it would be wicked to carry such an infection back to the household and the village. Messages, at least, she would be able to send, and medical help could be summoned. She knew that the worry James must already be feeling could only be increased by knowledge of their state, but it could not be helped.

Very early, when the dawn was no more than a dim greenish glow on the eastern horizon, she heard a footstep outside the door, and the faintest suggestion of a knock. At once Anne left her unquiet bed and wrapped herself in her cloak before creeping to open the door. Delamere, already dressed, waited in the passage. He held a flickering candle which underlit his face in an eerie way and hightlighted the planes of cheeks and brow with gold.

'How is she? Have you slept at all?'

'Yes, I have slept, and so has she. She is — well, no better, but not a great deal worse either, I am pleased to say. You are setting out now?'

'Yes, now that the fog has lifted I must not waste any time. I shall be in Dorchester as soon as may be. Is there any doctor there that you trust, that I may send out to you?'

'I have never had dealings with him, but I have heard that Dr Fletcher is a good man, if he will be willing to come.'

'He will be willing.' His tone left her in no doubt that the doctor would have no choice in the matter. 'What else may I procure for you? If there is anything to be bought I can have them sent at once, before I go on to Minterne Abbas.'

Anne, who had already been hoping for this, gave him a succinct list, not forgetting lemons. 'As for my brother. . .oh, you must tell him the truth, of course, in every detail. I am afraid he will be much distressed, but I hope that the relief of knowing that we are safe here will give him some comfort. Ask him, if you would, to have the maids pack up some clothes for me — they will know what to send — and give him my dear, dear love. It will be hard for him, but you must do everything you can to prevent him from coming here. We do not know how such infection may be carried, and it may even be that it can spread from the garments of those who have been near it. I cannot risk him carrying it home with him.'

'In that case I shall not enter the house, since I too may be carrying it.'

'Yes. . .when you reach the manor, you must be sure to change and bath at once, and burn everything that you have worn here. Then you may go where you will.'

'I shall do no such thing.'

'But. . . Mr Lydford, and his sister?'

'Will be in no danger. I will send for some clothes, and come back here.'

'Come back? No, there is no need. You must not take the risk.'

'And leave you here alone, with a sick girl to nurse? I would not do that to the merest acquaintance, leave alone. . . No, it is no use arguing with me. You will not change me when my mind is made up.'

'I know it,' she said, with a rueful smile. 'But——'

'But nothing. I shall be back with you as soon as may be.' Whatever else he might have said was cut short by the appearance of Mrs Carter. He kissed her cheek, and was gone. The two women looked at one another.

'You're a lucky girl, my dear,' said the landlady.

'Oh, yes, I know,' said Anne distractedly. 'He is a very good brother.'

'Yes, if that's what you choose to call him,' said the other. 'Though mark you, if any brother of mine had looked at me the way he does at you, my mother would have been in a rare old taking! No——' she held up a meaty hand when Anne opened her mouth to speak '—I asks no questions. I can see well enough that to let it be known that you are brother and sisters is best for everyone, and I know you well enough to believe that there's no harm in what you're doing, though why the three of you should be junketing around the countryside, with no more than one bag of luggage between you, is beyond me!'

At this forthright speech Anne drew the landlady into her room. Arabella still lay quiet, and in a low voice her sister told Mrs Carter the true tale of their exploits.

'Well, I'd guessed mostly as much, for all those fibs you told me. Running off to London on her own, the naughty puss! And her with no more idea how to take care of herself than the kitten in the kitchen!'

'Rather less, I should say,' agreed Anne with a sad smile. 'All we can now hope for is that she is not too severely punished for her folly. I know that she must be worse than this before she is better.'

'Aye, no need to tell me that. But you and me together, miss, we'll cheat the devil of his due yet, you'll see. And to think we have a real lord staying here! And me scolding him, like as if he was just a man! Not that he isn't, of course, but. . .well, I just hope he didn't take offence. Now, I'll be away to fetch you some hot water. A real live lord, and staying here! Just wait till I tell Carter that!'

The morning seemed interminable. Dr Fletcher, sent hotfoot from Dorchester by Delamere, arrived betimes and was fortunately not affronted at being used as a parcel carrier also, Delamere having handed him several bulky packages and a basket of lemons and oranges. Anne was fulsome in her apologies.

'I'm afraid he was so worried about my sister that he did not think how far beneath your dignity it is to be acting as a common carrier!' The doctor laughed.

'As to that, I'm not one of your fine London fellows, you know! I've carried stranger things than a few lemons in my gig, and between you and me, my dear, they're likely to do as much good to her as anything else I can bring. If you want me to bleed her, I will, but I doubt it will do more than weaken her, and the fever is not great.'

'Oh, no, please do not. I have never known it to help in such cases.'

'Sensible girl. You'd be amazed how many people expect me to cup them for anything from a broken leg to a headache, and seem to think I'm not doing my job if I refuse! I have something that will soothe her throat and make it easier for her to drink and take some light nourishment, and I will leave you a draught and some drops to give her when the fever mounts. Mrs Carter here is an excellent nurse; you may have faith in her. Be sure to take care of yourself — it will not do for you to be collapsing in exhaustion just when your sister most needs you to see her through the crisis!'

He left, promising to return the next day unless he were sent for sooner.

Arabella lay quietly in the bed, half asleep for much of the time. Bullied by Mrs Carter, Anne put on her cloak and went outside to get some air and exercise, leaving the landlady sitting beside her sister. Such members of the hamlet who were about stared at her in fascination, but all the children had been warned not to approach her, so it was far from the cheerful walk she would have had in her own village, where everyone she saw would have greeted her and passed the time of day.

She walked as far as the road, and could not help watching and listening for a moment, though she knew it was far too soon for Delamere to have time to return from Minterne Abbas. The sound of wheels that sent a tingle through her for a moment turned out to be no more than a farm cart, plodding its way with a load of sacks — a farmer sending some of his newly threshed wheat to be milled, perhaps. She watched it out of sight, then turned back.

During the afternoon he returned, but by then she was too busy to hear his arrival. Arabella's temperature had risen sharply, and she was halfway delirious, trying to throw off her bedcovers and fighting when Anne tried to replace them. Whereas earlier she had complained of being cold, and had huddled beneath the quilt, now she was burning up. Anne sponged her with tepid water, which brought some relief, and was trying to persuade her to drink the lemonade Mrs Carter had made when Delamere strode into the room.

He took in the situation with one glance, and came to the bed.

'Arabella!' he said firmly. 'Arabella, be still and take your drink.' Miraculously his deep tones seemed to pierce her clouded brain. Arabella opened her heavy eyelids, and a little smile stretched her cracked lips.

'Edward,' she whispered. He came to her side, and took her hand.

'Yes, it is I. Now I am going to lift you up, while Anne gives you your drink. It will make you feel better, and do you good.' Obediently she drank, then closed her eyes as he laid her back. 'Good girl. Now you may go to sleep.'

'Thank you,' said Anne, in heartfelt tones. 'I could not make her mind me.'

'It is no more than the stronger tones of a man's voice,' he said. 'She is worse?'

'A little, but no more than I expected. But tell me — my family? Have you spoken to James? How are they all? Is he very angry, and worried? Did he guess what had happened?'

'Gently, gently!' He took her hand and drew her to a seat by the window. 'I cannot answer so many questions at once. All your family and friends are well, and all unite in sending their love to you both, and good wishes for a speedy recovery. Your brother, in particular, was insistent that I should tell you not to worry. He sends you his fondest love, and a letter which I will give you presently. As you expected, I had my work cut out to prevent him from riding straight over here at once; only by making him see how much extra burden of anxiety it must put on your shoulders could I persuade him to stay at home!'

Anne's eyes filled with tears, and she fixed them on her lap.

'Had he been very worried?' she asked huskily.

'A little, of course. But as I had hoped, my man and Lydford between them persuaded him that with my help you would soon find Arabella and save her from her folly. When we did not return that evening he was naturally alarmed, but I am happy to say that he tells me he reposed complete confidence in me.' His voice exuded a parody of self-satisfaction, and Anne had to smile. 'Luckily, the fog that kept us here yesterday was pretty general over all the country, and no one wondered that we did not come back. Now, of course, his only concern is that Arabella should make a safe and quick recovery.'

Anne felt as if a burden had dropped from her shoulders. In all her life she had never before had cause to fear her brother's anger. This time she had known he would blame himself most bitterly for not having been able, somehow, to prevent Arabella's flight, and she had dreaded this more than anything else.

'Did he say anything about. . .the future?' she asked, wondering if he would now refuse to permit Arabella to return to her uncle's in London.

'Many things. But we will not discuss that now.'

His face was serious, but there was a warm smile in his voice and Anne felt a glow of warmth steal up to her cheeks. She raised wondering eyes to his face, eyes that were shadowed with the violet bruises of a sleepless night, but which had regained the golden flecks in their warm amber depths that had delighted him before.

'You have gold-dust in your eyes,' he murmured. 'Anne, if you look at me like that, I ——'

At that moment Arabella cried out, and the hands that had been imperceptibly stealing towards one another dropped. The wild rose colour died out of Anne's cheeks as she turned towards the bed, where her sister was struggling to push aside the covers and get up. The movement made her cough, which hurt her throat, and while Anne dealt competently with all these ills Delamere sat back in his chair, biting back the words that had so nearly come leaping to his lips. One could scarcely find a less opportune moment for a declaration, he thought drily.

He drew out James's letter and laid it on the table. They had been forced, for reasons of prudence, to converse in the garden with the space of several feet between them, so it had been scarcely possible for anything of a private or personal nature to be discussed. Nevertheless, he had made sure that Anne's brother was aware which way the wind was blowing. He returned secure in the knowledge that no objections were likely to be raised in that quarter. In fact, the only objections were likely to come from the lady herself. And, of course, her sister.

And who would have thought, he said to himself with a smile of self-derision, that the great Lord Delamere, the object of who knew how many matchmaking mamas and fashionable beauties' wiles, would find himself staying, by his own choice, in a country ale-house in order to be with a small, unfasionable and damnably sharp-tongued young woman, with no fortune and of no more than respectable family?

At that moment the object of his passion turned and, with eyes that scarcely noticed his presence except as someone who might be useful, requested him to fetch various items from her luggage in tones that were tantamount to a crisp order. Mrs

Carter, entering the room at that moment, gave a shocked gasp.

'You can't talk to him like that, miss, and him a lord!'

'Oho, so that cat has been let out of the bag, has it?' he asked with some resignation, having a clear idea of the added discomforts his elevated status would earn him. Anne glanced round guiltily.

'Yes, I'm sorry, I forgot to tell you. But in fact Mrs Carter had guessed a great deal of it for herself, and it seemed simpler to tell her the truth. She said you didn't. . .we didn't behave like brother and sister.' A swift blush rose to her cheeks, and she turned back to the bed. 'But if I might trouble you, my lord, for the lavender drops, and the balsam?'

He grinned at Mrs Carter before she could remonstrate again.

'Madam, your *most* obedient servant,' he said in servile tones, and went.

CHAPTER THIRTEEN

THAT night followed the pattern of the previous one, different only in the degree of Arabella's illness. Anne, knowing that she could not go a whole night without sleep after her disturbed rest the previous night, consented to lie down on Delamere's bed for the first part of the night, while he sat with Arabella and Mrs Carter. Rather to her surprise, she slept deeply, with her head buried in the pillow that had known his face and that still carried the faint scent of the bay rum he used. When Mrs Carter came in at two o'clock to waken her, as they had agreed, she felt refreshed and invigorated, but one sight of her sister's face banished whatever optimism she might have woken with.

Arabella lay sunk in a sleep that more nearly resembled unconsciousness, her breathing harsh, with an occasional little moan on the exhalation. The pink rash, which had started on her hands and feet, had spread up her limbs and only her face was left. That, however, had fierce spots of feverish colour burning high up in the cheeks, while the area round her mouth was blue-white with the classic pallor of the disease.

'She's not changed for some hours now, and at least she's no worse. I don't think we've reached the worst of it yet, but she's fighting, bless her heart,' whispered Mrs Carter. 'Will you be all right alone, miss, or shall I stay with you a while?'

'No, thank you, Mrs Carter. You must have your sleep too. I shall be quick enough to call you if there's any change.'

'Very good, miss.'

Delamere stood irresolute. Like most men, he had no knowledge of illness other than the distant memory of his own childhood ailments. He felt helpless and, because of that, angry.

'There must be something that can be done,' he said in a low, tight voice. 'What of the doctor? Why did he not return this evening? Did he leave anything for you to give her?'

'Yes, he did, and he would have come if I had sent for him,' said Anne, wiping Arabella's face with a dampened towel and moistening her lips.

'Then why in heaven's name did you not send for him?'

'Because in my judgement there is nothing he could do. There may come a time, in the future, when a cure may be found for such diseases, but for now constant, careful nursing and a strong constitution are the only weapons we have, and at least we have those in full measure.'

'Yes. I'm sorry.' He beat his fist into his palm in frustration. 'It is only. . .she is so young, and so lovely. . .'

'And will be both still, God willing,' said Anne with more confidence than she felt.

'Yes.'

For the first time in his life he was unable to say what was in his heart. If Arabella should die. . . he could not help believing that some of the responsibility must be his. Carelessly he had flirted with her, meaning nothing but to please a pretty child, and so caused her banishment from London. Then, worse than that, he had followed her to the country only to fall, with one sickening headlong rush, in love with her sister. And, perhaps because he loved her in a way that had never come to him before, he found himself unable to gauge Anne's feelings for him. There were times, like that afternoon, when he was sure that she felt for him as strongly as he did for her. Then, at other times, she seemed to close herself off from him with a completeness that argued a heart-whole self-control.

That she held him responsible for her sister's presence in the country he knew full well. It followed, then, that if Arabella should die. . . Could she ever forgive him? Could she ever bring herself to admit to love for the author of the family's unhappiness? Or would she withdraw into her spinster cares, and devote herself to her brothers and, eventually, their children?

Most of the time he was confident in his love, but at this hour, the time when the human spirit was at its lowest ebb, he felt far less sure. If he could but ask her, talk to her. . . Unthinkable, at the bedside of a possibly dying girl. Without another word, he turned and left the room. Anne stared after him, and her eyes filled with tears.

Unconsciously she had become accustomed, during the time when they were pretending to be brother and sister, to expect his kiss of greeting and farewell. That he should omit the caress now, when she had most need of his love and support, argued that she had been mistaken after all. It was Arabella that he loved, Arabella's whose state made him forget everything except his own fear and misery, Arabella who occupied his every thought. And how much more likely that was, after all. Even as sick as she was, her sister's beauty shone out in the dingy room like a rare jewel set in rusty iron.

Well, if it was Arabella that he wanted, then it was up to Anne to see that she survived for him. Loving him as she did — and at last she looked deep into her own heart and acknowledged that there was no part in it that was not filled with his presence — it was unthinkable that he should not have anything, everything that his heart desired. Even if, in giving it, her own heart was broken forever.

Doggedly, through the rest of the long night, Anne fought for her sister's life. Tirelessly she sponged the burning skin and dried it again. Whenever Arabella roused even a little, she lifted her against her shoulder and with painstaking care dribbled warm milk laced with sugar and brandy between her lips, to give her the strength to go on fighting, and lemonade to cool her fever. When the girl cried out against the phantasms of delirium Anne held her close, rocking her like a baby and singing the murmurous lullabies that once, so long ago, her mother had crooned to her.

So the night passed, and in the morning Delamere, looking at Arabella, felt encouraged.

'She is a little better, don't you think? I believe she is not so bad as last night.'

In response to his voice, Arabella lifted reddened eyelids and fixed her eyes on him. A minute curve of her lips indicated a smile.

'There! You see! She knows me!' Her eyes fell closed, but he was triumphant. Anne and Mrs Carter, with more experience than he, glanced at one another but said nothing.

Not long afterwards there was a clatter of hoofs outside, and a familiar voice calling her name.

'William! Oh, it is William!' cried Anne, running to the window. Through the thick glass she could see his face looking anxiously up at the windows, and she tapped to get his attention, then waved. 'He must not come up here!' she said hastily. 'I will go down, and speak to him outside. Oh, where is my cloak?'

The visit, bringing as it did all manner of loving messages and attentions from home, did much to cheer her spirits, although she would have given anything to be able to embrace her brother, and feel the comfort of his strong arms round her. He would happily have forgotten the danger but she was stern with him, reminding him that not only his own health, but that of others in the family, depended upon their being sensible.

She sent a guardedly optimistic message about

Arabella's progress, and waved William farewell through a haze of tears. Her eyes were pink when she returned upstairs, and Delamere had to call on every ounce of self-possession within him to prevent himself from gathering her into his arms. Instead, he was brisk with her, insisting that she drink a glass of wine, and making her eat a meal, though the food, even the little delicacies that had been sent by Mary Sudbury to tempt her appetite, almost choked her.

During the afternoon the doctor visited again. He, like Anne, was unwilling to give an opinion one way or the other, but said that on the whole he was hopeful. Delamere was inclined to be short-tempered with him, and it was clear that he did not think that enough was being done. After Fletcher had taken himself off Delamere was all for posting at once to London, and bringing down the finest physician he could lay his hands on. Anne longed to kiss his frowning face and smooth away the lines of tension and worry. But her caresses, she thought sadly, were not the ones he wanted, so she confined herself to soothing him with her usual calm common sense, and pointed out that, even if it were possible to persuade anyone to come, there would be no chance of their returning soon enough to be of any help.

'But I must do something! I can't just sit around here, like a stock!'

'Why do you not return to Minterne? Or even to London? Now that we are settled here, with Mrs Carter to look after us, we are scarcely in need of protection,' she said reasonably, her heart quailing at the thought of his going.

'I could not bear to,' he said simply, and she could not argue with him. Had the positions been reversed, and it was he who lay at death's door, no consideration in the world would have induced her to leave him, to forgo sharing with him what might be his last hours of life.

After that they spoke little, each lost in thoughts that could not be spoken. When, as she had done the night before, Anne went away to snatch a few hours of sleep, she longed for the luxury of shedding the tears that burned behind her eyes and ached in her throat. She would not allow herself to do so, however, and lay rigid on the bed, willing herself to sleep. At last she did so, and did not know that she wept in her sleep. Delamere, creeping in to make sure that she was all right, found her with the tears trickling slowly down her pale cheeks. With infinite gentleness he dried them and, unable to deny himself, bent to kiss her lips with an almost imperceptible touch.

Anne stirred but did not wake, muttered a few incomprehensible words and flung out her hand. He took it in his own and held it gently. His touch seemed to soothe her and she subsided back into sleep. For a few minutes he stayed where he was, motionless at the bedside and watching her. She was peaceful, and reluctantly he tucked her hand back beneath the rug that covered her, and left the room.

When Mrs Carter came to call her later, Anne

took one look at her face and jumped from the
bed.

'Is she worse?' She was already tying the ribbons
of her kid slippers as she spoke, having laid down
fully dressed in expectation of a summons.

'The fever's very high; she's burning up with it.
I think you should come, miss.'

It was as Mrs Carter had said. Arabella's skin
was so hot that Anne could feel the heat coming
from it from several inches away. Even in so short
a time the flesh seemed to have melted away,
leaving the fine bones sticking up through blotchy
pink skin. Arabella lay without moving, her shallow breaths barely lifting the bedcovers.

'We must get the fever down. Is there any ice to
be had?'

'None, miss. It's too early in the winter. The
well water's near as cold, though.'

'Then we must make use of that. Where is Lord
Delamere?'

'I sent his lordship away, seeing as how we'd
need to strip the poor young lady. In any case, a
man like him's no manner of use at a time like
this, begging your pardon, miss.'

'No, you are right. I know how much he feels
for her. . .' For a moment Anne's voice shook,
then she took a grip on herself and concentrated
on the matter in hand. 'Do you send for cold
water, if you please, and as many towels as you
can spare, Mrs Carter. We must not lose any more
time.'

For more than an hour the two women worked

together. Taking off the fine cambric nightgown, they laid Arabella on towels and laid other towels, wrung out in icy well water and folded into compresses, against the burning skin. As the damp towels warmed they replaced them with others, and with others again.

At last, Anne put her hand on Arabella's forehead. Her fingers were icy from wringing out cold, wet towels, though the rest of her body was hot from working.

'The fever is down, I think,' she said doubtfully.

'Even if it were not, we would have to stop,' said Mrs Carter. 'I doubt if she could take much more of this, so weakened as she is.'

Taking away the damp towels, they pulled a sheet and a single blanket up over the still figure. Anne took her sister's hand in her own, the little bones feeling as light as a bird's. There was no response to her grip, and the pulse when she felt for it was slow and faint.

'Arabella!' Anne leaned down and called in her sister's ear. 'Arabella, wake up! Wake up, Arabella!' Not a tremor crossed the closed eyelids that domed over sightless eyes. Again and again she called, but there was no response, and already it seemed that the spirit was withdrawing from the motionless body, withdrawing from life.

Anne's face was drawn with anguish. Mrs Carter put out her hand, mottled and red, and patted her consolingly.

'I'm sorry, my dear. I'm afraid she's sinking.

You mustn't blame yourself; you did all that you could, and more.'

'She must not die. I tell you, she must not die. Send for Edward.'

'His lordship? At a time like this, and her with no more on than a new-born babe?'

'What difference, if she's dying? Besides, she's covered decently enough. Fetch him.'

'But. . .'

'Do as I bid you!' snapped Anne, her patience breaking.

'Yes, miss.' Mrs Carter, who had worked along-side Anne as if the sick girl had been a child of her own, was wooden. Anne's face softened, and in her turn she put out a hand to the other woman.

'I beg your pardon,' she said simply. 'I should never have spoken to you so, when you have been so good a friend to my sister and me. But. . .he must come, you see. I have done my best to save her for him because he loves her. It may be that he can call her back. If not, he has the right to make his farewells. So please, Mrs Carter, will you go and call him?'

The landlady stared at her silently for a moment, a little puzzled frown between her brows. This was not at all how she had read the situation, but it scarcely seemed the moment to argue the point. Besides, it was true that once before the sound of Delamere's voice had roused the girl. Catching her breath on a little sigh, she went.

Anne knelt by the bed, holding and stroking the

little hand that lay so lax within her own. She did not turn when she heard the door open and the sound of Delamere's footsteps cross the room. She could not bear to look at his face, to see written on it the blame that she felt within herself. He came to stand behind her, and she almost shrank from his presence.

'You sent for me?' His voice was low, as if he thought he might disturb the silent girl.

'Yes. Her fever is down, but. . .oh, Edward, she is slipping away. I cannot do any more.'

'Oh, my dear. . .' Aware of his every movement though he was not within her sight, she felt him reach out to comfort her. She slipped under his outstretched arms.

'No! Don't touch me!' How could she explain that even now, in the presence of his dying love, she could not trust herself not to fling herself into his embrace, to clasp her arms around him so that he could not help knowing her feelings? 'Call her! Call her back!'

'I?' he sounded dazed.

'Yes, you! It may not be too late, if we can only rouse her. She does not hear me, but you. . . Oh, take her hand, here, here, and call to her!'

She lifted Arabella's limp hand up to him, and laid it in his, which came up to accept it. As his fingers closed around it she could have howled like a dog, and she snatched her own hands away as if they had been burned and backed away from the bedside. She felt Mrs Carter's strong arm come up to steady her, and was grateful.

He knelt as she had done, Arabella's hand disappeared inside his own, and leaned forward until his mouth was almost next to her ear.

'Arabella!' His voice was clear and sonorous. 'Arabella! Arabella!'

Anne's own hand was pressed tightly to her mouth, not even aware of the pain as her teeth pressed into flesh. If it were me, she thought, if it were me, his voice would bring me back from the edge of death and beyond, were it no more than a whisper.

'Arabella! Arabella! Arabella!' Insistent and steady as the tolling of a bell, he called to her. 'Arabella! Arabella!'

The room was so silent that the sound of his voice seemed to echo round it. There was a faint sigh, so slight that Anne would have thought that she had imagined it if she had not seen Arabella's breast rise and fall. Exactly so had Anne seen a dying child draw in one last, long breath before letting go the frail thread that held him to life, and she felt the tears start down her face again.

'She has gone,' she whispered.

'No! Mrs Carter's voice was low, but triumphant. 'Wait! Look!'

Another breath lifted the bedclothes, and another. A faint tinge of pink flowed up Arabella's face beneath the waxy pallor. Tripping and stumbling in her haste, Anne ran to the other side of the bed and took the other hand that still lay on the smooth surface of the folded sheet. Her fingers trembled as she pressed them to the inside of

Arabella's wrist, the gap between bone and tendon clearly defined by the wasted flesh. Beneath her fingertips the pulse seemed to grow stronger even as she stood there.

'You've done it,' she whispered. 'She's come back. Oh, Edward! Call her once more!'

He did so, and this time the eyelids flickered, and then parted. As unfocused as a new-born baby's, Arabella's eyes drifted round the room, then settled on Delamere's face. Her lips parted, and they saw her neck strain as she tried to speak.

'Lift her up, my lord,' said Mrs Carter. 'Lift her up, and let's see if we can't get some of the brandy and milk into her.'

He held the slight figure against his shoulder and carefully, drop by drop, they trickled the life-giving fluid between her lips. At first some of it ran out again at the corners of her mouth, but then she swallowed. Painfully at first, but then more easily, until almost a full cupful was gone. Then Arabella smiled, turned her face a little, and was still.

'What is it? She hasn't. . .?'

'No, my lord! She's asleep, that's all! Lay her down again; she'll sleep for a while and it will do her all the good in the world, you'll see.'

Obediently, still in a daze, he did as he was told, and stood looking down at the sleeping girl. Then he raised his head and looked across the bed at Anne.

'My dear,' he said. She smiled tremulously at him.

'She will live,' she said simply. 'I am so thankful.' There was a deep gladness in her voice, because she was able to say it and it was true. All along, when it had looked as though the battle might be lost, she had feared that somewhere deep inside her was a devil that could rejoice at her sister's death, at the death of a rival. But there was no devil after all, and she was more grateful for that than for anything. She could even smile at him, and wish them well in her heart.

'There now!' Mrs Carter was smiling and wiping her eyes at the same time. 'It's morning, and we never even realised!' It was true. When she drew back the curtains the sky was pink and gold with the dawn, and the world was filled with the sounds of another day beginning. 'Now, you sit yourselves right down and I'll fetch you up some breakfast, if that girl has kept the fire going in the kitchen range, like I told her to!' She bustled off, with no hint of tiredness.

'Come and sit down, my dear. You look so white, it frightens me.' He held out his hand, but she slipped past him and sat in the window-seat. He came and stood beside her, and together they looked out at the dawn.

'My brothers,' she said. 'We must get word to my brothers.'

'I will ride over as soon as I may. Shall I bring James back with me? He longs to come.'

'Not yet.' It seemed so natural that he should refer to her brother by his first name that she scarcely noticed it. 'She will sleep for most of today, and there is still danger of infection. In a day or two, when she is stronger, we may move her into another room while this one is cleansed, and he may safely visit. I long to see him so much, I do not think I could bear it if I must keep a distance between us!'

'I know,' he said, with feeling. His hands were gripped together behind his back, and his eyes devoured her hungrily. Half turned away from him, she was silhouetted against the dawn, its colours mysteriously dimmed by the heavy old glass but still glowing with opal hues. She was thinner than before, he thought with compunction, the old cotton gown she wore hanging in unbecoming folds from shoulders slender as a child's. Her soft hair was twisted back in a careless knot at the nape of her neck that was half undone, and beneath it the soft line of her throat was so innocent and yet so seductive that he felt that if he once touched his lips to it he would never leave off kissing, until it were to kiss her lips. She seemed completely unaware of him, but, although he knew the moment might be ill chosen, the pent-up emotions of the night must have some outlet, or he thought he would run mad.

'Anne. . . Anne. . .' He dragged himself away from her, lest he seize her bodily in his arms and carry her away. Restlessly he paced to the fireplace, and pushed at the logs with his foot. 'Anne, my darling, forgive me for choosing this moment, I am a boor, what you will, but. . .' Heavens, he was babbling like a green boy in the throes of his first infatuation! He pulled himself up short. 'Dearest Anne, you cannot have failed to see that, to me, you are the most precious, the most desirable, the most wonderful. . . Oh, Anne, I love you so much. Say that you will marry me, darling! Say that you love me, at least a little bit! No, not a little bit, that will not suffice me! Say that you love me as much as I love you! Anne! Anne?'

Her silence mocked him. She did not speak, or even move. Humiliated, he stood by the mantel-shelf, scarcely believing that it was possible that he could love so much without any return. At last, he made himself turn and look at her. She did not move, and he walked back to her filled with hurt anger.

Then he reached her side, and he stopped dead. Self-deprecating laughter made his shoulders shake. His beloved, the first woman to whom he had ever proposed, the only one he had ever professed to love, sat with her head leaning against the bunched-up curtain. Her eyes were closed, and she was fast asleep.

'Oh, Anne, my darling girl,' he whispered. He reached out as if to touch her, then thought better of it, and whirled on his heel and almost ran from the room.

'Carter! Have my horse saddled!' he called as he hurried to his room. This was decidedly not the moment for a declaration, but he must do something. So, lover-like, he must needs fulfil his lady's wishes. He would ride to speak to her brothers, and later, when the time was right, he would try again. And that time, he promised himself, she will not fall asleep. Laughing, he ran down to the stable.

CHAPTER FOURTEEN

BOTH Anne and her sister slept through most of the next day and night, waking to swallow the cups of beef tea and egg posset that Mrs Carter decreed for them, and then slipping thankfully back into slumber. Edward Delamere rode as he had promised to Minterne Abbas, where his news was greeted with joy and relief and he was required to recount, over and over again, the story of the recovery. His own part in that happy ending he modestly suppressed, but the very fact of his presence was felt by all to be an act of the greatest kindness. Once all the interested parties had been satisfied, he requested the chance of a private interview with the rector.

'If any conversation may be said to be private, when I am obliged to keep a distance of several feet between us, and am moreover unable to come inside your house,' he said ruefully.

'Oh, dear me, yes! It does seem so very ill mannered to keep you outside! Surely you might come in just for a moment?'

'Your sister would never forgive me if I were to do so,' said Delamere. 'And. . .and I would not wish to do anything that might give her the slightest cause to be displeased with me.'

'Ah,' said James. 'Of course.' His expression

was non-committal—so much so that his lack of expression said more than the most knowing of looks might have done. Delamere's lips twitched. He was becoming increasingly fond of this simple country parson, whose innocence of the ways of the world was so refreshing and was, from time to time, tempered by a profound wisdom and knowledge of human nature in its highest and lowest forms.

'Perhaps we might take a turn round the churchyard?' suggested Delamere. It was a place that was open enough to make it impossible for anyone to be within earshot without being seen at once, and it was, besides, a place where no one would be surprised to see the rector walking.

'Of course.' The two of them walked up and down the neatly scythed paths, which were wide enough to permit them to keep a distance of two or three feet between them, and spoke earnestly. An observer, had there been one, might have understood something of their feelings from their attitudes and movements: one could have seen pleasure, anxiety, annoyance, and even resignation. There was, however, no one to see them.

As a result of this conversation, Delamere returned to the inn in a thoughtful frame of mind. He had ridden slowly, leaving his horse to find its own path and letting his mind chew over the various possibilities before him. Loving Anne as he did, he yet felt that in many ways she was a mystery to him: he was bound to accept her brother's opinions on the subject. There was also the problem of Arabella.

'There is no possibility of Anne accepting you,' James had said firmly, 'if she thinks that by doing so she is depriving her sister of the man that she loves.'

'But I do not love Arabella! I never have done, and what is more I do not believe that she loves me. My position in the world may have dazzled her, young as she is, into infatuation, but not love.'

'Oh, I quite agree. And so would Anne,' added the rector surprisingly. 'But that is not the point, is it? The point is that Arabella *believes* that she loves you, and I am afraid she has never before been denied anything that she wants so she believes also that you must love her. And of course your constant presence over the last few days will not have done anything to disabuse her mind of this idea.'

'Before she fell ill, I proposed to Anne in her presence. I should not have done it, I know, but it was half in jest and half in anger, because Arabella was trying to use our mishap to push me into proposing to her. She was quite hysterical, and I am afraid it brought on the beginning of her illness.'

'She had already taken the infection; it would have done no more than precipitate matters. And Anne?'

'She did not believe I was serious,' admitted Delamere wryly.

'No. She is entirely lacking in that kind of confidence in her own powers to please. It is, of course, one of her great charms.'

'Yes, it is. And then the next day Arabella seemed to have no recollection of what had passed. Whether she will remember it now. . .'

'Very likely not. If she has been as sick as you say, both her mind and body have undergone a great trial. Who can say whether this might not, in the end, be the making of her? A soul, tried in the furnace, you know?'

He looked hopefully at Delamere, his simple faith in the ultimate goodness of all things sent by God shining in the hazel eyes that were, though darker, so like his sister's.

'Perhaps,' said Delamere, doubtful but unwilling to cause him pain. 'But what am I to do meanwhile?'

The rector was sympathetic, but firm.

'The one thing you must not do is to show, by word or look or deed, your feelings towards Anne. In Arabella's weakened state it would be most prejudicial to her recovery, and nothing could be more likely to turn Anne against you than that. If, in some way, you can make Arabella see that she does not love you. . .well, then there will be nothing more to do than to give you my blessing.'

By the morning of the next day Anne pronounced herself perfectly fit again, and she resumed the nursing of her sister that Mrs Carter had carried out the previous day. Arabella was still inclined to sleep for an hour or two at a time, but her wakeful periods were longer. Anne kept her quiet and cheerful, speaking only of trivial matters, and talking much of the past, the distant days when Arabella had lived at home and they had all been children together. Delamere sat quietly, when he was with them, and contributed little to the conversation, though he watched how Anne avoided looking at him, while Arabella on the contrary allowed her glance to slide towards him as often as possible.

By the next day Arabella was well enough for him to insist that her sister leave her for a while. He had arranged for his servant to bring a curricle, and before Anne knew what was happening she was carried off by Mrs Carter to be dressed in freshly laundered clothes before being driven off to Minterne Abbas to see, at last, the rest of her family. Arabella pouted prettily.

'But how shall I manage without Anne?' she asked.

'You will have to make do with me, and of course Mrs Carter,' said Delamere firmly. Arabella, leaping instantly to the conclusion that he had engineered the whole thing in order to be with her, smiled up at him through her eyelashes, and Delamere's heart sank. It was, of course, quite true, but in a sense far different from what she imagined, and now it was up to him to make the most of his opportunity.

Arabella, recovering rapidly, was already beginning to be bored, and was quite willing to be entertained with conversation. Delamere, how-

ever, was unaccountably unwilling to provide her
with the kind of flirting and light-hearted teasing
she was used to from gentlemen. Indeed, he even
had the temerity to scold her like some kind of
disagreeable old uncle when she complained about
her pitiable state, and even was unkind enough to
tell her that it was entirely her own fault, and that
if she had not behaved like a spoiled child she
would not have put herself, and the rest of her
family, through so much worry and discomfort.

'But. . .but I *wanted* to go back to London! You
said yourself that I would be better suited to that
kind of life!'

'I did, and so I still think. But we may not
always have just what we want, you know,' he
informed her austerely.

'I don't know why you should say so,' she said
sulkily. 'It does not seem to me that you ever have
to do anything you do not wish to.'

'Does it not? You could not be more mistaken.
I am frequently obliged to do things that I do not
at all enjoy. It is one of the consequences of my
position in the world.'

'But you're a lord!' she said naïvely, and he bit
back a smile.

'Of course I am. And for that very reason I
must fulfil the duties that my title lays upon me.'

'Like sitting in the House?' she hazarded.

'That, yes. It obliges me to be in London when
I should rather prefer to be in the country.'

'In Dorset?' Her pique forgotten, she was prepared for a compliment.

'Not necessarily,' he said, in quelling tones. 'Do not forget that I have a country seat and estates there. I visit them as often as I can.'

'Oh, for the shooting, I suppose,' she said carelessly, knowing the ways of the great and fashionable, 'and for a few weeks in the summer, at the end of the season. It must be charming!'

'It is, but that is not what I meant. I have farms to manage, I am a magistrate and must perform the duties that that involves; I am required to be there for some part at least of each month.'

'Oh.' She was thoughtful. 'Poor you.'

'Not at all! I delight in it, and enjoy my life there! Of course, the house is a little inconvenient, being so old, and it can be very cold and draughty in the winter months, but I assure you I never regard it!' He spared a thought for his mother, who would have been shocked and indignant to hear him say such a thing of the home which, under her supervision, was both warm and commodious.

'And have you pleasant society there?' she asked, daunted but pursuing.

'Pleasant society? Oh, very pleasant, though rather elderly, I fear! There are one or two residences that are no more than an hour's drive away, and several more if one travels further.' He ruthlessly suppressed the memory of the several elegant establishments within no more than a few minutes' drive of his home, and ignored the existence of three or four younger friends. 'I do not visit them a great deal,' he said with perfect truth.

'How, then, do you fill your evenings?' Arabella was staring at him in horrified fascination.

'Why, with books. My father left an excellent library, and it has been my pleasure as well as my duty to add to it. I am never so happy as when I have a book in my hand.'

'I am very fond of novels. . .'

'Novels? All very well in their way, I suppose, but I prefer something with more meat to it. Philosophy, for example. And natural sciences.'

Arabella, whose governesses had given up the unequal struggle to persuade her to read anything that did not involve a pretty romance, with a few mysterious castles and sinister apparitions as seasoning, looked dumbstruck. Delamere, almost hating himself, continued.

'Of course, when I marry. . .'

Arabella put her head a little on one side, fetchingly.

'You will naturally wish to change your mode of life?' she asked hopefully.

'By no means! I was going to say, I expect to spend even more time there! Marriage, after all, brings children, and I mean my children to be raised, as I was, in the healthy air of the country, knowing all its simple pursuits and simple pleasures. I doubt if I shall ever wish to visit London from one year's end to the next!'

'Not even to attend the House?' asked Arabella in fading tones.

'Not even that. I shall consider myself more

usefully employed tending my acres and raising my family.'

'I think,' said Arabella faintly, 'that I am a little tired now. I should like to go to sleep.'

'Of course. Unless you would like me to read to you?'

'No!' The word was almost a shriek. 'No, thank you,' she added more moderately.

Delamere left the room. He wondered what the rector would have thought of so much deliberate bending of the truth, and was thankful that the only witness to his duplicity had been Aggie. Detailed by her mistress to keep the proprieties by sitting in the corner while Delamere was in Arabella's chamber, she had been enjoying the unaccustomed luxury of idleness by sitting, her mouth slightly ajar and her eyes fixed vacantly on the window, in a pleasurable stupor. The mending that her mistress had left for her lay forgotten in her lap, the thread grey and knotted, and it was doubtful whether she had listened at all, or would have comprehended more than one word in five.

When Anne returned at the end of the afternoon, glowing with the pleasure of seeing her family and satisfying herself that they were truly none the worse for her enforced absence, she found her sister in a strangely silent mood. It was obvious that there was something on her mind, but when they were alone at bedtime and Anne tried gentle questioning Arabella merely shook her head, and sighed.

'I was just. . .oh, Anne, I do so wish to go back to London,' she said pathetically.

'I know, my dear,' was the gentle response. Arabella's eyes filled with tears.

'That sounds so very ungrateful, I know,' she said through quivering lips, 'and indeed I do not mean it so! You have been so very good to me, and I have not deserved it! I know I have behaved very wrongly.'

Anne did not seek to deny it. She put her arms round her sister and hugged her.

'My dear, you were very foolish, but who should know better than your family that you did not mean any harm? You have been punished enough already, and no one will scold you. I know you are not happy at the rectory, and though we were pleased to have you there we would not keep you against your will!'

'I loved being with you, and James and William and Henry! Indeed, if only we could all live together in London, I think my happiness would be complete! Only. . .only. . .'

'Only you are not made for country life. You do not need to tell me that!'

'Is that very wrong of me?'

'Why should it be? A strange sort of world we would have if everyone wished to live exactly the same as everyone else. Now let me tell you, dearest, that James has had a letter from your uncle this very morning! He was much shocked to hear of your illness, for James had naturally written to him, and since all our friends at home have preserved the greatest discretion I do not think your uncle need never learn of this little — adventure of ours. He writes that he will come to fetch you the very minute you are well enough to travel, and that he intends to take the whole family to Brighton, so that you may profit from the sea air. What do you say to that?'

'To Brighton! Oh, Anne!' Arabella's face was pink with excitement. 'How I have longed to see it! And though the Prince will not be entertaining, I suppose, it is sure to be quite gay, is it not? They hold subscription balls twice a week, you know, and one may meet the world and his wife there! Only think of it!'

'You may well see all your old friends and acquaintances, I suppose.'

'Some of them, at any rate,' said Arabella carelessly. 'But what I really want, at the moment, is to meet new people! One may be quite deceived, I find. People who appear to be. . .well, amusing. . .turn out to be quite different underneath when one's eyes are opened!'

'Indeed?' Anne was amused. 'And who has caused this sad disillusionment?'

'Well, I do not think I should tell you,' said Arabella naïvely. 'You know,' she added after a pause, 'I do not think I should like to be betrothed just yet, after all. I think it would be more fun to be presented first, and enjoy the pleasures of the season.'

With a wise nod she snuggled down into her pillow, and within a few minutes was peacefully asleep. Anne, torn between tears and laughter, sat watching her for a few moments, then sought her own bed.

The following morning, Anne noticed that her sister's behaviour towards Delamere had completely changed. Though polite, and perfectly pleased to see him, she treated him almost as if he had been James, or someone even older. Anne busied herself with some needlework at the window-seat, and kept her eyes firmly fixed upon it.

'Now, how may I entertain you?' wondered Delamere, when the courtesies of morning greeting had been gone through. 'I have some delightful books that were sent to me from London the other day. Perhaps you would like me to read to you?'

Anne would have opened her mouth to agree with pleasure, but she was forestalled.

'Oh, no, thank you very much,' said Arabella carefully. 'It is so kind of you, but. . .but I could not think of allowing you to tire your voice!' Anne, who knew that Arabella liked to listen to someone else reading a novel to her, was surprised.

'Have you a headache, dear?' she asked in concern.

'No. That is, yes, perhaps a little. I believe I should like. . . I should like to be quiet for a little while.'

'In that case, perhaps I might take Anne for a walk? It is such a bright day, and I am sure she would be better for the exercise,' said Delamere carefully.

'Oh, no. . .' said Anne.

'What a good idea!' exclaimed Arabella at the same moment. 'I am sure she would like that, wouldn't you, Anne?' Common civility forced Anne to agree, and rather against her will she found herself, a few minutes later, walking down the lane.

It seemed strange to be alone together, without the distraction of Arabella's health and the neutral topic for conversation that it provided. Anne felt very conscious of Delamere and refused his offered arm, walking apart from him and keeping her eyes on the ground as though picking her way.

'It is a delightful day, is it not?' asked Delamere in urbane tones.

'Delightful,' she answered repressively. 'Lord Delamere ——'

'So formal, Anne?' The tone of his voice brought the blood to her cheeks, but she turned away her face a little and continued.

'Edward, then. Though really it is a habit we should long since have discontinued. How people would stare to hear us address one another so, when we have only been acquainted for so short a time.'

'Let them. Why should we care? Besides ——'

'What have you been saying to my sister?' she interrupted rudely.

'I? Nothing at all. At least. . .'

Anne stopped and faced him. She could not

bring herself to look up into his eyes, so fixed her
eyes on his coat buttons as she had done before.

'I believe you have said something to make her
unhappy,' she continued doggedly.

'Does she seem unhappy?' He sounded surprised and even a little amused.

'No,' she admitted, 'but. . .there is a difference.
She seems so very odd when you are with her!
Have you quarrelled?'

'Far from it.' There was laughter in his voice
now. 'On the contrary, I think we are more in
agreement now than we have ever been.'

Anne's throat felt tight; it seemed as though she
could not breathe at all. Unable to speak, she
waited.

'We are agreed, you see, that we do not suit
one another. Not in so many words, of course, but
I can assure you that Arabella now feels, as I do,
that our interests, our characters, our lives—in
short, everything about us—are so dissimilar that
we could never be happy together. We find,' he
continued suavely, 'that we do not love one
another. In fact, I don't believe we ever did.'

Anne found that she had breathed in after all,
and that the air was stuck in her chest so that she
thought she might explode. She breathed out with
a gasp.

'Oh,' she said, foolishly.

'Oh, indeed. Is that all you have to say, Anne?'

'Of course it is,' she said, with some difficulty.
'What else could I say?'

'Well, what about, "Naturally you do not love

one another. You may not love anyone but me"? That would do, for a start,' he suggested helpfully.

'As if I could!' she exclaimed. 'How could I say such a thing?' Her cheeks burned fiery red as she thought how very easily the words could have slipped from her tongue.

'Very simply, if you meant it.'

'It would be most unladylike,' she said primly.

'Perhaps, but would that matter? I would not tell, if you did not. Come now, shall we take it word by word? I shall help you.'

Her heart beat so fast that she thought it must stifle her, and a little bubble of happiness was growing inside her. He had spoken only of her own love, however, and no word of his own feelings. Was he — could he still be behaving from motives of chivalry alone?

'I wish you would not tease me,' she said. He could see little of her face, hidden as it was by the brim of her bonnet — those wretched bonnets of hers! he thought with a flash of amusement — but he could read her uncertainty in the set of her shoulders, and the way her gloved hands unconsciously gripped one another. He put out his hands, and took hers in a gentle clasp.

'I know, but it is irresistible. Oh, darling Anne, I love you so much! Surely you must know that? I should think everyone else does!'

Her hands twisted in his as though they wanted to escape, but when he slackened his grip the slender fingers twined, almost shyly, with his.

'No,' she said simply. 'No, I didn't know. I. . .

hoped you might,' she finished shyly. He let go of her hands, and snatched her into his arms, and she came to him without any false assumption of modesty. Her hands lifted of their own accord to clasp the lapels of his coat, but she still could not quite bring herself to look him in the face. Even now, she half feared what she might read in his eyes.

'My dear little love,' he said tenderly. 'I believe I loved you in the very first instant that I saw you. And you were so cross with me! Will you ever forgive me for teasing you the way I did?'

'I expect I shall. But. . .'

'And you will marry me? Tell me that you will, Anne. Tell me that you love me.'

She did not raise her head, but spoke to his chest.

'But what about James? How can I leave him with no one to care for him and run his house?'

'James, unless I am very much mistaken, is going to find himself married to Emily Lydford before he is very much older. You may safely entrust him to her.'

'Really? How delightful. Her brother does not make any objections?'

'None in the world that I know of, and if he should do you may rely on me to remonstrate with him. Now, Anne. . .'

'But there is William. . .'

'I shall buy him a commission, since that is what he wants more than anything. He does not need you, darling, but I —— '

'And poor little Henry,' she said meditatively. 'He is so young, and an orphan too! You would not ask me to abandon him, would you? I am all the mother he has ever known.'

'Henry shall go to school, and he may live with us in the holidays, if he chooses.' He felt her shoulders shake, and looked suspiciously down at the top of her head. 'Confound this bonnet, I cannot see your face at all,' he said. 'Dash it all, I believe you are teasing me! You hussy!'

She raised a face that was bright with laughter and glowing with love. Before he could move she pulled the ribbons of her bonnet undone and threw it away.

'Is that better, Edward?' she asked demurely.

'*Much* better,' he assured her. She would have told him then that she loved him, but there was no need. He bent his head to kiss her, and there were no more doubts or questions any more. Her lips were as hungry as his, and her body melted against him without any reserve.

'My darling Miss Mouse,' he whispered, when at last his lips left hers. She smiled.

'I thought you had promised not to call me that any more?' she reminded him.

'Did I? Perhaps I did, but I don't mean to keep my promise. It reminds me of how we first met. Do you mind?'

'No,' she said. 'I'm afraid I don't mind at all. I don't mind what you call me, if only you will kiss me again.'

So he did.

LEGACY *of* LOVE

Coming next month

SEVENTH HEAVEN
Elizabeth Bailey

London 1783

'Wild to a fault, all of them. And quite penniless!'

Naturally, when eminently eligible Lady Louisa Shittlehope
arrived in town for the season, the four Berowne bachelors
wasted no time in knocking on opportunity's door... But after
a year of wealthy widowhood, Louisa prided herself on
having become adept at discouraging such attentions. And
yet, in Septimus Berowne, seventh-born, and rock of the
clan, Louisa found a man who, for the first time, made her
feel like a woman. Was it possible that he could want her for
more than her money, after all?

THE CAPTAIN'S LADY
Paula Marshall

New York/London 1891
(Book 1 of Trilogy)

Gerard Schuyler, back in New York from England for his
grandfather's funeral, was astounded to see the old man's
young mistress appear at the funeral. It was rare enough for a
woman to run her own newspaper business in 1891, but her
relationship with 'the Captain' had made her notorious!

At the will-reading, Gerard went from astounded to furious
when he heard that the Captain had ensured Gerard wouldn't
receive a penny of the huge fortune, unless he married
Victoria within three months. Somehow they had to come to
terms, but what kind of marriage could it be, with this very
secretive woman...?

LEGACY *of* LOVE

Coming next month

MARI
Donna Anders

Hawaii 1867
(Book 1 of Duet)

When she fled her grandfather's tyranny, Mari Webster knew she had burned her bridges. But her life began anew the day she sailed into Honolulu harbour—and saw her future in the eyes of Adam Foster.

Half-Hawaiian Adam Foster was lost the moment he laid eyes on Mari. And when his fellow islanders warned him against mingling with a foreigner, he dismissed their worries as foolish fancy. But Adam soon questioned his irreverence and wondered if the paradise he had found in Mari's arms could survive the wrath of the pagan gods.

THE LOVING SWORDS
Marjorie Burrows

Montana 1876

Clemma Wells had only meant to buy time with the desperate story that she was carrying Will Brandt's child. She never suspected that Tom Cord would offer to marry her. If she told the truth now, she would be sent home in disgrace, and what would Cord do when he found out that their marriage was based on a lie?

She owed her life to the renegade Brandt, but his actions had branded her a fallen woman. Torn apart by her own stubbornness and pride, Clemma struggled with her decision. For it was becoming increasingly clear that it was to Tom Cord she owed her heart...

FOUR
HISTORICAL
ROMANCES

&
TWO
FREE GIFTS!